THE HANGING SHED

'An impressive example of what's now called "Scottish noir" . . . we might just have found a new Ian Rankin.'

Daily Mail

'It's the first literary outing for this latest addition to Scotland's proud tradition of fictional sleuths, and if the strength of his debut is anything to go by, we'll be seeing a lot more of Douglas Brodie.'

Observer

'Riveting and arrestingly violent, it's an on-the-edge-of-your-seat thriller, and Mr. Ferris has confirmed himself as an exciting and original voice in the crime noir genre.'

New York Journal of Books

'Writing in the great Scottish tradition of mystery and adventure, Gordon Ferris is the natural heir of Stevenson and Buchan – great feel of authenticity, and a terrific narrative drive.'

Val McDermid

Also by Gordon Ferris

DREAMING OF A SONG
TRUTH DARE KILL
THE UNQUIET HEART

THE HANGING SHED

GORDON FERRIS

McArthur & Company
Toronto

First published in Canada in 2011 by
McArthur & Company
322 King Street West, Suite 402
Toronto, ON M5V 1J2
www.mcarthur-co.com

First published in Great Britain by Corvus,
an imprint of Atlantic Books Ltd.

Library and Archives Canada Cataloguing in Publication

Ferris, Gordon, 1949-
The hanging shed / Gordon Ferris.

ISBN 978-1-77087-074-1

I. Title.

PR6106.E769H35 2011   823'.92   C2011-904297-5

Cover photographs © Getty Images
Cover design: www.headdesign.co.uk
Printed and bound in Canada by Trigraphik LBF

10 9 8 7 6 5 4 3 2 1

Big thanks to:
Tina Betts, my diligent agent; Becci Sharpe at Corvus, the first
Brodie fan; Nicolas Cheetham at Corvus for taking the leap;
Richenda Todd for incisive editing and knowing too much about
boats; Sarah for insights and unstinting support.

I'll take the big sordid
dirty crowded city.

Raymond Chandler, *The Long Goodbye*

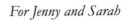

For Jenny and Sarah

ONE

There are no windows in a hanging shed. Only a sadistic architect would provide a last glimpse of the fair green hills. The same goes for paintings or potted plants. You're unlikely to divert the condemned man from the business in hand with a nice framed 'Monarch of the Glen' or a genteel aspidistra. Besides, he'll only visit once. Wearing a hood.

Before the war I was taken to the hanging shed of His Majesty's Prison Barlinnie. Years after, I can close my eyes and recite every dismal detail and dimension as though they were tattooed on my eyelids.

Think of a clutch of grey monoliths scarring the countryside on the outskirts of Glasgow. Each solid rectangle studded with tiny barred windows, the roofs festooned with Victorian chimneys. Like houses drawn by an obsessive child. The whole ugly mass surrounded by a tall grey wall. Focus in on the central courtyard and the building known as D Hall. Inside is a standard prison set-up: a high vaulted chamber with galleries facing each other across a gulf. Cells stud the walls on each level. Metal decks bridge the galleries. Metal staircases connect the levels.

There is one special cell on the third floor. Its occupant has nowhere to go except across the short bridge and through the plain wooden door on the other side. Take the walk. Go through the door. Eyes open.

Inside, the air is inert and the white walls press inwards. In the centre, set in the floor, is a trapdoor. Alongside, and surely connected, stands a lever. There are three square holes in the ceiling directly above the trapdoor. You can see the long retaining beam in the room above. A noosed rope dangles from the beam through the central hole. The two other holes gape invitingly, ready for rush hour in the hanging shed, three at once. Jostling for position on the trapdoor.

Today a lone figure stands on a chalked T in the centre of the trap. A broad leather strap binds the upper body. A hood covers the head. The noose is draped over the hood and round the neck. Soft leather coats the noose. No abrasions here for a tender neck. The noose is held in place by a brass slip to make sure it tightens quickly and efficiently. To snap rather than throttle. The mark of a civilised society.

A man in a blue uniform walks across the echoing floorboards. He grips the lever and grins. There is a shocking clang and thud and the trapdoor falls open. The joist in the room above gives out a tortured creak as it takes the weight. The figure plunges into the void of the floor below where a slab waits. The rope hardens and trembles like a plucked guitar string. The guard sneers at the white faces of the four new constables being shown round for their edification. He signals to the guard below to take down the dummy.

I can conjure it now, lying on my back, rocking in the top bunk of the overnight train to Glasgow. But this time the dummy has a face. Beneath me and all around me I feel the Royal Scot hurtling through the night, steel wheels clacking remorselessly on the rails. Occasionally the great beast splits the tomb-black landscape with a midnight shriek and I listen for an answering call that never comes. I'm going home for the first time in two and half years, and the thought of what I have to face there fills me with a hot mix of anger and dread. I take another pull at my cigarette and watch the tip glow and die, and the smoke drift and swirl away.

Four carefree days ago I was sitting in my wee attic room in South London. I was having a good spell. Almost a week of sleeping better and drinking less. Maybe the two were connected. My newly polished shoes – army indoctrination – were sitting by the door ready for their sprint to Fleet Street. The spring sun was already banking through the skylight window. I was hunched over the table nursing a second mug of tea while reading yesterday's *Times* and my own paper the *London Bugle*. Know your enemy, my old drill sergeant used to say. Besides, I enjoy the adverts on the front of the *Times*. In their way they give as clear a picture of Britain as the inside news pages. Stories of a hard-up country where *gentlemen* were selling their *fine leather gloves,* or where an *ex-officer, RAF, DFC would make excellent private secretary.* Where trained mechanics were searching for work as drivers, and war heroes were on the lookout for *gardening jobs or other manual exercise.* The fruits of victory were bitter enough for some.

I supped my tea and counted my blessings. In the last month I'd started to get a steady trickle of freelance assignments from the *Bugle* and there was a chance of a full-time job. I was making enough money to afford food, fags and Scotch, not necessarily in that order. But at least I would no longer simply be drinking away the last of my demob money. Two weeks ago I'd dragged my flabby body round to Les's Boxing Academy on the Old Kent Road and – aching limbs apart – I was already getting back a sense of physical well-being. Something I hadn't felt since the build-up and hard training for D Day. After a few days of the glums last week I was daring to hope that I was nearing the end of the tunnel. Sunshine on my face would be good. Such was my upbeat mood that I'd been crooning along with Lena Horne and whistling a tuneless descant to Artie Shaw on the Light Programme. Even my first fag tasted sweet instead of just satisfying a craving.

Then the phone rang down in the shared entry.

I glanced at my watch. It was just after seven-fifteen. Someone was starting early. I knew Mrs Jackson wouldn't answer it unless she'd cranked up her hearing aid; I wondered why her daughters had bothered getting the phone installed. Her voice was so loud it made the device redundant. The other three households in our entry rarely got calls, but we were all happy to chip in to pay for the rental. I sprang to my door, still in my slippers and collarless. I could have done with another fifteen minutes of paper-reading and crossword-filling, but maybe the *Bugle* was calling. I dived down the three flights of stairs and grabbed the shiny black set.

'Yes, hello? Brodie here,' I gasped.

'Is that Mr Douglas Brodie?' A posh voice. A professional voice. An operator's voice.

I got my breath back. 'Yes, that's me. Doug Brodie.'

'Please hold the line, I have a call for you. Go ahead, caller, please put your money in now.'

I heard the clank and rattle of coins going in. Several. At least a bob's worth, which meant long distance. My mother using her neighbour's phone? An accident? Bad news comes early. A man's voice started up. Scottish accent, *West* of Scotland. Like mine. Like mine used to be.

'Is that you, Dougie boy?'

4

A bucket of ice splashed down my neck. No one called me Dougie now. It had been Brodie for a decade. The voice scratched at my memory, but I couldn't put a face to it. *Wouldn't.* My mind simply rejected the likelihood. For it was an impossible voice from the days of bows and arrows, spots and whispering girls. Of fist fights that ended in bloody lips and trembling anger. Of a great betrayal that gnawed at me still.

'Who's this? What's happened?' I pressed my palm against the wall for support, feeling the cool plaster suck at the heat of my hand.

'That's a big question,' said the voice.

My mind was fumbling with memories. The timbre and cadence were heavier and slower but, oh, so disturbingly familiar. I knew who this was, but didn't, couldn't believe it. How could it be him?

'Let's keep it simple, then. Who … are … you?'

With new strength: 'Don't tell me you don't know me, ya Proddy sod?'

That did it. The mocking West of Scotland greeting. I saw his face, a wee boy's face. Pawky, we called it, cheeky, with his big silly grin and his fringe of black hair. We played soldiers back then, erupting from our trenches against the machine guns of the Boches. Seeing who could die on the barbed wire with the greatest panache. Shug Donovan – or Hugh, when we started going out with girls – beat us all. He'd fall in a cartwheel of melodrama, great anguished cries and flailing arms. He grew tall and handsome, black hair and blue eyes, like an advert for a Celtic bard. The girls loved him and his easy smile. I hated him for the same reasons, especially for the one girl that fell for him.

I hadn't seen him since I left Kilmarnock for Glasgow University back in '29. I heard odd snatches about him from my mother down the years, though she knew I hated every mention. He was a journeyman cooper at Johnnie Walker's at the same time I was making my way in the Glasgow police force. In '39 I went into the army, the Seaforth Highlanders, my dad's old regiment, though I was a lowlander. Donovan ended up in the RAF, Bomber Command. A tail gunner. A guaranteed way of getting yourself killed for real. Which was exactly what happened.

In a letter from my mother in 1943 I was told that Hugh Donovan had died in his bomber in the flames of Dresden. My first ungracious thought was: Serves you right, you sod. Then remorse made my cheeks burn. It prompted me to write to his mother saying how sorry I was to hear the news. But the guilt of that instant wasn't so easily erased.

'Shug? Is it *you*?'

'Aye, Dougie, it is.'

'But how, what the hell? I thought you were dead!' My voice cracked and echoed round the empty entry.

'So did I, old pal. So did I.'

'But this is great! Just fantastic!' I could stop feeling bad about him, about how we'd left things. Time to move on.

He cut in. 'Dougie. It's no' … It's no' great at all …'

TWO

The train roared through a station, lights flickering briefly before we plunged back into the dark. The sour scent of cheap Scotch tinged the air. The bloke in the bunk below had sucked patiently on a half-bottle to get to sleep. Mother's milk where he came from; *we* came from, I reminded myself. I'd resolutely declined when he'd passed the bottle up to me. To prove I could. Now I wish I'd taken a slug or two. My brain was fidgeting. I lay in the dark and lit another fag and thought about going home, and what I meant by that.

There was Kilmarnock, the place where I was born and grew up. And there was Glasgow, where I'd gone to university, studied languages and, in a fit of rebellion, joined the police. A town and a city a mere twenty miles apart, but they might as well have been on different continents. It wasn't just that I left my boyhood behind on the short train journey from Kilmarnock. It was as though someone had carelessly spliced two strips of films together from entirely different movies. The lead character had changed, as had the supporting cast and the entire plot and arc of the film. The one connecting thread between the two places was the language of the script and the sharp-edged humour and brashness of the West Central Lowlands. Where no German spy could mimic the tortured

7

accents. His request for a pie and a pint in any of the hard pubs that littered the slummy landscape would have earned him a good kicking before being handed over to the comparative safety of the polis.

I'd last been in Kilmarnock in late '43, on leave from my regiment, proud to bursting of the 2nd lieutenant's pips on my epaulettes and the North Africa ribbon on my chest. The dull khaki of my battledress tunic was outshone by the strong blues and greens of the MacKenzie tartan in my Seaforth kilt. I rolled off the train with my kitbag over my shoulder and my tam-o'-shanter pitched at a suitably jaunty angle on my head. I was the picture of health. My leg had healed. Army training and the residue of the desert sun had honed me into a lean brown warrior. I bounded down the steps of the station and out into Kilmarnock's high street. The heavy swing of the kilt made me lift up my head and push out my chest as if I was on parade. I marched down King Street with its stout Victorian façade, and strolled nonchalantly one full time round the cross – the town centre, with its statue of James Shaw in the middle of it.

I caught the smiles on girls' faces: *See you at the Palais on Saturday, then?* And the nods of welcome from the old men: *You've done your time now, laddie, just like us in the last one.* When I thought I'd earned enough silent plaudits, I sauntered back up the Foregate and up the Gas Brae. I was held up briefly at Barclay's yard as they trundled a new locomotive across the main street and on into the run of rail tracks that would channel it into service. The driver nodded and winked at me and I was eight again and enthralled by the giant metal wheels and the massive boiler.

I was marching into my own past, shedding the years with every step, casting off the veneer of learning, city airs and cynicism, and three years of hard fighting. On up to Bonnyton. On the left, climbing up the hill, smart rows of smoke-black sand-stone terraces. Opposite, on the right, a clutch of older, sorrier tenements where the mining community clustered and from where, each day, the buses picked up the lines of men and ferried them off to dig the black seams below the fertile Ayrshire hills. I turned right and marched through the rows of grey tenements and across the drying greens. Washing flapped on the lines strung between the communal poles. The smell of washed linen anywhere in the world would take me back to that spot in a heartbeat.

She was there behind the net curtains, looking for me. I saw the twitch. Sure enough, she was out in a moment, her tiny frame all mobile and flapping, and her white hair shining and lifting in the warm breeze. A lifetime ago it had been red as rowan berries. For a while it seemed I'd inherited her wild colour. But as I grew my father's black bristles counterattacked and turned mine to a compromise shade of dried blood. Only my morning stubble held the memory of her oriflamme. And his dark eyes, his height and miner's shoulders won out against her grey eyes and elfin figure.

'Hello, Mum,' I called, and waved. I dropped my bag and held out my arms.

She scooted towards me, not sure where to put her hands, on her face, outstretched in front of her, or clasped in some inner prayer. The hero's return.

'Oh, Douglas, Douglas. Look at you! Ma wee boy!'

The tears were already coursing on her cheeks. And my eyes were wet by the time she clasped me to her. She felt like a bird, so light and bony. She smelt as she always did, a mix of coal-tar soap that she scrubbed her face with, and lavender from the sachets she hung on her handful of clothes. The very essence of home. I breathed it in, and was a child again. Some of the neighbour women poked their heads out, just by accident of course. But they were all beaming, glad to see one of their sons returned in one piece. Though most of their menfolk had been in reserved service down the pits, there were enough that hadn't come back or had come back maimed.

The one black mark on the day, on all my days now, was the absence of the big man with the coal dust stamped in his hands and on his forehead in a line below his helmet. My father. Three years after his death her red had turned to snow as though she had no further need of it. My mother and I would visit his grave in the afternoon with flowers. Me in my uniform still, to show him what I'd become. What he'd made me. But unable now to delight in the banter over our shared uniform. No chance now of him saluting me with an insolent grin to show that a sergeant could honour a son even though he was now a bloody officer.

This homecoming would be different. I'd lost that bounce and sense of invulnerability that had swept me home two and a half long years ago. My skin had a London pallor and my shock of mud-red hair bore stubs of grey on my sideburns. Only thirty-four, one year short of the biblical halfway mark, and already on the downward slope.

This summons was too soon. It felt like I was rushing pell-mell towards a nexus in my life of dark threads spewing from my past. I wouldn't have been surprised if the conductor had appeared with red-hot coals for eyes and an announcement that the next stop was purgatory.

Hugh Donovan had survived the war and was calling from a pay phone in the visitor section of Barlinnie Prison, Glasgow. The Bar–L, the Big Mansion House, as we used to call it. Thanks to my own problems I'd missed all the furore north of the border. Certainly missed the trial and the verdict. Hugh wanted to see me, to convince me of his innocence. But why me? Why call the man he shafted, the man who still nursed rancour for what he'd taken from me? Why the hell would he think I'd care whether he was guilty or not? Just when I was getting my life back in some sort of order, he kicks up the pieces and I lose the pattern again. And by the sound of it, and from the enquiries I made later that day, he was guilty as sin. It had taken just four months from his arrest in November 1945 to conviction and sentencing.

The judge at Glasgow's High Court had donned the black cap. In just over four short weeks, on the spring morning of 30 April, they would hang Hugh Donovan by the neck until he was dead.

Good riddance.

THREE

I must have dozed. The rhythm of the train had finally pushed me into a deep sleep studded with crazed dreams of riding in a landing craft, slap, slap, slapping through the waves towards the roar of a mighty waterfall. Now the change in rhythm brought me back to the surface; the train slowed, the wheels clacking at walking pace. I peeled back the curtain in the carriage and saw a grey dawn over a brown cityscape. A sluggard river stretched away through the girders of a bridge. I knew exactly where we were. Soon enough the pillars of the station were flicking past the window. As I struggled from my cot and dropped to the floor, the brakes were applied and we ground and huffed to a stop in St Enoch's station, Glasgow.

I quickly soaped my face and skimmed my razor over my chin. I dressed, put on my hat, grabbed my little case and left my travelling companion to groan his way out of his stupor. I wasn't smug. It could have been me last week. I walked past the towering wheels of the Royal Scot and resisted giving her steaming flanks a pat for getting us safely here on time. All around the familiar accents of home burst on my ears like rain after a long drought.

Two young men slouching by: 'Ma heid's gowpin', so it is.'

'Nae wunner. Ye were stocious last nicht.'

'Ye wurnae exactly singin' wi' the Sally Ally yersel'.'

A conductor in uniform giving a trainee a clout on the ear: 'Tak' a tummle tae yersel', ya glaikit wee nyaf.'

Two old women with string bags and bare legs knotted with veins: 'See you, Ah says. If that was ma wean, Ah'd a gi'en her a gid skelp in the lug.'

'Aye, ye cannae ca' yir ain mither a wee hairy, neither ye can. Even if she is, Jessie ...'

It took me a minute or two to tune in, like finding the Home Service on a crystal set. But then it was like music. Scarcely Brahms, more Buddy Rich, all hard edges and rhythms. My spirits rose despite my mission. I was back among kin. It brought me unexpected pleasure and sharp regret that I'd put off this return for so long. Tonight I'd catch the local train back down to Kilmarnock and give my mother a surprise. But this morning I had a date with a murderer.

I dropped off my case in the left-luggage office and came out through the great blackened Victorian arches of St Enoch's into the bracing Glasgow air. Ten degrees cooler than the lucky south-east of England, but with the great marching skies that I'd forgotten. The air was tangy with the reek of house and factory fires but the steady breeze up the Clyde was keeping the smog away. There had been days before the war when the only way you could tell if a tram was coming was by its bell sounding through the murk.

I stopped and looked around. It was as though the war hadn't happened. No signs of bomb damage, and a bustle and an urgency that London lacked. As well as being a mainline station, St Enoch's was a tram and trolley terminus, so I shouldn't have been surprised, but I felt as if I'd walked on to the stage of a mad ballet of machines. The square was heaving with the great cars, their network of overhead wires like a drunken spider-web. There was even the choice of an underground: the Glasgow Subway, but that would have taken me round in a circle south under the Clyde, then west to Govan, back north over the river to Partick, and east again to where I stood. I could have walked from here to the Eastern Division police station in Tobago Street. My first job. But I'd save that pleasure for later.

I got help from a patient tram inspector who reminded me of the colour coding system. I made him repeat his directions and started what seemed like an epic journey east out of the city along the Edinburgh road and then north-east to a quiet suburb with open fields beyond. I changed trams twice and then took a bus. I got off it at the terminus and walked down Lee Avenue. Already I could see the bulk looming over the few houses. Finally I saw the whole massive set of blocks sitting at the end of this forsaken avenue like a disused factory. Which I suppose it was. His Majesty's Prison Barlinnie takes men in and processes them. They go in defiant or terrified, and come out angry or broken, but certainly paler and thinner. Some, like Hugh Donovan, never come out, but are interred in unsanctified ground in the yard near the hanging shed.

The prison cast a long sullen shadow. I began to feel guilty as I walked towards the huge metal door in the centre of the six-storey grey-stone building. I hadn't done anything, but the sense of oppression made me check off my past sins to see if any were jailable crimes. One or two perhaps, but who would know? I felt watched all the way. When I got to the man-sized door set into the giant-sized gate, a grille opened.

'Visitor?' asked a head with a cap on.

'I'm here to see a prisoner. I made an appointment.'

'Name?'

'Mine or the prisoner's?'

There was a narrowing of eyes. 'Both.'

'I'm Brodie. Here to see Hugh Donovan.'

'Donovan, is it? Well, you'd better be quick,' he said with a malevolent grin.

He slammed the hatch down and then opened the door. He stood back to let me step over the threshold. I walked in and stood in a narrow alleyway with a further metal-grilled gate ahead and an office either side. Two other guards in black uniform stood casually in front of the inner gate.

'This way, *sir.*'

The guard who'd let me in walked off in front of me and began a slow ritual with multiple keys through several inner gates and doors. There was a familiar smell: like the cells in Tobago Street nick writ large. Floor polish, fag smoke, male sweat and, from one branching corridor, the pungent smell of cooked greens. We fetched up outside a door marked 'Mr Colin Hislop, Deputy Governor'. I was shown inside. It was an outer office with a pale secretary manning the defence of the inner sanctum. I was made to wait the obligatory twenty minutes before her desk buzzer went and she showed me into the deputy's presence.

He was a careworn clerk in a bad suit with too much in his in-tray and not enough in his out. He took off his glasses and we shook fingers over his pile of papers.

'I'm sorry to be taking up your time, Mr Hislop.'

He looked despairingly at his paperwork for a long second. 'It's perfectly all right. It was important I saw you. Donovan's request that you visit him was, shall we say, unusual.'

His accent was curious: local, certainly, but trying to gild the working-class vowels with the drawl of Kelvinside. Like a mutton pie coated in cream. Then I wondered how mine sounded after all this time mixing with the regimental accents of Sutherland and the Hebrides. Maybe we both sounded like phonies.

'Unusual? Why?'

He dug in his drawer and pulled out a paper. 'His application said you're an old friend and that he wanted to see you. Is that correct?'

Old friend was pushing it, to put it mildly. Old foe, old adversary, old *I wouldn't piss on you if you were on fire* would be more accurate. Which made me wonder again at my being here.

'We grew up together. I only heard about the trial and verdict four days ago. When Hugh phoned me.'

'Yes, quite. Prisoners in his – category are permitted one such call a week.'

'So, may I see him?'

He pointed his finger at the papers in front of him. 'It says you attended Glasgow university then became a *policeman*, a detective sergeant with the Glasgow constabulary.' Said with disbelief as though you'd have to be daft to toss away a good education to pound the beat. He had a point. 'Then you joined up. The Seaforths? A *battlefield* commission, I gather?' He sniffed, as though he personally would have turned it down. Not that he'd been within five hundred miles of action. I felt my anger levels pick up.

'I don't know what you're reading there, but the commission was confirmed. As was the next. It was *Major* Brodie, acting Major. I reverted to Captain when I demobbed.' Why should I care what this little prick thought of me? But it seems I did.

He went on as though I hadn't spoken, 'Now you're a *reporter*, I believe?' Said like *wife-beater*.

'That's right. Where did you get all this?'

'We can't be too careful. In the circumstances. I contacted the Glasgow Chief Constable's office.'

Hislop began to look ever more uncomfortable and put his specs back on. To stop me hitting him, maybe. 'What I'd like to know – *we'd* like to know – is why you want to see him. What I mean to say is, we don't want any more *headlines*. Do you see?'

I stared at him. So that was it. 'I'm here in a private capacity, not a reporter. The London papers don't cover regional stuff.'

He gripped his typed sheet for comfort. 'Well, of course, it's just with your police affiliation, and all the fuss we've had ...'

I cut in, exasperated with all this shilly-shallying. 'I'm just a friend. Wanting to see an old pal. I wish I'd heard sooner, before the trial. Are you refusing to let me see him?'

Off came the glasses again. 'No, no, of course not. It's just ... with so little time the appeal, et cetera ... we don't want any problems. Do you see?'

I didn't feel like being helpful. 'I don't think I do.'

He pushed back his chair. 'Perhaps you haven't been aware of the uproar there has been in Scotland? The public were, shall we say, quite upset by it all. We don't want to stir things up, do we?'

I noticed sweat beading his thin top lip. My, my, Shug, look what you've done. 'Mr Hislop, all I'm asking is to visit a man who has four weeks left to live.'

'Quite, quite.' Hislop fussed around, moving some papers on his table and generally making me want to grab him by the lapels and give him a good cuff round the ears to spur him into action. Finally he leaned over to his desk buzzer and when his pale assistant responded he told her to arrange for me to see Hugh in the visitors' wing.

'Half an hour only, Mr Brodie. And of course – ahem – we will require you to be searched beforehand. If you don't mind. Can't be too careful, you know ...' He trailed to an end and I left him to gnaw at his desk or whatever he did to control his inner rages. Practise his elocution perhaps.

FOUR

different guard escorted me through the warren. Our feet rang out on the tiled floor as we headed towards the cells. We came to an open space with a line of seats jammed against a counter. Above the counter, and coming down to rest on it, was a six-foot-high metal grille. I could see other chairs facing these on the other side. I was motioned to a seat. There was no other visitor. I sat and lit a cigarette, taking deep drags to calm me down. Beyond, on the other side, a door swung open about twenty yards away. A guard stepped forward, looked around and then motioned to someone behind him. A shackled figure shambled forward, head bent to the floor. He wore grey overalls and chains round his wrists and feet. Another guard followed him out. They pointed to me and waited for the prisoner to lift his head and step forward.

I didn't recognise the creature who stood, uncertain, by the door. His head was still bent but there was no shock of black hair. The scalp was bald with livid patches. This wasn't Hugh Donovan. There'd been a mistake.

Finally the figure shuffled towards me. He stood for a moment facing me through the grille. I stood up, my legs shaking. He twisted into the seat opposite mine and sat bent over his knees, his forearms resting on his thighs and his hands clasped together. Keeping his head bent, he began rocking backward and forward. He might have been praying. He needed to, if this was Donovan, and he'd done what they said did. But it wasn't Hugh's head.

I gazed at his tortured skull. Red and white, marbled and distorted as though the skin had run. Which of course was what had happened. I had seen it before on some Spitfire pilots, young men, handsome young men, whose faces had melted in the flames of their cockpit. When the Perspex cover caught light, there was no putting it out, and little chance of wrestling it open without serious burns if your plane was spiralling towards the ground. I suppose the same applied to a tail gunner if your Lancaster had taken hits from phosphorus shells. I sat down and placed my forearms on the bench that ran under the grille through to his side.

'Hello?' I tried.

'Hello, Dougie.' He still didn't look up, and the voice was slow and dull. But this was Hugh. 'Thanks for coming.'

'Hugh, look at me.'

For a moment he did nothing. Then he slowly lifted his head. I'd been steeling myself but it wasn't enough. I stopped breathing. It was a clown's face, badly made up. Hairless, seamed and ridged like a child's bad attempt at a patchwork doll. One ear, the right, was missing completely. The nose was vestigial. Then he smiled. It was the worse thing. A twisted, lopsided desecration of that beautiful grin. At least he had his sight; those bright blue eyes of his seemed to mock me from behind a mask that he would take off any minute now. He'd giggle, and then we'd both laugh at the great wheeze. But this was no faux-face from our boyhood guising at Hallowe'en. I couldn't help myself. The tears sprang.

'Oh, Christ, Shug. You've been through it, old pal.'

I reached out instinctively with both hands and clamped them through the grille. He looked at them, smiled that perverted smile again, and put out his own withered limbs. He touched my fingers and then pulled away. I saw the guard on his side step forward and shake his head at me. I pulled back.

'You wanted to know why I never got in touch …' He sounded as though he was speaking from beneath the sea.

'Hell, Shug, none of us are as braw as we were.'

'I'll swap you ony time, Dougie,' he said softly.

We held each other's eyes for a minute longer till we both got embarrassed.

'Tell me, Hugh.'

He looked up again. His blue eyes beseeched. 'I never killed those weans, Douglas. And certainly no' that wee boy, Rory. As God's my judge, I never killed him. How could I kill Fiona's boy?' I saw his eyes mist and wondered if this was another of his big lies. Perhaps the biggest.

Hugh and I had grown up playing together even though he went to the chapel and I went to the kirk. He lived in the next close. He'd call me a Proddy sod and I'd call him a Papish pig. And we'd punch each other on the shoulder to see who could stand the pain the longest. Our friendship survived Orange marches through Kilmarnock when the drums and flutes and orange sashes would clear the streets of left-footers like Hugh. It survived us going to separate schools where the religious differences were drummed in deep. We got looks down the main street, him in his black blazer and me in maroon.

It survived some of the battles we had at the local dance hall – the Air Training Corps hut – the Attic – Protestants squaring off against Catholics instead of enjoying the girls and the dancing. Hugh left school at fourteen like most of my pals, and followed in his dad's footsteps into an apprenticeship in the cooperage at Johnnie Walker's. I stayed on at the Academy thanks to a Co-op bursary, aiming for my Highers. It wasn't my choice. My father, through his coughing, vowed I'd not follow him down the pits.

Hugh and I stayed in touch. He brought his girlfriend, Maureen, to the Attic one night. They'd been to St Joseph's School together. And Maureen brought her sister, Fiona. Fiona, with heavy black hair flowing halfway down her back. With the upright head and slim musculature of a dancer. With dark lashes sheltering Celtic-black eyes.

The way she looked at me that first night was all challenge and light, as though she was waiting for me to say something stupid. I don't know what I said. It couldn't have been too daft. We danced like dervishes then and every Saturday after. Her hair swirling and tossing like the mane of a black stallion. It was unusual then and maybe still. Catholics winching Protestants. Something you hoped the war would have blown away for ever. We'd see. The Montagues and Capulets had it easy. We became an item in that reckless summer. We were both fifteen and I was harpooned by the love of my life.

The four of us remained inseparable through the following year, me at school, the other three out earning their living. My pockets were usually empty except for the coppers earned on my paper round. Fiona was a mill girl like her mother and sister before her. I got catcalls from her pals if I picked her up after work, me in my school blazer and she in her pinny, shaking her hair loose from her headscarf. The gentlest jibe was *professor*. It didn't seem to matter. We were in love and even the entreaties of her priest and parents to give up this scandalous affair went unheeded on into the spring of '29.

Until I learned of a different arrangement. I heard it first from Maureen, her face burning with bitterness. Hugh and Fiona had been meeting secretly for months. Suddenly all the little evasions made sense – her too-tired-to-meet-after-work rebuffs, the going out with her pals excuses, the perpetual washing of her black mane. I caught them together walking hand in hand in the Kay Park, their mouths feasting on each other. I stepped in their path. I wasn't sure what I was going to do: punch him; slap her; kill them both. In the event they froze and looked at me with such pity that I turned and walked away. Hugh called after me: how sorry he was and how they hadn't meant it to happen. I *should* have hit him.

Seventeen years ago. And you know what? It had hurt for seventeen years. It still hurt. What does a seventeen-year-old know of love? Everything and nothing. Nothing about the longueurs of married life. Nothing about the dips and doubts, the chains and ties. Everything about the spark and fire of a kiss. The agonies of *does she, doesn't she?* The racing blood, the utter certainty, the high passion. Why should a teenage love count less? It's unconstrained, insane. It lacks adult defences and cynicism. First love is engraved on a developing heart. Like carving the letters on a tree and years later finding them swollen and proud on a mature trunk. Knowing they would last the lifetime of the tree. Longer than your own.

There had been girls since. Kind women, bright women, teasing women, women who wanted a life with me. I was too busy, too fussy. Fiona cast a long shadow.

I looked at the wrecked face in front of me. Beyond punching now. I hadn't spoken to him or her since that day, just heard of their continued passion through others. Until she married someone else. Why? And why not me? Not even third best? And bore her husband – the jammy sod – a son. Why not mine, Fiona?

Did that have any bearing on the murder of her wee boy? The Hugh I'd known hadn't had it in him, not for Fiona's child, for pity's sake. Surely? But I'd seen the hardest of men turn into gibbering wrecks after two days of bombardment in a desert foxhole. Hell, I still jolt awake wrapped in sweat-soaked sheets, with Panzer tanks rolling over me. How would being burnt alive affect you?

I'd phoned an old contact in the Glasgow police. He told me that five boys had gone missing over the past year, three in the East End, two in the Gorbals. Only the last one had been found. Fiona's son Rory had been discovered in a coal cellar at the back of some tenements. He was naked and dead. He'd been raped, God help him. The following morning Hugh Donovan had been arrested in his single-end in the Gorbals. There was hard evidence all over the house that Hugh had killed the boy, including the boy's clothing. And here was Donovan telling me he didn't do it. Despite what he'd done to me, I wanted to believe him, wanted to believe that no one I knew was capable of such horror. But the facts said otherwise. And there was motivation: sick revenge on a faithless lover and her dead husband.

'Tell me everything, Hugh. How did the boy's clothes get into your flat?' I took out my reporter's notebook and a pencil, to encourage him to talk. It usually works.

He was shaking his head, holding his face in his hands. 'It's going to sound stupid.' His eyes looked hunted. He flung up his hands. 'I don't know, Dougie! I just don't know! I don't know how they got there, and that's the truth!'

'What do you remember? I mean what was the last thing you recall before ...?'

'Before they found me there? And took me away? Took me here?'

I nodded.

'Look, I'd better tell you a wee bit about the last few months. How I ran into Fiona again.'

This is what he told me. These are the notes I took, good ex-copper and budding crime reporter that I was.

FIVE

Hugh Donovan kept his hat on and his collar up in all weathers. Even in pubs; no, especially in pubs. He didn't want to put off his fellow drinkers. It was a habit he'd started the day he'd left the hospital at East Grinstead and taken the train north. Donovan was terrified. He'd spent nearly two years cloistered in Professor Archie McIndoe's revolutionary burns unit. Nineteen operations on his hands and face and he still looked like something stitched together by a one-handed seamstress. This wasn't to malign McIndoe's now legendary skills. It was a recognition of the starting point.

Hugh should have got off at Kilmarnock but he took one look at the familiar smoke-black sandstone of the station and kept going, kept right on the extra twenty minutes to Glasgow. No one was expecting him in Kilmarnock. His father was dead and his mother had stopped visiting East Grinstead months ago, *too stressing, all those poor boys wi' ruined faces*. She'd gone a bit doolally lately, Hugh had thought. He had five older siblings but they'd scattered to the winds in search of work or husbands.

He turned south as he came out of the St Enoch's and walked over Jamaica Bridge spanning the Clyde. Hugh knew little of Glasgow, but enough to know that the Gorbals was an area where a man could lose himself and not stand out too much among the other ill-favoured folk crowded into the four-storey tenement blocks. It had always been Hugh's experience that the people at the bottom of the heap were the most forgiving and accepting.

He found digs in Florence Street; a one-room single-end next to the room and kitchen of a family of five, four kids and a widow whose wage-earner had died in a shipyard accident. The 'houses' shared a toilet on the outside landing on the second floor of the sandstone tenement.

Hugh checked into the local post office and began collecting his army pension. He found Doyle's pub on his second day and it became, through convenience and its anonymous cubbyholes, his evening haunt. Sometimes his lunchtime haunt too. He had no further thought to his future than to lie low, not bother anyone, see how it went, maybe get a wee job. The wee job that turned up became the heart of all Hugh's future problems.

Hugh could ignore the looks. He could hide in quiet corners. He might have been happy enough to drift through his days like a wraith. But the physical pain was often beyond bearing. As the flesh had healed – haphazardly and multi-hued – the nerve ends too came back to life, back to haunt him. Instead of being cauterised by the ravening flames, his nervous system kept telling his brain to move away from the terrible heat. Kept sending waves of invisible fire over his face and limbs.

It had been expected and McIndoe had lined him up with a letter to take to the Glasgow Royal Infirmary to ensure that Donovan would have a steady supply of painkillers. But bureaucracy had stood in the way. The National Health Service existed only in newspaper reports forecasting the effect of the Beveridge proposals. If they were to be believed, in another couple of years Hugh would receive all the pain relief he needed from a free national medical system. It seemed unlikely. And as of today he lacked a local sponsor to have him taken on the books of the dispensary. But an ex-army doctor took pity on him and agreed to give him morphine injections once a week on a Monday. Tuesdays were bliss for Hugh. Wednesdays were bearable. All the other days were nightmares waiting for Monday to come round.

He added Scotch. It brought temporary oblivion, but soon the sawing at his frayed and burnt nerve ends cut through and jolted him awake to a pain–filled hangover. Sometimes his moans woke the folk in the next flat and they banged on his wall till he quietened.

So the man he met in Doyle's one night was as much a saviour as Christ himself. He sold dirty brown lumps of chemicals that you heated till liquid and then injected into a vein. The relief was instant. Like a balm administered by God himself. Stronger than the hospital version, it helped Hugh bridge the gap from Wednesday to the following Monday. Indeed, for an hour or two Hugh Donovan was transported, beyond pain, into a land of utter bliss. It was unsurprising that he began taking it daily. Unsurprising that his entire paltry war pension went on the heroin salve. Inevitable that the daily fix wasn't enough. His body demanded more than he could afford. His saviour helpfully explained a solution. Hugh began to sell the stuff and take his commission in kind.

'You became a junkie? And you sold the stuff! For Christ's sake, Shug!'

He gazed at me with his tortured eyes. 'I saw your limp. Wounded?'

I nodded. 'Sicily. It's fine mostly. Just when I get tired.'

'Did they give *you* morphine?'

I remembered with all the warmth of a love affair, the blissful floating feeling of the first shot from the medic as they hauled me into the ambulance. I scarcely felt the bumping and crashing as we swayed down the pitted roads. There were many more injections, each taking me off into a wonderland of sweet comfort and happiness. It took a while to do without it.

'Sorry, Hugh. It's just … *Selling* the stuff?'

He shrugged. 'I thought I'd go mad with the pain.'

'What about the boy, then? What about Fiona?'

It was pure chance. He glimpsed her coming out of the Co-op in Cumberland Street. It was her familiar walk that caught his eye. But she had a child by her side, a lad of maybe six or seven. Celtic-dark like his mother. A sweet wee face too. He pulled back into a shop doorway as she went past. He heard her tell the boy to pick up his feet, and he knew her voice. As unobtrusively as he could, he followed her along the cobbled streets to a close in Kidston Street, which ran at 90 degrees to his own Florence Street. He watched her vanish inside and wondered what her husband was like. He wondered if I had kept in touch.

He took to hovering between Cumberland Street and Kidston Street. Over the coming weeks he must have seen her four or five times, usually with the boy, never with a man. Once he followed them to the benches under the trees in Hutcheson Square. He sat on the other side and pretended to read a newspaper. But his talent as a scout was soon laid bare. He'd waited till she walked round a corner before crossing over and peeking round it. She was waiting for him, two yards away.

'Mister, Ah don't know who you are but if you don't stop following me ah'm getting the polis.'

Hugh slumped against the wall. 'Sorry, missus. Sorry. I thought you were someone I knew.'

'Oh, aye, and who would that be?' She folded her arms.

Hugh turned and made to walk away. But she took two steps and grabbed his arm. He turned and faced her and said, 'Fiona MacAuslan.'

Her hand flew to her mouth. 'That was my maiden name. How did you ken? Who are you, mister?' He lifted his head a little. She could see his eyes under the hat. 'Oh, dear God, is that you, Hugh Donovan? Is that you?'

'Aye, Fiona. Sorry to have frightened you. Ah'll no bother you again. Sorry.'

'You'll do nae such thing, Hugh Donovan.' She reached out and held his elbow again, stopped his retreat. Tears were already running down her face. 'You'll take some tea.'

They met once or twice a week after that. Fiona's husband had died in the push through the Ardennes. She got a small war widow's pension. She lived near her mother and had a part-time job at Miss Cranston's tearoom in Buchanan Street. Her mother picked up the boy, Rory, after school. At first Hugh's face made the boy hide behind his mother's skirts, but soon, with the capacity all children have for absorbing change, Rory accepted him and ignored his blistered skin. Hugh taught the boy card games and made him giggle. Hugh clung to these moments like a rope in a gale. It helped him reduce the intake of heroin, even lessened the amount he would push. Until the world crashed around him.

She was in the street, calling Rory's name, when he turned the corner. She was wild with fear, storming this way and that. There was already talk of this being the third or fourth child that had gone missing. The neighbours were out and soon there were little groups of women combing the closes and the washing-filled greens round the back. Rory had been out playing. His pals said a man with a hat and a coat had called him over. Rory had taken his hand and walked off. They hadn't seen his face. Could have been anyone. Could have been him, they said, pointing at Hugh in his buttoned-up coat and hat. Fiona looked at him in a funny way for a second and then went back to her raging worry.

The police came and took notes and tried to calm the now hysterical Fiona. Her panic was infecting the whole neighbourhood. The press was ramping it up too. Headlines about the 'Gorbals Ghoul' were selling newspapers like the announcement of D-Day. A day passed, then another, then nearly a week had gone by and there was no sign of the boy or of the four others. The police interviewed everyone, including Hugh, in the first couple of days. They spent longer with him than anyone. He didn't have much of an alibi for his time. How could he? They searched his room, it didn't take them long. They found nothing.

Until the morning they burst down his door and found Hugh Donovan unconscious from a drug overdose. He was still dressed but his clothes were caked with coal dust. Under the sink was a bucket full of evidence. They dragged him from his bed and gave him a good kicking to wake him up. They called him an animal, a child molester, a murdering bastard who would rot in hell. They handcuffed him and dragged him out of the flat on to the landing. As an afterthought they read him his rights and arrested him for the kidnap and murder of Rory Hutchinson, and the kidnap and disappearance of four other missing boys.

SIX

I looked at Hugh with a mix of despair and disgust. I couldn't comment on the four missing boys. But all the evidence in the world pointed to him having abused and killed Rory in a drug frenzy. What other conclusion could a jury come to?

The rational part of me wanted to ask where he had kept the lad while the coppers were searching his tiny room the first time. Didn't the neighbours hear something? But surely to God Hugh had never been a homo? Far less fancied wee boys? Was it some stupid revenge on Fiona for having married someone else and having a child by him? But rationality was crowded from my mind with the image of that poor raped child. He must have read my face.

'I never touched him, Dougie. On Fiona's life. I'm no' that kind of a guy. You ken me.'

I nodded. I thought I had known him. Like a brother. Then he stole my girl and smashed the trust. If he was capable of that, he was capable of becoming a drug addict, pusher and murderer, in my admittedly prejudiced book of crimes against Douglas Brodie.

'What *do* you remember? Of the day before? Up to the time you were picked up.'

'Nothing much. I did my usual. I needed a fix and went to

one of the pubs I use. It was the Mally Arms near Gorbals Cross. I got enough for me and a bit to sell later, maybe six hits in all.' He could see what I was thinking. 'But, Dougie, I wouldnae take the lot at once. I never do. Just enough to keep me going. Enough to keep me sane.' His poor face was twisted now with the pains racking him. It would be part burning nerves and part withdrawal pains. I stood up. He needed help.

'You need a doctor.'

'No! They'll just knock me oot! That's what they do. He gi'es me too much. To stop me screaming. To stop me upsetting the screws. For the last couple of days, waiting for you, I've refused to take their jab. So I could talk. Explain to you. Bastard said: Good, I should suffer in hell for what I did. But I never touched him, Dougie!' His face ran with tears.

I studied his poor hands for a while. I didn't get it.

'So why are you telling *me* this, Hugh? What's the point?'

'I wanted *someone* to believe. Someone to know I didnae do it. Just someone. After I'm dead. Ma life's shite, Dougie. But I don't want everyone to think this.'

The silence hung between us at the thought of what was to happen a month from now.

'But *me*?' I asked. 'We were hardly best pals, at the end there.'

'I know. And that's the other thing. We used to be the best. I was a stupid prick, Dougie. I couldnae help myself over Fiona, that's the truth. But I should have. She was yours.'

I'd waited a long time to hear his apology, but it hardly registered now. He had nothing I wanted, nothing I could envy.

'That's by with,' I said, waving my hand – and almost believing it.

'You're the only pal that mattered, Dougie. An' I fucked it up. I didnae want you to hear about me and just write me off. I wanted you to know. To believe.'

33

'I'm not into belief any more, Hugh. I've given up all that stuff.'

For a moment there was something of the old Hugh flitting across his eyes and mouth. 'Ya Proddy sod! I always said it wasnae a real religion.'

I smiled and shrugged. 'I gave *him* enough chances to prove himself. But there's just too much ... too much shit, Hugh.'

'You should have been brought up a good Catholic. You don't get a choice about believing.'

'Even now?'

'Even now. There's a priest that comes by. From my chapel. Actually it's a help.'

'Maybe I was with the polis too long. No belief without proof.'

'OK wi' me, old pal. Besides ...'

'What?'

'You wi' your fancy university education and being a big man in the polis. I need a Sherlock on the case. I thought maybe you'd have some ideas.'

I shook my head. 'We don't have much time.'

'*We*? I sure don't.'

I looked long and hard into those blue eyes and wondered if I had enough magnanimity in me to spend precious time on a hopeless quest on behalf of a man I'd come to hate. 'Why should I?' I meant, why should I do it for you? He saw my thoughts.

'Don't do it for me, Douglas Brodie. Nor for Rory, even. Though that's plenty. A maniac like that will do it again. Another wee boy...'

I left Hugh nodding away and wringing his hands. He'd put a load on my back and I was minded to fling it off. If no one else was asking the hard questions, why should I? I had a life to lead and it wasn't here, chasing ghosts. I felt soiled with travelling and with exposure to new horror. I'd had my share. I walked away from the prison, walked until I came to the first tram lines. I boarded a majestic 'Coronation', climbed upstairs and pulled out a much-needed cigarette. By the time I was coming into the city centre the air was thick and blue with the other smokers, mainly older men on their way back from picking up their pensions. I dragged deeply on my fag, wondering where the hell to begin if I took it on. But mainly wondering why I should bother with such a hopeless case. Why I should care. I looked out the window and saw a pair of wee boys playing marbles in the dust. Their grey shirt-tails hung out and their feet were bare and filthy.

Pals for life, Dougie? Pals for life, Shug.

SEVEN

By the time the train reached Kilmarnock it was smirring, that fine West of Scotland rain that doesn't seem much at the time, but soaks you as thoroughly as falling in a river. I pulled my mackintosh out of my case and put it on. The road up to Bonnyton was achingly familiar but it looked more rundown, the sandstone blacker. Maybe it was the rain. I felt the now familiar black mood descend and I fought to banish it. I didn't want to spoil my homecoming. But as I took the hill my stride grew shorter, my gait slower, as though the rain was lead. I paused under the railway bridge and smoked a fag until I got hold of myself.

It was a bleak return. I was in civvies this time, the kilt handed back last October together with the major's crowns. It would have been nice to have had just one last saunter down the High Street in full dress uniform in my acting rank before they bumped me back to captain on demob. Sporting the medal ribbons of the Africa Star, the Italy Star and the France and Germany Star, like the awards at primary school for spelling, writing and sums. To have dropped casually into the Wheat-sheaf, and bought a round or two for my old mates, and let them mock me gently: 'I hope the guy was deid when you stole his uniform, Brodie.' Or: 'I didnae think the Catering Corps gave oot medals.' And so on, and so on, but seeing in their eyes just a hint of the envy or admiration that they'd rather die before admitting.

It wouldn't have the same impact to roll up in my demob outfit and explain exactly what a freelance journalist did for a living. They'd call me the 'paperboy' or ask why I couldn't get a full-time job. They'd mock me all the harder when I said I specialised in crime reporting, and that there was more to it than sitting in the Old Bailey fleshing out lurid stories of straying spouses being caught *in flagrante delicto*. The phrase always made me smile: *while the crime was blazing*. It conjured images of wild passion and pounding bed springs. The truth was usually duller: it was generally a set-up in an accommo-dating hotel to get a divorce. The 'lovers' would be found in their underwear, waiting for the photographer to show up. At which point they'd grapple a bit on the bed and look as enamoured with each other as two strangers could in front of a grinning audience.

Then there was the limp from the shrapnel I took in Sicily in '43 after chasing Rommel up the North African coast. The leg wounds earned me two pleasant months in a hospital in Alexan-dria and a ticket to officer training back in Blighty. When I kept up the exercises the limp didn't show. But since I'd got back to London last autumn, I'd let things slide. If I wasn't exploding at the bureaucracy involved in getting my hands on my demob pay or a nice bit of bacon, I was sunk in gloom feeling sorry for myself. I'd meet a girl in a pub and we'd get on great until I went into one of my fugues and spoilt it all. My local quack said I should buck up and prescribed iron tonic. He said it was normal, that London was full of men like me. Which would explain the punch-ups I got into in the bars I frequented.

I blamed it on the extra four months I served after the

fighting stopped last May. It was my own fault. My hitherto underused German was no sooner on display at the surrender of the 15th Panzer Brigade than I was seconded to the clear-up task force interrogating Nazi camp commandants and SS zealots. While my regiment was shipped home to be showered with the roses and kisses deserving of heroes, I was noting down the forced confessions of psychopaths and fanatics. Useful training for a journalist, I suppose.

They let me home to a bitter autumn. *A cold coming we had of it, just the worst time of the year for a journey ...*

I chose to be demobbed in London. A grateful nation gave me a Burton's suit and trilby, a good mac, a solid pair of shoes and enough money to keep me drunk for as long as my liver lasted. Whenever I sobered, the tremors started. Whenever I slept, storm troopers came for me with slavering dogs and whistles. My language skills seemed to have improved – the nightmares were in German.

It was easier to stay drunk, skulking in south London, feeling sorry for myself, plunging in and out of black moods. Waking up with lead weights on my chest. Suffocating in my dreams. A few times the neighbours knocked on their ceiling to complain about the noise, like murder was being committed. I thought they were imagining things until I woke to the sound of someone sobbing and found it was me. Christmas came and went and winter ate into my battered bones. I hunched over tepid briquettes with a quilt round me gazing into the glow, looking for my future but only seeing my past.

I wanted to go home to Scotland, but how could I face them in this state? A wreck. A drunk. Just a liability to my mother. I fended her off with letters but I knew from the tone of her replies she was worried sick. They were even asking about me at her kirk. Where was her wee boy? The bursary winner, the scholar, the one that escaped. What was I up to? Why didn't I come home to see her? Throughout, she never stopped going, never explained, never sought comfort or understanding from a soul. She'd never needed anyone's approval except that of her man, my dad. And she was as certain of that fifteen years after his death as the day he'd married her.

But I hadn't been completely forgotten. I was demobbed at the same time as the Guards brigadier who'd run the interrogation programme out of Berlin. He'd been given his old job back: on the board of the *London Bugle*. We had a beer. We had several beers. He got his editor to fling me some crumbs and keep flinging them at me until one day as the year turned I caught one. I managed to stay sober long enough to crack out a thousand words on black marketeering. It didn't take much footslogging round my favourite bars to get the ammunition. The *Bugle* seemed to like the article, well, half of it anyway. They asked for more and I was beginning to scribble irregular pieces on the darker side of London life. I'd even started going to Les's boxing gym to get my leg moving again and help soak up the anger that seemed always on tap.

So this cry for aid was premature. I wasn't ready. Guilt hung about me like a shroud. Guilt about how I'd loitered in London and not come home to see my mother. Guilt about how I'd let myself go. Guilt that I'd made it home and scores of better men hadn't. Guilt that my first feeling in response to Hugh Donovan's summons had been anger. I stabbed my fag out and marched up the hill.

EIGHT

There was no welcome flick of the curtains from my mother's tenement. For a minute I panicked, thinking the worse. But of course she wasn't expecting me. I went in the close and up the single flight of stone stairs and knocked on the door. Nothing. I knocked louder. Then I checked my watch. It was half past one. Tuesday. I left my case by her door and hung my dripping coat on the doorknob. I walked down to the entry and out the back. Sure enough. I could hear the noise of splashing from the brick wash-house. Smoke was coming out the open door.

I stuck my head in. It was the witches' scene from *MacBeth*. My mother was standing wreathed in steam next to a cauldron – the washing bine: the big metal dish that sat on a waist-high brick column. Underneath, a coal fire spat and glowed and boiled the water. My mother wore a headscarf and a pinny. Her blouse sleeves were rolled up and her arms were red and wet with suds. She held a sheet in both hands and was rubbing it up and down the ridged washboard that protruded from the bubbling pot. Behind her, one of her neighbours, Mrs Cuthbertson, was grinding the big handle of the mangle and pulling through another sheet. A steady cascade of water filled a wooden basin below the mangle. My mother's face was puce but she was happy in her work, humming away to herself.

She looked up and her face lit. She flung her hands to her face, stopped and dropped them to her apron. She dried them and shot round the bine to me. She clutched my arms, afraid to get me wet against her soaking washday clothes.

'Douglas! You should have phoned. I've nothing ready. I havenae baked a thing. Are you all right? Is anything the matter?'

'Mum, it's OK. Can I no' visit my mother without it being a national disaster?'

She looked up at me, her face losing its smile, tightening. 'You've come about Hugh, haven't you?'

Later, I heard her version of the story as we sat quietly sipping tea in front of the coal fire in the back room. It felt, as it always did, like being wrapped up in a cosy blanket. A tiny place. Two rooms, front and back, with the scullery leading off the back room. As the light fell outside, I got up and lit the gas mantles to send a soft glow around the room. The clock on the mantelpiece beat out the rhythm that had measured out my quiet boyhood absorption in a new book from the library. I prodded the fire so that the glow illumined the big black metal fireplace. We sat either side of it, mimicking the Wally dugs whose black china eyes gazed down on us from the mantelpiece. She'd drawn the curtain across the bed-in-the-wa' and the room tucked itself round us. It was a world away from a cold cell in Barlinnie.

'You don't seem that surprised, Mum.'

'About two weeks ago, Jessie Cuthbertson got a telephone call asking for me. It was a secretary from a solicitor's office. Wanting to get in touch with you. Jessie had your number in her book and she gave the woman it. I hope you don't mind?' she asked anxiously. 'We've got a note of the name.'

'Of course not. It was fine.'

She nodded. 'That poor wee bairn. And him Fiona's boy too. The trial was in all the papers here, once they found he was a Kilmarnock man.'

My stomach flipped. It was one of the few times my mother had ever used her name in this house. Going out with a Catholic lassie had been as counter-cultural as voting Tory. Hugh had got past the religious censoring by dint of being a neighbour's child.

'Did you not think I should know?'

She looked embarrassed. 'You had enough troubles. I thought maybe you'd heard and decided to say nothing. You don't phone that often. Oh, I know it's such a fuss.'

It was true. It involved me phoning Mrs Cuthbertson and her running up the stairs and getting my mother to come down. And my mother then panicking that I needed to call her and her shouting down the line because she was so far away. Trauma all round rather than a casual kindness. Letters were always easier somehow, and more lasting. I reread hers at least two or three times, just to hear the gossip about the town. But clearly there were some things that weren't for writing down.

'My fault, Mum. You know what I'm going to do? I'm going to get the phone put in here. And don't you worry, I'll pay the bills.'

She looked startled and anxious. 'Oh, I don't want that thing going off in the middle of the night. What would I use it for anyway? Everyone I need to talk to is just a walk away. Except you, of course.'

We had some more tea and then she looked me in the eye. 'Did he do it, Douglas?'

As usual I'd underestimated my mother's ability to absorb the unthinkable. She was taking it calmly and sensibly, as though Hugh had been caught plunking school.

42

'It's hard to draw any other conclusion.'

'But?'

'But there are a lot of questions.'

'What like, son?'

'The big one is *why*? Why would Hugh do such a thing? The boy was missing for a week. They searched Hugh's room early on and found nothing. Then they found the body in the coal cellar outside Hugh's tenement, and found Hugh up to his oxters in evidence linking him to the murder. Where was he hiding the boy all this time? How did nobody see him, hear anything? Who told the police to look there? What about the other four missing boys? If it was Hugh, how did he keep them quiet? Why did he dump Rory's body where it could be found? Carelessness or arrogance? Maybe they asked all these questions at the trial and the answers still added up to him being guilty. I don't know.'

We sat in stillness for a while, each of us, I'm sure, imagining that wee broken body lying in the dark. And wondering about the missing lads. Her hair shone silver in the flickering light. She shook her head, as though puzzled with the badness in the world.

'When is it?' She meant when would they hang him.

'Four weeks. April the thirtieth.'

'What will you do?'

Not *it's no business of yours; keep away from this because mud sticks; what will the neighbours think?* No question that I wouldn't, shouldn't, get involved.

'I don't know. The odds are against him. So is time. I'd just be wasting my efforts.'

'But you said there were questions.'

'But who's going to answer?'

She must have read something in my face. Even before I

admitted to myself. She nodded. 'Just like your dad. He always had to know.'

'If Hugh didn't do it, somebody did.'

'It's not about Fiona, is it?'

'No, no. That was a long time ago.' I hoped I sounded convincing.

'I'll make up a bed in the front room. It's back to sharing the scullery, son.'

I shook my head. 'Just the one night, Mum. I'll get digs up in Glasgow for a week or two. That's where I'm going to be spending my time. I'll visit a lot, though.' I smiled to soften the blow as she failed to hide her disappointment.

NINE

By practice, Hugh Donovan's defence counsel had been picked by the solicitor appointed to Hugh by the court. I travelled back up to Glasgow and trekked round the hard streets of the West End to find an advocate called Samuel Campbell, working at the offices of Harrison, Campbell, MacLane. It was the name left by the secretary who'd phoned my mother. I'd used Mrs Cuthbertson's phone first thing to fix an appointment and get the address, but I hadn't anticipated how far along the Great Western Road I'd need to travel. Especially carrying a suitcase. I was getting hot, bothered and asking myself for the umpteenth time why I was doing this for Donovan.

Scottish advocates, if I remembered from my sergeant's exams, were self-employed members of the Faculty of Advocates. I assumed Campbell was using his old office at the solicitors he'd trained with. I found the nameplate on the side of a sandstone pillar on a fine Georgian townhouse. The terrace sat on a side road back from and looking down on the Great Western Road itself. They must have made wonderful homes a hundred years ago, but now most of them were given over to offices.

Inside was less pretty. The carpets were worn and the chairs sagging. So was the woman in the receptionist's chair. She managed to achieve looking bored and harassed at the same time and directed me to sit and read some of the pre-war magazines while I waited for the lawyer. I sat and smoked and fidgeted, wondering what this bloke Campbell expected of me. Then a woman appeared from down a dark-panelled corridor to take me to him. She was slim, blonde and bespectacled with a careworn frown. Her boss was giving her a hard day.

She strode towards me and stuck out her hand. 'Sam Campbell.'

I was on my feet and shaking her hand before I could wipe the surprise off my face. Her eyes registered a habitual weariness at the puzzlement she provoked in folk meeting her for the first time.

I smiled warmly at her to compensate. 'Brodie. I'm here about Hugh Donovan, Mrs Campbell.'

There was no answering smile, just a shrug. 'I know, Mr Brodie. We spoke this morning. I left my number at your mother's. And by the way it's Miss.'

Her tone was schoolmarmy and her face registered at best disinterest, at worst hostility. I could see why she'd been left on the shelf. 'Well, *miss*, I've come at your bidding. How can I help?'

She cocked her head to one side. 'Frankly, I don't know, Mr Brodie. It wasn't my idea. My client seemed to think there might be some advantage in it.' She made it plain that she found *that* idea pretty bizarre.

Don't ever believe that Scotland doesn't have a class system. That we're somehow immune from England's stratification by birth and vowel sounds. For one dizzying moment, her cultivated accent pushed me right back to my first days and weeks at Glasgow University, surrounded by so much privilege and gentile upbringing that I could hardly open my mouth for fear of sounding like an Ayrshire farmer. When I worked up courage to ask a girl out I felt like Rabbie Burns arriving among Edinburgh's society: patronised. Samantha Campbell with her common touch – call me Sam – opened old wounds.

I felt my ears heating up. Then six years of soldiering cut in. I'd led a company of 250 fighting men. Accents meant nothing. Only actions. Only whether you got up out of your foxhole and charged when the piper blew.

'He was my friend. Is,' I added.

'He needs one,' she said dryly. 'Come on.'

She turned and led the way down the gloomy hall and into a gloomy room. Despite bookcases filling the walls floor to ceiling, there was no room for the piles of papers bound in red ribbon and marching inexorably across the floor. She climbed nimbly round one pile and dropped into her seat. I did the same on my side of her desk. She had only one file on it. It didn't take much talent for upside-down reading to read Hugh Donovan's name across it. While she leafed through the file, I sat getting more and more huffy at her being so offhand with me. I'd made this pilgrimage to her office on behalf of her client whose neck I'd wanted to wring for half my life. Why should I make any effort to prevent someone else doing it for me? Officially.

I studied her. Several years older than me. Late thirties, maybe forty, but far from the dour old man I'd been expecting. She was no doe-eyed dolly, but then she didn't seem to be trying. Face pale and devoid of all make-up so that the freckles stood proud on her nose. I bet they annoyed her. Short ash-blonde hair pulled hard back behind each ear with kirby grips. Blue eyes obscured by thick glasses. Slim figure in grey cardigan and skirt. Maybe ten years ago she'd been the cliché of the mousy librarian who could turn into the slinky vamp, in the right light, with the right make-up and with the right amount of beauty sleep. Maybe a week's worth.

She looked up and pulled off her specs, showing the dark rings of tiredness and the beginnings of lines at the corners. 'Finished, Mr Brodie?'

'Sorry?'

'The inspection.'

'It's my job.' I hoped she hadn't been reading my mind.

'Oh, yes. The crime reporter.' She made it sound like a distasteful hobby, like eating your own toenail clippings. Hislop was one thing but why should a bloody lawyer be so snooty about what I did? I was getting fed up with this. I didn't need to be here, especially for a back-stabbing bastard like Hugh Donovan. I stood up, my anger at the whole damn thing boiling up inside me. Enough.

'Shall I come back when you're having a better day?'

She coloured. The pale skin glowed over her cheeks and on her neck. She rubbed the bridge of her nose where it was marked by her specs. 'You're very touchy.'

'I don't like being anywhere under sufferance.'

'Sorry, sorry. Please sit down.' She took a deep breath and placed her hands flat on the table as though to support her tired body. 'I shouldn't have been so rude. It was Hugh's idea but I *am* glad you're here. I'm at the end of my tether. You're my last resort.' She smiled ruefully.

'Things are that bad?' I whistled.

She ignored my sarcasm. 'That's if you're willing to help?'

I shrugged and retook my seat. 'How?'

She tapped the file. 'We have an appeal in two weeks' time. I've got nothing.'

'Two weeks!'

'You weren't that easy to track down!'

'What are the options? I mean what possible grounds?'

She raised three fingers. 'One, a wrong decision on any question of law. Two, the verdict of the jury was unreasonable, or not supported by the evidence. Three, miscarriage of justice. I can't see any one of them applying here.'

'Do you think he did it?'

She sat back. 'That's irrelevant. I'm an advocate. My job is to defend.'

'But it must add a wee bit of conviction, make you more determined, if you genuinely think your client is innocent?'

She was reddening again. Not a useful faculty in an advocate, I'd have thought. Or a poker player.

'I put everything into this case, Brodie. Absolutely everything. No one could have done more.'

'You could have got him off!'

'I got close!'

'What do you mean?'

'Didn't you know? It was a majority verdict.'

'A majority?' I was astonished.

'I thought you were once one of Glasgow's finest? This is Scotland. A jury comprises fifteen men and women drawn randomly from the public. You always get a result. Even if it's not the one you want.'

I'd forgotten; been away too long. 'What were the numbers?'

'We'll never know if it was fourteen to one or eight to seven. The court won't say.'

I sat stunned. 'But surely they can't hang a man if eight think he's guilty and seven don't. Can you? Surely?'

'Oh, yes, they can. They do. And they will. Unless we can find something new to put in our plea.' She waited for me to say something smart.

'Any chance of a cup of tea?'

49

'I'll see if I can disturb the sleeping dragon out there.' She got up and went out. I heard a brief, sharp exchange, and then she was back.

'It'll come. Eventually. I hope you're not allergic to strychnine. Now, where were we?'

'At the risk of being boring, can I ask you again if you think he did it? I haven't seen Hugh since our teens. We parted on bad terms. I've been dragged up here to try to help him. As of now, I've seen nothing, heard nothing that suggests he's other than guilty. I'd just like to know what you think. You, more than anyone, will have sifted the evidence. I need some … encouragement.'

She pulled her glasses down her nose. Her clear blue eyes focussed fixedly on mine. 'I think Hugh Donovan is innocent. OK?'

'OK. Until proven otherwise.' I took out my notepad. 'You'd better start with the trial. What was the evidence?'

She opened the file at a document with tab on it. 'This is a summary of the trial report. Not that I need it.' She looked up at me and held up her left hand with the fingers and thumb splayed open. She closed down her pinkie with her right hand. 'First there are the clothes with the blood on them.'

'The child's clothes?'

'The child's *and* Hugh's.'

'Both of them?' Damn.

She nodded. 'The child's shirt and short trousers, simmet and pants. No socks or shoes. He was playing barefoot. A lot of them do over there.' She nodded towards the badlands of the Gorbals. 'Saves the shoes for school. The clothes were found rolled up in a bucket under Hugh's sink in the flat. A stupid place to hide them. But there they were. And the blood matches the boy's. A rhesus positive.'

'Common enough round here, as I recall.'

'Agreed. But they were wrapped inside a shirt of Hugh's.' She raised her hand to stop me asking how they knew it was Hugh's. 'Inside the collar was a label. They'd put it on in the hospital so the patients wouldn't lose their clothes. It said "Cpl H. Donovan, RAF".'

Of course. They'd done it with mine when I was convalescing in Alex.

She went on, 'He says one of his shirts was stolen.'

We both raised our eyebrows. 'What else?'

She sighed and pressed down a second finger. 'The murder weapon. A knife wrapped up in the same bucket. It had the boy's blood on it too. A bread knife, so the serrations held the stains very nicely thank you.'

'Prints?'

'A smudged set of Hugh's on the handle.'

I winced. 'You've seen his hands. He couldn't hold a knife.'

'The prosecution implied he could if he wanted to. The jury seemed to agree.'

'Anything else? Witnesses swearing they saw him killing the boy?'

'Nearly.' She lowered a third finger. 'Knowledge of the crime scene. Hugh knew a couple of things that only the murderer or his accomplice could know. The number of stab wounds: seven. That the body was naked. And that there were signs of strangulation.'

'Christ.'

A fourth finger dropped. 'There were also traces of heroin in the boy's body.'

'Dear God! But that doesn't tie the murder to Hugh,' I said desperately.

She raised one eyebrow. 'But you can imagine what a meal

the prosecution made of it. This junkie forcing himself on an innocent child. Turning him into a ravening dope fiend like himself. The jury's eyes were rolling around like a game of bools.'

'Did they know that Hugh used to go out with her?' I choked on her name.

'The boy's mother, Fiona? Yes. It just gave the jury something else to nibble away at. Jilted lover, betrayal of the woman who befriended him, et cetera. Hugh said you knew her too?'

Oh, yes, Fiona. I knew you. I nodded. 'Is that it?'

She turned her extended thumb down, leaving a clenched fist. 'Just one more teeny wee thing. He confessed.'

TEN

rubbed my face with both hands. Short of a Pathé newsreel
showing Hugh murdering the boy, this case was as watertight as a Clyde steamer.

'To all five?'

'Just Rory.'

'Duress?' I tried.

'Do you mean is it likely he was forced to confess? Yes. I have
absolutely no doubt. Around here, your former colleagues are
not known for their compassion towards child molesters, far
less child murderers. When I first saw Hugh, his face – such as
it is – was badly bruised and so was his body. Resisting arrest,
they said. By the time he got to trial the marks had pretty well
vanished. And of course the police claimed they'd used kid
gloves.'

I nodded. It wasn't new. I'd seen plenty of interrogations that
involved gentle persuasion with a truncheon or a boot. Disillu-
sionment was one of the reasons I joined the army, not that I
found many choirboys among my fellow NCOs.

'Did he retract his confession in court?'

She leaned towards me, and shook her head. 'Not as such.
Hugh was – is – a sick man. Half the time he doesn't know what
day it is. They gave him some painkillers during the trial but

either too little or sometimes too much. And there was something about him. A sense of fatality. He just wanted it all over with. The trial. The pain. His life.'

'The poor wee bastard.'

'That he is,' she said. We were silent for a moment.

A thought struck me. '*Were* there any witnesses? Anyone hear anything? Hugh says he lived up a close. Rented a single-end next door to a family. A mother and four kids. What did they have to say?'

She shook her head. 'The police took a statement from them at the time, just after his arrest. They said they saw nothing, heard nothing.'

'Did you question them? At the trial?'

She sighed. 'They weren't at the trial. They'd vanished.'

'Vanished? How do you mean? There were five of them, were there not?'

'Seems they were evicted a few weeks before the trial started. No forwarding address. No one knows where they went. It happens. The police say they exhausted all lines of inquiry. Convenient eh?'

'Smelly.'

There was a tinkling of china behind me and then the door was bashed back. The receptionist came in bearing a tray and a grudge. She plonked it down with an unnecessary clatter and 'Yer tea, miss' and returned to her lair. For the first time Samantha Campbell and I smiled at each other. It made her look younger.

'What do you think, then?' she asked.

'I think we're in bother.' I slurped at my tea. 'Can I read the trial report myself?'

'Help yourself.' She swivelled the papers round to face me. 'I'll leave you to it. I'll be back in an hour. I have another client to see.'

I leaned over the desk and began reading and flicking through the papers. She'd summarised it well. It all stacked up. The verdict seemed a foregone conclusion. And yet, and yet, the very neatness and comprehensiveness of the proof was too good to be true. If I'd wanted to build a procurator fiscal's case I could hardly have done better. Was it just *too* pat? Why had Hugh not got rid of the bloodstained clothes? Or the knife?

Then there was the question of when the boy had died. He'd been missing for a week. Six and a half days. Last seen on the Monday around teatime with his pals, then found at eight-thirty the following Monday morning by the coalman come to deliver some more bags to the coal cellars behind the tenements. The police pathologist reckoned he'd been dead for two to three days. There was very little blood in the coal cellar. It was likely that the boy had died elsewhere and been dumped. So where had Hugh – or the murderer – hidden the boy for three or four days? Surely not in his single room? The police had searched it early on. Could he have kept the kid quiet for four days? Not a whimper? Using the heroin?

Reading the detectives' reports, I recognised several names. The Chief Superintendent in charge was George Muncie. I remembered him from before the war, a big florid man, with red hair and a temper to match and a high opinion of himself. He ran my old Eastern Division as his personal fiefdom. Reporting to him was the case officer, Detective Chief Inspector Willie Silver. He must have got over his drink problem to have risen from detective sergeant in '39. Or maybe he'd got better at hiding it. As Sam Campbell had put it, 'Glasgow's finest'.

'Anything?'

I turned as the lawyer came back to her office. 'I need to get below the words here. I need to speak to people, find out what the forensic boys *thought* rather than just what they wrote. I don't like this gap between the boy's abduction and his death. Where was he? Did you ask Hugh?'

'Of course. So did the prosecution. And the judge. He had no answer.'

'Well, I guess he wouldn't, if he didn't do it.'

'The prosecution just claimed he was covering up his bestiality or at best was in a drug-induced stupor. Either way he was a sick animal for whom hanging would be a mercy.'

'This heroin habit of his. Did they ever find his supplier?'

'I don't think they looked. Is that relevant?'

'I have no idea. It's just a loose end. Another part of the jigsaw. Hugh didn't have contact with many folk. One of them was the supplier. It might give us a picture of his movements that week.'

'Anything else?'

'Witnesses? Friends?

'The only one who seemed to stick up for him was his priest, Father Cassidy. He kept telling Hugh he believed he was innocent. But even *his* faith seemed to waver as the case went on. But he still goes to see him at Barlinnie. He might be able to point you at other people who knew Hugh. Including the pusher. I'll give you his address.'

She scribbled his name and address on a sheet of paper, tore it off and handed it to me. I looked at it. She was staring at me.

'What?'

'My turn. From what you've just read, what's your verdict?'

'If I was on the jury? And only using the evidence? Guilty.'

'But?'

'As an ex-copper with a suspicious mind, it's a little too watertight. I've never seen such an open-and-shut case.'

'Can you suspend judgement?'

'I'm not sure why.'

'Will you at least stay and help?'

I thought I'd hardened myself to pleading eyes. But reading the trial papers had set up an itch I needed to scratch.

'I suppose it does. For a few days anyway. I'll need to get the rest of this week off from my boss at the *London Bugle*.' I was pretty sure I could make up the time by working late or week-ends, as long as I could knock up five hundred words of fearless crime reporting to keep my editor interested. I had a couple of half worked-out ideas that didn't require more research. I could write about Hugh's predicament but it would have little interest for London readers. Besides, I'd just tie myself in knots wondering whose side I was on. Little chance of journalistic objectivity. And it would feel like I was using him.

'Just use the phone here.'

'I'm also going to need digs for a few nights. Any suggestions?'

She looked at me coolly for a long few seconds.

'Do you snore? Get drunk and fall downstairs? Leave clothes on the floor? Leave toilet seats up?'

'I can't swear to the loo seat, but no to the rest. Though I'm not teetotal. Is this a temperance hotel you're suggesting?'

'I couldn't make that claim. My folks left me their house. It's fairly big. There's a spare room and bathroom. In truth, there's a choice.'

Was she just trying to make up for the initial brusqueness? I doubted it was animal passion. No need to lock my door at night. She didn't look much like a man-eater. I hesitated. I didn't want to be under constant inspection by this tough spinster who looked as if she had a preference for cold baths and hard beds. Cold beds, certainly.

'Neighbours?'

She stood up, riffled through her bag and placed a key on the table. 'It won't be the first time I've scandalised them. If your reputation can stand it, so can mine.'

Scandalised the West End? Not washing her milk bottles would be enough. 'What do you charge?'

'Hand over your ration book and one pound ten for a week's grub. Nothing fancy. The bed's free, if – and only if – you come up with something new for the appeal. Deal?'

'Miss Campbell, it's a deal. Thank you.'

'Call me Sam. Everyone else does. Do you prefer Doug or Douglas?'

I shrugged. 'Most just call me Brodie.' Only my mother used my first name. And Hugh, of course. I wasn't about to get intimate with Samantha – call me Sam – Campbell.

'Brodie it is. Are you going to try to see Father Cassidy now? Leave your case and I'll take it back with me.'

'Sure?'

She pointed at the corner. She scribbled her own address on a sheet of paper, together with the numbers of the trams that ran by. It was further into the city and up on the smart hillside of Kelvingrove Park. Very nice. I left her gazing at her piles of paper as though by sheer force of will they would file themselves.

ELEVEN

The Gorbals were legendary. In Kilmarnock, among the private pink and red sandstone houses that laced the better streets, the very word was synonymous with dirt and degradation. Even the working class of Kilmarnock, my class, in our roughcast council estates, gazed down with shaking heads on our brethren just up the Glasgow road. The worst waster in the most run-down part of Kilmarnock clung to his illusion of being a rung above his counterpart south of the Clyde – a speculative ranking based on the size and numbers of rats patrolling the outside toilets.

For really it was only a question of scale. You'd find TB, rickets, polio and malnutrition in any sizeable Scottish town. It was just that those Glasgow wastelands stretched over a quarter of central Glasgow and were as densely packed and aromatic as a giant box of herring. And whereas Kilmarnock had its fair share of louts ready for a rammy on a Friday night, the Gorbals were infested with razor-wielding gangs like the Beehive Boys. If disease didn't get you, a knife would. In the *Kilmarnock Standard* we'd read of bottle fights at the Glasgow dance halls and knew that there would be Gorbals' thugs behind it, yet taking a tram ride through the area with your eyes part closed would have left the impression of wide streets

and fine Victorian sandstone buildings, a township that should
have turned out model citizens.

A closer look uncovered the deep problems: cobbled streets
full of patched holes and covered in filth because the Corpora-
tion dustmen couldn't be persuaded to visit without an armed
escort; families living ten to a room; sewage systems literally
bursting at the seams; and mass unemployment and illiteracy.
For the last hundred years the Gorbals had been a magnet for
the dispossessed. Jews fleeing Russian pogroms, Highland
clearances, Irish tattie famines and, lately, Nazi persecution.

I saw the bad side first hand in the thirties when I was
drafted in to help a team of detectives from Southern Division
in Craigie Street track down a gang of rapists terrorising the
streets. They'd wait for a gaggle of lassies to come home from
the dance halls – the jigging – and pick off one of them as she
entered the dark close of her tenement. There was enough
amorous activity going on in every entry across the Gorbals on
a Thursday night (winching night) for muffled shouts and evil
grappling to go unnoticed – until the morning and the girl was
found battered, weeping and bloody in the stairwell.

But my abiding memory was the stench in the worst of the
closes. The smell of urine and rubbish. The hot, steamy reek of
humanity piled on top of each other in the houses themselves.
Cooking, defecating, procreating, fighting: like a troop of Nean-
derthals.

And yet, and yet ...

If you looked past the gang warfare, the drunks and the no-
users there was a pride and a dignity about so many of the
people, especially the women, the mothers. Aged thirty and
looking sixty after rearing eight weans, she should have given
up long ago. Instead she'd drag her kids to the kirk, steal a
shilling from her man's drinking money for a few ribbons for

her daughter's sixteenth birthday, stitch and mend clothes till there were more mends than original. And stand with blackened eye and bruised mouth, refusing to bring charges against her drunken husband, instead helping him home from the nick to start the cycle all over again.

And they'd dream, these stubborn women, they'd dream of one day walking out of the Gorbals. A wee place of their own, maybe down by the coast, at Irvine, or Saltcoats. Or if they couldn't make it themselves, then maybe one of the kids would get a trade, break free, allow them to visit them in *their* wee hoose. That would be grand. I wondered how Fiona had got used to it. Would she stick around now?

We Protestants attended the kirk. The Catholics went to the chapel. This Gorbals chapel had been built of the same red sandstone as every other building in the area. Like them it had acquired a black sheen of soot and grime blowing in from the chimneys and the shipyards and the factories around the city. The blast furnaces of the Dixon's Blazes just a mile away belted out enough fire and brimstone, night and day, to have smeared an inch coating over the entire Hutchesontown division every week. Even cleaned up, this chapel was no cathedral, just a simple pile of stones with a cross atop its peaked roof and some undistinguished stained-glass windows on its façade.

Inside was different. It was always a shock for a wee boy who'd grown up in the austerity of the bare wood and plaster of a Presbyterian church to be confronted with bloody icons and shimmering light from mass candles. The whole place looked like a fairy grotto to my eyes, though the scenes of blood and torment on the glowing glass screens were a far cry from Neverland. Why is suffering so attractive to the godly? We shiver at tales of Aztec priests and their penchant for gory offerings. But at the bloody heart of all Christian sects is the notion that God demanded the sacrifice of his son. As painfully as possible. I remember getting my ears clipped in Boys Brigade bible class for questioning one of the scriptures. How did it go? *For God so loved the world, that he gave his only begotten Son, that whosoever believeth in him should not perish, but have everlasting life.* Then he arranged for him to bleed to death on a cross for the delectation of the crowds. The minister shut me up with a pat on the head and a promise that I'd understand when I was bigger. Maybe I needed more time.

I made my way nervously down the aisle, not knowing whether to call out or sing hallelujah. The chapel seemed empty – apart from its gaudy spirits. I neared the altar and stood feeling sinful (which shows how the bloody thing works) while Jesus hung there silently censuring my failure to genuflect or light a candle.

'Can I help you?'

The strong voice came from the side. A man was walking towards me, wearing an ankle-length black cassock surmounted by a wooden cross on a heavy chain. A dog collar completed the outfit. He was in his late fifties or early sixties, about my height but thin as a blade. His hair was a grey brush swept back from a face that registered openness and warmth in contrast with the accoutrements of his demanding creed.

'Is it confession you want, my son?' he asked, drawing closer. His Irish accent became more pronounced.

'I'm not of your faith ...' I reached for a word that didn't make me sound as though I owed him obeisance. I failed. 'Father.'

'We all need to unburden ourselves sometimes. I am happy to listen. You look troubled.'

'I am troubled. For a friend. Hugh Donovan.' I watched his

face. The smile slowly dimmed to be replaced by a mouth stretched by concern.

'Then you must be Douglas Brodie. Please follow me.'

The vestry was much less gaudy than the body of the chapel. Bare, apart from the obligatory man being crucified, some books on a shelf, a small desk and two beaten-up armchairs. We sank into them. He leaned forward, his cross swinging out over his knees.

'He said you would come, Douglas. May I call you Douglas?'

No, you may not. 'I'm used to Brodie. And …?'

He smiled. 'Patrick will do. This is a terrible business. I never expected it to go this way.'

'You thought he was innocent?'

He nodded. 'I've known Hugh for about a year now. He's known great pain and temptation. I don't think I would have had his strength. Now he needs all his courage to get him through the next few weeks. And to face whatever God has in mind for him. It's good that he has a friend he can talk to at this time. Other than me, of course. I visit him as often as I can.'

'Next time, can you have a word with them about more pain relief? Unless you think it's God's punishment?'

Father Cassidy looked at me quizzically. 'The good Lord leaves mortal judgments to us. *His* judgment will come in the fullness of time.'

I felt foolish trying to provoke him. There's something about all men of the cloth, their quiet assurance and certainty, that makes me want to shake them. Just jealous, I guess. I finally lost all patience with superstition during my stints as a policeman and a soldier. Were the rampaging Derry Boys really a product of an all-seeing God? Were the concentration camps? If so, it was a queer way of showing love for the creatures built in your own image. Confronted by this grown man blithely uttering platitudes as though he believed every word, knowing he'd have an excuse for every Godly thunderbolt, labelled him – in my jaundiced view – an idiot or a charlatan. But I recognised that the same hard logic had made me substitute belief in a god – any god – for a belief in myself. That worked for a while. I blamed nobody but me for my failures and took quiet credit for my personal triumphs. But for the last six months, I seemed to have handed in my self-belief with my uniform.

'So what is your mortal judgment, Patrick?'

'If you believe all the evidence, then it's hard to go on thinking him innocent. But that doesn't mean I can't forgive him and offer him succour in his darkest hour.'

I wondered if Hugh had already known that hour. The first time he'd looked in a mirror after the bandages had come off.

'He still has an appeal,' I pointed out.

'Indeed. But Miss Campbell tells me she's got little new to work with.'

'I think that's why I was summoned.'

'*Do* you have something new, Brodie?' His shrewd eyes searched my face.

I shook my head. 'There are things that don't add up.' I explained the gap between the time of going missing and the time of death. 'But I don't have any leads. That's why I'm trying to talk to all the folk that knew Hugh. See if there was anything they can recall about his whereabouts that week.'

'It's a while ago now.'

'I know, but I'm desperate.'

He rubbed his chin. 'It was a difficult week. Fiona was distraught. I spent most of my time with her or out looking for the boy. Like everybody else.'

'You knew Fiona too?'

He smiled. 'There are not so many chapels round here. Yes, I've known her – and Rory, of course – for years. She lost her husband and now this.'

'God's will, eh, Patrick?'

The smile hardened. 'God gave us the freedom to choose our own path. It means we take responsibility for our actions and answer to Him later.'

'How does that help the innocent, like Fiona MacAuslan? Sorry, Fiona *Hutchinson*. It wasn't her fault her husband died in the war. Not her fault that her son was murdered.'

He pulled himself upright and clasped his left hand round his cross. 'We cannot know the mind of God. Sometimes from great grief a stronger faith grows.'

'That will be a great comfort to Hugh Donovan when they hang him!'

I hadn't realised how angry I was over this whole damn business. I was angry at being dragged up here away from the new life I was trying to construct in London. I was angry at having to rake over the past. I was angry at the mirror being held up to me here in my old stamping ground. Angry at reaching thirty-four with a great education and nothing to show for it. No wife, no children, no career, no peace. Angry at being so pathetic. We sat in awkward silence for a few seconds.

'I will help you in any way I can, Brodie. But I'm not sure how ...'

'This drug dealer. The one that hooked Hugh. Do you have any idea where I might run into him?'

'I don't have a name. But I suppose you could try Hugh's haunts. The pubs he frequented. Doyle's at Gorbals Cross. Or the Mally Arms.'

'What about the neighbours? The ones who mysteriously vanished after the murder. Do you know where they went?'

He shook his head. 'They weren't of my faith. I never knew them. But I'm afraid it's typical of life here. I hear they fell behind with rent.'

Ripples. Drop a pebble in a pond and watch the effect. It doesn't take much to snap the thin anchor chain of some people's lives, capsizing them, sending them tumbling and twisting off into the murk. I glanced at my watch. There was nothing else for me here except more platitudes. Whereas the bars were open in half an hour, and I had a legitimate reason for a pub crawl.

TWELVE

In one sense I was looking forward to a drink. The day's revelations had taken their toll on my equilibrium. In another sense I was wary of entering one of Hugh's watering holes. Before the war when I did my five-year stint at Tobago Street nick, drink was the blight of every evening shift. It wasn't so much in the pubs we had trouble but in the parks and walkways by the Clyde. Gangs of broken men getting tanked up on their own special brew: a mix of meths and cheap red wine that they called 'Jake' or 'Johnnie Jump Up'. It was hard to say which of the two ingredients was the real poison. I reckoned it was a recipe handed down from the Viking invasions. It would certainly account for the berserkers roaming the streets on a Saturday night.

Those that could afford to drink the real stuff – a half-gill of Bell's chased down by a half-pint of Tennent's – blew their pay packets at the weekend in pubs that were little more than tiled caves for garrulous drunks. Glasgow's East End and the Gorbals itself were littered with dingy wee hostelries that refused to serve women, as much from embarrassment as from sensitivity to the gentler sex. Not that any self-respecting woman would have demeaned herself by standing ankle deep in soggy sawdust amidst a jabbering crowd of flush-faced men in flat caps. A woman's role in the Friday-night revels was to stand at the shipyard gate, ready when the whistle went, to tackle her man and extract enough cash from his pay packet to feed her and her ragged weans for another week. I've seen six-footers reduced to shame-faced mumbling at the factory gate by a tiny wee fury wanting to know where he'd hidden the ten-shilling overtime she knew he'd worked that week.

So it was with some trepidation that I approached the bunker-like Mally Arms off Gorbals Cross. It was just past opening time but already there were a few old soaks at the bar. There was fresh sawdust on the floor and fresh tobacco smoke wreathing the air. There was nothing else fresh. Dark rings surrounded the corroded spittoons while a fireplace gasped out a thin trail of smoke from glowing dross. The chairs and tables had only recently been recovered from the wreck of the *Titanic*.

The bar itself was horseshoe shaped with a partition dividing the public from the saloon bar. The lounge had chairs with arms and lacked spittoons. The public had a dartboard and a snooker table whose green baize looked as if it had hosted the final Somme offensive.

I chose to pay a penny extra for a pint in the comparative luxury of the saloon and pushed through the dividing door. It was empty. I ordered a stout and picked up the *Racing Mirror* to see what I might have lost at Ayr. Not that I ever put a bet on a nag or a dog. Not since I'd heard from my dad about the tricks of the trade such as making a whippet swallow a packet of ten Woodbine before a race. I can't recall whether it slowed the poor beast down or fired him up. But it did seem to make a nonsense of the form guides. The paper was only of use as camouflage. I glanced at it long enough for appearances then called the barman over. I was taken aback to hear my accent dropping back into the nasal grooves of my boyhood. Self-preservation behind enemy lines.

'Got anything to eat here, pal?'

'Pies. The wife heats them up. Be ready in about ten minutes.'

'That'll do the job, fine. I'll start wi' the one and see how it goes.'

I whiled away the time with the racing horoscopes until a steaming plate came over the counter. It held a round mutton pie, sweating and drowning in its own juices. Its sides sagged under its own internal conflict.

'Sauce?' the barman asked, and plonked down a bottle of brown.

Surprisingly the pie tasted better than it had any right to. Maybe it was the sauce. Maybe it was nostalgia. I even contemplated a second one; this could be a long night and it was better to have some ballast on board, even at half a pint a time. I didn't want to be rolling into Sam Campbell's house singing 'Glasgow belongs to me'. Not the first night. Instead I got the man in conversation while the pub was still quiet. This was going to be delicate. I was relying on people's relish for discussing a hanging.

'Did you know this fella Donovan, the one that's to hang for killing that wean?'

He stopped wiping some smears on to his glass. 'Who's asking?'

'I used to know him. He ran about with a pal of mine.'

'Does that make him a pal o' yours?' There was an edge to his voice.

'Naw. No way. I just saw him about.' I wondered if tonight I'd beat St Pete's record for denying *his* friend.

The barman didn't look convinced. 'See if he was, then yon's the last drink you'll taste in here. I'll no serve any pal of that murdering bastard in this establishment.'

'I don't blame you. The guy was obviously a bampot. Did he look the type? I mean were you surprised?'

'You're not the polis, are you? Ah thought all this was by?'

I wondered if the smell of the uniform ever leaves you.

'No. But you've got a good eye. I used to be. Here in Glasgow before the war. Now I work in London. Reporter.'

'Christ, no' another one! They've been round here a dozen times.'

'This is personal. I'm just up visiting my mother. I was curious. He looked a normal sort of fella when I last saw him. They say he was badly burnt?'

The barman looked around and then leaned over the bar at me. 'Like a horror show. Poor sod. I suppose it turned him. Nae excuse, mind.'

'But he was a regular?'

'Oh, aye. He'd sit through in the public. Quiet in the corner. Never any bother. Kept his hat doon. Didnae want folk to see his face. Nae wonder. My wife couldnae handle it. I had to serve him.'

Now came the hard questions. 'Did he ever talk to anyone? Any friends?'

He shook his head. 'No' what you'd call friends exactly.'

'Fill me up. Will you take one yourself?' I pushed my glass over to him.

'I'll put one in the tank. A wee goldie. For later. Thanks.'

'But he had some acquaintances?'

He leaned even closer. 'There's always guys selling stuff roon' here.' He tapped his nose.

'What sort of stuff? Fags? Meat ...?'

'A' that. But if you want something special ...' He drew himself back. 'Anyroad, I've telt you enough. I don't know you from Adam.'

70

'Fair enough, friend,' I said. 'But, look, I've got a wee habit of my own. D'ye ken what I'm saying?' I tapped the inside of my arm. 'If you know anywhere I can get hold of some stuff, I'd make it worth your while.' I took out a ten-bob note and laid it on the counter. 'That's for the pie and your own drink. Keep the change.' I made to go.

'Hing on, pal.' He signed me to come closer. 'If you can wait till the morn's night, there might be somebody who can help. Different nights, different pubs. He comes by here on a Thursday. Regular as the coalman. About seven. OK?' He gave me the heaviest wink I'd seen since Max Wall at the Windmill.

I did my best to return the wink and went looking for Hugh's other pub in case it was its turn to be visited tonight. If I had no luck there I could come to the Mally Arms tomorrow night for a pie and a hit.

Doyle's bar at Gorbals Cross was scarcely more salubrious. But the clientele seemed less likely to fall down with consumption. The beer seemed less watered too. Maybe there was a connection. I decided to play this differently. People are always ready to talk to you in Scotland. Strangers will wish you a good morning so they can comment on the weather before getting on to the important stuff like football. Women will strike up an intimate discussion about varicose veins on the bus with perfect strangers. Put that same propensity in a pub, add alcohol and time on their hands, and you'll get their life story in a flash.

It was just after seven o'clock and I gazed through the fug looking for some likely candidates. I discounted the wee men dressed in their shabby work clothes stopping in for a snifter before facing their pale wife. I ignored the tables where there was a steady clack and slide of dominoes. I was looking for someone whose clothes were less frayed and slept in, who slipped around the room stirring the little groups like a breeze through trees, going about his dirty business, eyes swivelling. No one fitted the bill.

I sat down to wait with an abandoned copy of the *Daily Record*. I read it cover to cover. It didn't take long. Ink and paper were still at a premium and the *Record* was down to a dozen pages. So I read it carefully, especially the reports of local crimes, to get a feel for this mean city. Nothing much seemed to have changed since I was last patrolling the streets. The gangs were still in charge of the East End but seemed more organised and less given to mass razor battles just for the fun of it. Chief Constable Percy Sillitoe had taken them on and given them a good hiding in the years before the war. Sillitoe's Cossacks earned a justly feared respect with their mounted baton charges against rioting Orange marchers. But the gangs hadn't gone away. They'd metamorphosed into organised criminality, protection rackets their speciality.

Today's paper reported that internecine feuding had resulted in petrol bombs through windows and three men's faces being slashed to ribbons in a pub fight. No wonder the police had to be such hard men. There was no quarter asked or given out there. I never had any problem with meeting force with force. It was the only response gangs like the Norman Conks understood and responded to. But the unbridled power assumed by the police led to a widespread cavalier attitude to the application of the rule of law. Some units began offering their own insurance policies against raids by their fellow officers. Others took backhanders to avert their steely gaze from illegal gambling, knocking shops and smuggling through the port. It wasn't what I joined for. It wouldn't pull me back. Call me naïve.

I turned back to the news. Four men had died at a party in the Blackhill scheme; industrial alcohol had been the drink of choice. A child had gone missing in Govan. I hoped for a happier outcome than for poor Fiona's wean. And just reading the paper reminded me that I needed to get into the local archives and see the reporting coverage of Hugh's trial. I wanted to get a feel for the case. It was hard coming at it cold. The newspapers would tell me what we were up against trying to win an appeal. They would also chronicle the police procedure day by day, within the limits of reporting constraints.

I sensed a different current in the bar. I looked up and saw two men sidling up to people, saying a few words, getting a headshake, and then moving on. Twice a transaction took place. I waited at my table by the wall, half-engrossed in the paper. I looked up when a shadow fell across the table. He was young, badly shaven, with crossed, jumpy eyes. He nodded at me.

'A'right, pal?'

'Aye, fine. You?' I asked.

His eyes stopped and focused, sort of. 'You polis?'

What was it about my personal aroma? 'Not now. Used to be.'

He looked triumphant. 'Wance a polis, always a polis. You're no' from roon here.'

'Kilmarnock. But I live in London now. Just visiting a pal.'

'Oh, aye. Need anything while you're here? A wee set-you-up for your holidays?'

'What've you got?'

He sat down opposite me and lit a fag. 'Whit do you need?'

'The same stuff as Hugh Donovan.'

His smile dissolved and his eyes started their St Vitus's dance again. 'Who the fuck are you, pal? You *are* the fucking polis, are ye no'?'

'What would the polis want with you? Donovan's for hanging. They got what they wanted. I was just reading in here…' I tapped the paper, certain that my new friend hadn't been '…that he liked a wee hit now and again. It didn't take too long to work out where he might be getting it. So I thought I'd try out a couple of places round here. Seems I got lucky.'

'Maybe you are. Maybe you're not.' Suspicion had set his body jangling like a plucked harp. He looked round and signalled to his buddy to come over.

His pal was older and steadier. His left ear had a lobe missing and the scar ran on to his cheek. He sat down and inspected me. 'What's going on?'

'This yin's playing smart, so he is. He's no' from around here. Wants the same as Hugh Donovan, so he says.'

'Does he now. Would that be your face melted or your neck stretched?'

'That's a good yin, Fergie.'

'Shut up.' Fergie kept his eyes on mine and waited for my reaction.

'I was thinking more of some pain relief,' I said, rubbing my leg. 'Shrapnel.'

'We can make it hurt even more, if you're pissin' us around.'

'Look, if you don't want the business, forget it. You came to me.' I studiously picked up my paper and pretended to read. I heard the snick just before I could move. The blade of a flick-knife sliced up through the paper and left it hanging in my hands in two bits.

THIRTEEN

'You're not a reader then,' I said.

'What do you want? Specifically,' asked Fergie.

'The hard stuff, the Big H. What's your price?'

'Introductory price is a quid a shot.'

'Quality?'

'The best.'

'How do I know?'

'You don't. Until you try it.'

'Fair enough. One hit.' I began to dig into my pocket.

'Not here. In there.' He jerked his head towards the toilet. He got up and walked towards it, expecting me to follow. His cross-eyed pal sat grinning at me.

'You don't get twa invites,' he said.

I got up and walked after him, rolling up my sliced newspaper as I went. I pulled the door and went in. There was a second door in front of me.

'In here,' the voice called.

I pushed through the second door into a white-tiled room with a trough running at an angle along two of the walls and into a gutter. The stink of urine stung my nostrils. Fergie was waiting, back to the far wall, hands in his pockets. Behind me I heard the first door open again. I tightened my tube of paper

75

between both hands and moved further into the fetid room. As the second door began to open Fergie made his move. He drew his right hand out of his pocket. It held a black stub. He pressed the side. It snicked open. The knife gleamed bright and sharp in the dull air.

Fergie's eyes slid off me to the man behind me. I turned in time to see his pal raise a clasp razor and make his strike. I swung my rolled-up paper in a fast uppercut. Roll a newspaper tight and, point first, you have a tube as strong as iron. It took him right in the windpipe. His eyes bulged and he made a strangled gasp. The razor fell from his hand. He was dropping to his knees, gurgling, as I swung back to Fergie. The shock was clearing from Fergie's face and contorting into anger.

'Ya fucker, ye!' His arm sliced through the air at my head. I flung my left forearm up against his. I got lucky. Sort of. I hit his wrist. The knife popped from his numbed hand, glanced off my forehead and clattered to the tiles. I followed through with my trusty tube. It caught him on the side of the head, just by the ear. He tumbled against the wall and fell to his knees. I knew it wasn't a killer blow. So I stepped forward and kicked him in the belly as hard as I could. He doubled up on the piss-wet floor, floundering and sucking for air. I drew back my foot to kick his head in then stopped.

'Who do you work for?' I changed my aim and kicked him in the kidneys. He jerked and writhed.

'I said, who's your boss? The next one's your ugly face!'

He waved at me, gasping. 'You're. Fucking. Dead. Pal. You. Know. That.'

I stood back. I stamped on the hand that was wandering towards the knife. He squealed. I kicked the knife away.

'Tell me who your boss is.'

His face was engorged with rage and pain. 'You'll find oot soon enough, ya bastard!' I raised my foot so he could see the row of good metal tacks.

'Slattery. Dermot Slattery. That's who! Ask anybody around here. You'll soon ken who you've messed wi'.'

A name. A name I recognised from before the war. One of the top gangs in Glasgow. Let's see where it took me. I dropped my now bent newspaper and inspected the other man. He was choking to death. I leaned over him and ripped his collar and tie open. I pulled his head back to clear his broken air passage. It might do for a while. Something wet was dribbling into my left eye. I touched my head and found blood seeping down my face. I stuck my hankie on it.

'Call an ambulance for him, Fergie. And tell Slattery I'd like a chat. Tell him I'm an old friend of Hugh Donovan. The name's Brodie.'

I swung out of the doors and into the pub. There were expectant faces. Their stares changed to puzzlement and then turned away as I walked through them. A few began to head towards the exits. So did I. Outside I got my bearings and began to walk towards the address Samantha Campbell had given me. It was north of the Clyde, in the smart West End. A world away from the Gorbals slums.

It was ten o'clock when I found myself outside a terraced three-storey Georgian house in the commanding heights of Kelvingrove Park. A fine pile for a lawyer. I'm not the jealous type. But I imagine that the rise of Sam's family to this magnificence was a shorter journey than mine from Kilmarnock's tenements to … well, where, exactly? A rented flat in London? I bet she never needed a bursary to get to *her* academy, far less another one to go to university. I bet she slotted in as nice as ninepence to the social whirl at Glasgow. Born hearing the right accents. Growing up seeing the right manners. Wearing the right clothes. No, I wasn't jealous. Not much.

What I was was exhausted from the climb up the slopes. My head hurt and the pie and beer were sitting uncomfortably together. There was one faint light in a second-floor window. I climbed the three steps and used the big brass knocker. There was nothing for a long moment and then the door swung open. She inspected me for a second before standing aside.

'You look like you need a drink, Brodie.'

FOURTEEN

We sat on facing leather armchairs in a room filled with books. If ever I came into money, I'd have a house with a library. I'd sit there in my smoking jacket, with a good whisky in my hand, reading my way through the lot, starting from the top left.

She'd stoked up the fire and a warm glow dappled the room. Lumps of the real thing filled the scuttle. She must bribe her coalman. The book she'd been reading lay face down on a small table beside her. Rider Haggard, *Ayesha*. Her specs lay on top of it. I held a cold cloth against the cut in my head. The bleeding had stopped and the swelling was going down. In my right hand I fingered a heavy cut-crystal glass of good Scotch. My stomach felt easier. The pie and beer mix had succumbed to superior force. I'd just finished my story, and she'd just taken a big gulp of her own whisky. I like a girl who likes fine Scotch and takes it with water, not ginger.

'Good God, Brodie! Do you know who Dermot Slattery is?'

'In my day, before the war, he ran one of the biggest gangs. But I've lost touch.'

'Well, while you were off fighting for King and Country, Slattery was consolidating his grip on the underworld. The man's a total maniac. But an efficient maniac. He runs a razor gang that controls every dirty racket south of the Clyde. They've tried to pin murder charges on him three times to my knowledge.'

'I remember one of those trials. He had a good lawyer.' I didn't mean it as barbed as it sounded, but she handled it well.

'An advocate's job is to defend. We don't judge. He had the best. Laurence Dowdall, QC. I've seen him in action. If Adam had had Dowdall on his side, he'd still be in the Garden of Eden.'

'Better than you?'

She looked at me askance. 'You don't think a woman can do this job, do you, Brodie?'

I weighed my answer. 'Sam, it's not your sex. It's your experience. How many murder cases have you defended?'

She took another slug of Scotch. 'This was my first as lead, all right? But I've acted as junior advocate on plenty of others. And just to remind you, I turned an absolute certain guilty verdict into a majority!'

'How did you get the case?'

She inspected her glass, surprised that it was empty. 'That's a better question. I just got the call from the Faculty of Advocates in Edinburgh.'

'Why *you*, do you know?'

Her fine jaw jutted forward. 'I guess my time had come.'

'Do you really believe that?'

She got up like a jack-in-the-box. She walked to a table where a decanter sat, and poured herself another whisky. She added the same again of water. She brought the decanter over and splashed some into my glass. She walked over to the fire and stood, arms crossed round her slim torso, looking into the red embers.

'Do you know what I really think, Brodie? I think they chose me because they expected me to fail.' Her voice was weary and a little blurred.

I kept pushing. 'When did you think this? Before the trial? After? Why did you take it on?'

She turned, her face flushed and glowing. 'Because I needed to show them! Why do you think? And, by Christ, I nearly did!'

Breakfast was toast and milky tea taken in a rush. Sam looked strained in the morning light, her hair damp from the bath I'd heard her run at 6.30 a.m.

'Remind me to have more water with my Scotch, will you, Brodie? Or maybe just the water.'

'Head?'

'Eyes. Right between them.' She shook her sleek head, pushed on her specs and became the plain lawyer again. 'What now?' she asked, picking up an ancient leather briefcase and heading for the door.

'I'm going to read the papers.'

She looked quizzical.

'Down at the library. I'm going to soak up the atmosphere of the trial. See who was saying what. You get a different perspective from the pages of the fourth estate.'

She nodded. 'Makes sense. Kind of. Then what?'

'Then I'm going to look up some old pals. Could you get your helpful secretary to make an appointment this afternoon?' I gave her two names.

She wrote them down and glanced at her watch. 'Let's meet at my office at end of day. See what you've got. I need something. Anything!'

God Bless Andrew Carnegie. The man was mad for libraries, and Scotland – his birthplace – benefited enormously from his largesse. They say it was conscience money for the way he treated his workers in his American steel company. But he gave wee boys and girls like me a lust for knowledge beyond the bare bones of classroom teaching. His millions helped feed a hunger for the written word in Scotland that turned us from a nation of hard-working peasants and fishermen into an industrial force that helped shape the world. Or it did before the Depression.

The library I knew best, apart from the university one, was at Townhead, a half-hour's walk into and across the city centre on this blue-sky morning. By the time I was on my approach to the fine red sandstone pile I'd warmed myself up nicely and eased arm muscles stiff from my altercation in Doyle's.

I fondly inspected the building. There seemed to be no bomb damage, and the two statues stood proudly in their niches along the line of the parapet. Stepping inside to the solid carpentry and shining counter was like coming home.

I told the librarian I was researching a book about the trial and wanted access to the newspapers for the period of the trial and one month either side. So from November 1945 through to today, 4 April 1946.

He gazed at me over his half-specs. 'Do you know how many newspapers we take each week, sir?'

I shook my head.

'Fifty-five. Do you want them all?'

'Let's start with the *Glasgow Herald* and the *Scotsman*.' For the facts. 'And the *Daily Record* and *Glasgow Gazette*.' For the gossip.

I found a seat in the Reading Room under the great arched ceiling. Light streamed in from the roof-lights and boxed my wooden desk in sunlight. It raised nostalgia for university days, before the bloody war, before ... before this nightmare. In front of me would be a pile of French or German literature. Everything from Hugo to Euken, Dumas to Kafka, not newspapers with hysterical tales of child molestation and murder. I should have gone into teaching as ordained by my school rector and university tutors. There was even the offer of an assistant lecturer's position at the university. But the devil in me baulked at continuing a life buried in books. I'd grown up during the Great War, seen my father come back with medals, sergeant's stripes and a cough. Our tenement square was full of miners and miners' sons who braved death every day. My notion of what made a man was laid down early. It didn't involve conjugating irregular French verbs. I was twenty-one, robed and capped with learning, but untested.

Percy Sillitoe was recruiting men to enforce civilised behaviour on Glasgow's mean streets whether the mean citizens wanted it or not. I had a thirst for engaging with the real world for a few years before sinking back into the sweet embrace of intellectual argument and sentence parsing. I hadn't counted on a second world war breaking out. I had no idea just how much I would be tested.

A trolley arrived and the library assistant began piling the big heavy binders on my desk. I lined all four up in front of me. I planned to do a daily skim of each to get the different textures of the day. I opened up each folder at Thursday 1 November 1945 and plunged in.

FIFTEEN

At first there was little but post-war news, stories of ration-book counterfeiting and troops still coming home from the fronts all over the world. Then came a snippet about a child missing in the Gallowgate and a big search, but nothing hinting about the horrors to come. The *Gazette* made the only connection with three earlier reported missing kids in Bridgeton and Hutchesontown but consigned it to the back pages. I wondered if my fellow journalists thought there was no mileage in slum kids vanishing, as though family disasters happened too often to be newsworthy.

Then midway through November came a report of Rory's disappearance and suddenly other papers noticed. But it had taken five to go missing for them to see a pattern emerging. It was hard to say which came first, the newspaper speculation or the mob hysteria that was growing in the gossiping alleyways of the East End and the Gorbals. When Rory was found, and the details of his broken and naked body were disclosed, all hell broke loose. It was on the front pages under banner headlines. The police were under fire and were coming up with a stream of plodding platitudes that fooled no one.

When Hugh Donovan was arrested, the dam broke properly. The police were crowing and the papers were baying for blood.

A more moderate tone crept in as the trial started. They had no choice: Scotland's courts were jealous of their ability to host a fair trial. Any intemperate speculation that affected the possible outcome would have brought down the wrath of the judiciary. Mind, it didn't stop a good editor from fuelling the flames with innuendo and comments prefixed with that get-out-of-jail word, 'alleged'. And, of course, they were allowed to report the day's proceedings during the trial.

My head was buzzing and my eyes aching as I sat down in the tea shop in Sauchiehall Street for lunch. I sipped at my cup and chomped into a cheese sandwich. Beside me were my notes. I had four pages distilling six months of reporters' stories, some of which were models of objectivity; many simply echoed the lynch mob in shrill prose.

One thing was clear: Rory's abduction tapped into a ground-level panic in Glasgow about a monster who was snatching children. Rory's disappearance was the final spark that lit the tinderbox. Fiona Hutchinson turned her frenzied search into a front-page rallying point. The sudden newspaper pressure on the police to find the boys ratcheted up fears in every house-hold across the city. It could be their wee Archie next. From a brief mention the day after the boy went missing to banner headlines took only ten days. I kept hoping to find a photo of Fiona, but perhaps the papers had been warned off about prej-udicing the case. A pity. If she'd kept her looks, her tear-stained face would have sold extra editions by the cartful.

Within the week the stumbling desk sergeant filling the role of police spokesman had been replaced by Detective Chief Superintendent George Muncie himself. Muncie had never knowingly stepped into the shadows when there was a glimmer of limelight left to capture his hawk-nosed profile. The words 'major manhunt' and 'no stone left unturned' poured from his fleshy lips in an endless stream of pompous clichés. I never understood why reporters loved him. Maybe they were just taking the piss.

By one of those quirks of divine comedy the hunt was being led by detectives from Eastern Division, my old nick at Tobago Street. It was on their patch the first two kids had gone missing, and they were just the other side of the Clyde from the Gorbals where Rory had been abducted. They were working closely – they said – with the Cumberland Street police, but that probably meant both teams slagging each other off for failing to make headway and being ready to nab the glory if one did. It also gave the newshounds access to two teams of coppers who'd say anything to make it look like progress to cover their own backsides.

By the time they found the body, half of Glasgow was out looking for the weans, Rory included. The other half was stuck at home, guarding their terrified kids from the 'Gorbals Ghoul', as he'd now been christened by the *Gazette*. The pressure was on Muncie and his boys to deliver, and into their laps fell the poor racked body of Hugh Donovan. Within hours Muncie was crowing – in sombre and portentous tones, of course – about the remarkable detective hunt that had led to their apprehension of a suspect. It made it sound as if there'd been a mass clear-out of deadwood among the ranks of Glasgow sleuths and the repopulation by honours graduates of the Sexton Blake academy. Which frankly was a pile of horse manure.

The 'suspect' was held initially at Cumberland Street, then he was transferred to Tobago Street so that the lead team could get the kudos. But the gang of howling vigilantes outside the jail – women in curlers and aprons carrying noosed lengths of rope from their washing lines – forced them to transfer Hugh to Barlinnie 'for his own protection'. En route, his van was pelted with rotten food and cobbles, and by clever accident a cameraman from the *Daily Record* managed to catch a photo of Hugh's melted face to nicely underscore everyman's image of an ogre.

Before being driven off to the Bar-L, they'd given Hugh one outing. Muncie proudly announced that they'd taken the suspect back to the scene of the crime and that significant new evidence had come to light as a result of yet more fine police work. Was this what Sam had said about Hugh having 'knowledge of the crime scene'?

The trial itself had the same mob baying outside for justice, by which they meant a good hanging. There was no mitigation for his war exploits. No balancing of the scales with recognition of what he'd given for his country. Inside, the Procurator Fiscal constructed a Clyde-built case from the piles of evidence available to him. The wonder of it was that the jury took three days to come up with their verdict, and then chose to give a majority decision that would take Hugh to the scaffold. The defence counsel, Advocate Samantha Campbell, scored two clever goals.

First she tore apart the evidence given by two of the detectives. Detective Sergeant Bill Kerr swore on oath that Donovan had made his confession *before* being taken to the crime scene. Detective Constable Davy White said he'd first mentioned the seven stab wounds and the naked body *at* the coal cellar. He claimed that Donovan had then, through feelings of remorse, made his confession when he'd returned to the cells. Sam had got the pair of them so tongue-tied that they'd been shouting at each other at the end of it. I wondered what their notebooks said.

The second and crucial way in which Sam undermined the prosecution was in the sequence of events and the handling of the bloody evidence. The scientist from Glasgow Forensic Medicine Laboratory told the court that the body of the child had been dumped in the coal cellar two to three days *after* he'd been killed. This was apparent from the lack of blood in the cellar and the state of decomposition.

Under interrogation, the policeman – a local bobby called Robertson – who'd made the initial search of Hugh's flat the day after the boy had disappeared swore that he'd searched the tiny space from top to bottom, including under the sink. He claimed to have seen no sign of any blood-soaked material in a bucket, far less the boy himself. So where had the boy been held?

Within twenty-four hours of the boy's body being found, so was the bucket, brimming with murder weapon, bloodstained clothes from the boy and Hugh, and Hugh's fingerprints. Sam rightly asked why would a murderer keep the boy a prisoner for a few days in some as yet undiscovered location, then kill him, dump the body somewhere else and then cart all the evidence back to his flat? Why wouldn't he have left the evidence in this mysterious other location? Why hadn't the police searched for it? And if he was responsible for the other missing children, where had he kept them? Why provide this evidence? Naturally the prosecution couldn't bring charges for the abduction and murder of the first four boys. No bodies had turned up. But they certainly sprayed round the innuendo like muck on a farmer's field.

Sam used it as a lever. This time she had Muncie himself in the stand. He'd started off in his usual preening way to show how clever he and his team had been and ended up apoplectic in the dock shouting that there was no other location. He as good as accused the poor plod who'd made the first search of being incompetent and having failed to spot the boy, who'd no doubt been trussed up and gagged in a cupboard or under the bed. The judge had to admonish Muncie from shouting at the defence lawyer and calling her a silver-tongued mischief-maker who was twisting the words of an honest policeman.

Sam Campbell had made her point. It was just about conceivable that Hugh Donovan had been set up. That the murderer had inserted the evidence in his flat to incriminate him. She made a brave attempt to explain away Hugh's shirt with the bloodstains as having been stolen from the washing line in the back green. She also got the fifteen members of the jury thinking about the state of Hugh's hands. She made him show them to the court. I could picture the revulsion all round the room as he stuck out his burnt claws. She asked him to clench his hands and he couldn't. She asked him if he had any fingerprints left after his heroic exploits in Bomber Command. He said he had some on his right hand but grasping a knife with one hand was impossible. She spent some time reminding the jury how he'd earned his dreadful wounds in the tail turret of his RAF bomber.

He couldn't recall a thing about the night before he was arrested, except he'd taken some of his 'painkillers', maybe too much. And that in that state it was perfectly possible for someone to have entered his flat and planted the evidence.

It was a brave try, Sam, I thought. But the prosecution kept pounding away at the piles of evidence and the confession. Hugh never quite managed to retract his confession, just told the court that he'd said anything to be left alone. When they introduced the forensic discovery that the boy's body bore traces of heroin, it should have been a unanimous verdict of guilty. Sam's closing speech about this heroic warrior who'd given his all for his country must have been a cracker to leave enough doubt in a few minds. She was even getting to me. The circumstances of finding the body and then – conveniently – the evidence were simply too pat to be true. They searched the tiny single-end once and found nothing. They searched again and found a bucketload of incrimination. Why would Hugh do that? Why would he drag the body to the coal cellar? The lack of blood round the body made it as clear as daylight that the slaughter had taken place elsewhere. It stank of a frame-up. But by whom? And why? Why would anyone have it in for a poor wee junkie like Hugh? I'd seen his hands; it seemed implausible that he could have wielded a knife, far less left prints all over it.

But if Hugh didn't do it, then, obviously enough, someone else did. It gave me a toehold. If there was another killer he'd kept the boy somewhere other than Hugh's flat or the coal cellar and probably killed him there. Find the location; find the killer. He had to be someone who knew Hugh, knew his habits – especially his heroin one – and was local. He – and I suppose it was a *he* – must have been able to identify Hugh's shirt on the washing line, steal it and cover it in the blood of the child. But wasn't that stretching things too far? A premeditated act of murder and incrimination? Could I conceive of a person who was so demented yet so calculating that he knew he was going to murder the boy and that before he slaughtered him he would have to pinch a shirt to catch the blood? It couldn't have been an afterthought to acquire Hugh's shirt: the blood would have congealed and dried within hours, and how would the killer have known he'd find just the perfect piece of incriminating evidence? Name tag and all? Maybe there were two killers? Or they had had some helpful assistance in planting the evidence from our guardians of the peace themselves ...

Which gave me my next stop.

SIXTEEN

'Where to, friend?' asked the taxi driver.

'Do you know Tobago Street police station?'

It caused a big sigh from the front seat. 'Intimately. Ah've bailed ma faither-in-law out o' there on many's the occasion. Drunken aul' sod …'

He gave me his troubles for the next ten minutes of our journey. I contributed with a random few *tsks* and *ayes* out of politeness. But my attention was on the fair city streets that I'd pounded in my good black uniform a lifetime ago. I rolled down my window to sample the air and take in the smells and sounds.

There was nothing like the damage done to London. It was a struggle for German bombers to reach this far, and none of their daunting V1s or V2s made it beyond North London. Yet they had tried their damnedest to hit the shipbuilding capacity and ammunition production of the Clyde, and some stray bomb loads had straddled the residential areas in central Glasgow. The place that really took a pasting was the town of Clydebank. Back in March 1940, the Luftwaffe had filled their fuel tanks to the brim and swarmed across the North Sea. I might even have heard the murderous drone of their massing bombers while I lay in a French field as part of the ill-fated British Expeditionary Force. The bombers made it to Glasgow but missed the yards and instead razed an entire community. Only a handful of houses out of 12,000 were left unscathed. Hundreds of innocent folk – weans and women mainly – were blown to bits or crushed in the rubble of their homes. I wish I could say me and my mates in the 51st Highland Division took it out on the German army in return. But it didn't quite turn out that way. Not then. Not for *that* incarnation of the 51st.

I wrenched my thoughts back to the present. Outside the window of my taxi time had stood still. There were still groups of capped men huddling on street corners puffing on fags, waiting for something to come up at the yards. These were the unskilled, the casuals, the soldiers back from the war with no job and dwindling hope. It had the ominous tang of the thirties again, the years of the Depression and the Hunger Marches. Where were the laurel leaves and the spoils of victory?

The pawnshops with their three brass balls were doing a steady trade. The old gaffers handed over their wife's wedding ring on the Wednesday to tide them over till payday on Friday, then they liberated the abused gold bands on the Saturday. Weekend wives, these long-suffering women, some still wrapped in their plaids, oblivious to fashion as much as to the lengthening and warming days. Some of the younger women – Highland lassies mainly - had babies tucked inside their tartan rugs, tight-swaddled like papooses with only fat red faces on show.

Suddenly, out of a close, a squadron of kids with skint knees and holed vests shot into the street. Their leader ran with the balance of a Scotland winger taking on the English defence at Hampden. His right arm was outstretched and holding an iron bar which drove a black metal hoop. This gird and cleek was a top-notch affair. I'd made my own out of an old pram wheel with the spokes and tyre removed for the cleek. And for a gird, we used sticks torn from trees to propel the hoop along. This boy's must have been made at the yards; it was a blacksmith's job to fashion the ring of iron and fix one end of the gird to it with another smaller hoop. The best thing was the satisfying ear-splitting noise as the cleek clattered along the cobbles with a gang of shrieking tearaways whooping after it and demanding a 'shot'. I watched the yelling pack disappear down another close and wished I was running with them, starting again. But that's the kind of thinking that tortured me through the winter in London. Round and round. Replaying pivotal points in my life and taking a different path. Seeing where I'd end up. Almost anywhere better than the poky wee flat in a bombed-out city of strangers, with only my old pal Johnnie Walker to keep me company.

We juddered to a halt outside Tobago Street jail. It hadn't changed either. A squat rectangle of grey sandstone, built by the Victorians, manned by the Visigoths.

'You're no' the polis, are you?' He was regretting his intimacies.

'Sorry? No. Used to be. Not now.'

I paid him and got out. The sun warmed the street, and I was taken back ten years to my first day here in '33. Fresh from training, my new uniform smelling of warm serge. I'd checked my tie, made sure my cap sat square on my head and marched towards the big wooden door.

Now, I straightened my jacket, adjusted my trilby and walked quickly over the road and in through the doors. The clocks had stopped inside as well as out. Same solid desk and grille, same copper behind it writing in the charge book. He raised his eyes briefly then dropped them back to his work. But then the eyes came back up slowly and he scoured my face.

94

'Well, fuck me, if it isnae Detective Sergeant Douglas Brodie Esquire.'

'You're not my type, Alec. And it's just Brodie now. How are you getting on?'

Well, I could see. The three stripes on his arm looked white and new. He'd probably made it in the past couple of years. He'd arrived a new recruit, raw-jawed and gangly, in early '39, about six months before I resigned and joined up. He'd elected to stay on and see the war out on Tobago Street. It had clearly been the right thing for him. Might have been the right thing for me too. I'd probably be a detective inspector by now.

We threw a few clumsy catch-up questions to each other, neither listening to the answers, then Alec Jamieson, *Sergeant* Alec Jamieson, flushed and said, 'You're here about Donovan, the bloke who killed those wee boys?'

'He was only convicted for one murder, Alec. Anyway, you got the message?'

'Aye, we got the message. They're waiting for you roon' the back.'

Alec lifted the heavy wood barrier and let me through. He told a young constable hovering in the background to man the desk. We walked along the lino floor, my boots squeaking just as they'd used to as we headed to the offices round the back. Sunlight puddled the floor and climbed the walls where photos hung of former DCIs – a rogues' gallery if ever there was one. We stopped outside the office of the DCI himself and I looked quizzically at Alec Jamieson. He looked embarrassed and opened the door. The room seemed to have its own cloud system. It's amazing how much smoke three men can generate.

I'd asked Sam to get her secretary to fix a meeting with Detective Sergeant Bill Kerr and his sidekick Detective Constable Davy White. They were the pair of local cops who'd done the grunt work on the case and who'd been put through the mill by Samantha Campbell. I didn't know either of them and assumed they'd been posted to Tobago Street after I'd left. I guessed the two nervous-looking blokes in civvies standing either side of the desk were the happy pair. But sitting between them, hands clasped and propping his chin above his desk, was Detective Chief Inspector Willie Silver himself. In front of him a well-filled ashtray held a smouldering cigarette.

I'd known of Silver around Glasgow pre-war. He'd held various positions in nicks across the city, always managing to move on just before his drink problem got him thrown out. He was either a very talented detective or drank with the right folk to have survived this long, far less thrived. But he looked very sober indeed as he stared at me across his office. His eyes were close together above a large broken-veined nose. He raised his bottom lip and sucked at the ends of a smoke-stained moustache.

'You wanted a wee chat, Brodie?' he asked. His voice was deep and slow, like an undertaker trying to be sympathetic over an open coffin. I stepped forward into the room and took my hat off. Not deference, heat: the radiators were belting it out.

'It's the Donovan case. I'm an old friend of his. I'm helping Advocate Campbell with her appeal.'

'She needs it. *We* didnae find her that appealing, did we, boys?'

The two twitchy men twisted their faces in sycophantic grins.

'Yer right there, sir,' said the fat one to my left. I assumed this was Kerr. The senior one always speaks first. White, on my right, sniggered into his hand and took another drag on his fag.

'Sit down, Brodie. Sit down.' He pointed at the wooden chair in front of his desk. I parked myself in it and found it was a couple of inches shorter than Silver's. He looked down at me and smiled, or rather he turned the corners of his mouth up.

The rest of his face said, *I hate your guts, boy*. He introduced his minions. I'd guessed right about which was which.

'You know me, Brodie? From the old days, eh? I heard you were a good copper. Could have gone far. Why didn't you?'

'King and Country and all that.' I bit off the 'sir' that came so treacherously to my tongue.

'That's not what I heard. I heard you didn't like our style, how we did business around here. I heard you were a bleeding heart, Brodie.'

'Let's say I preferred to *look* for evidence, not plant it.'

The smirks and smiles left their faces. Silver's close-set eyes bulged.

'So, they were right. Is that what you're up to now, Brodie? That's what your girlfriend tried to imply, and now you're coming it too?'

'All I'm trying to do is get at the truth. I'm sure that's what you're after as well ... *Chief Inspector*.'

He sighed. 'Truth, is it? Is that what they taught you at Glasgow University, then? Fair turns a man's head, all that learning. Let me tell you what truth is, boy. Truth is here.' He pointed at his chest. 'I know the truth when I see it. I saw the truth in Donovan's eyes. He told me truly that he killed that wean. That's the truth the jury heard. And that truth will leave him swinging on a rope.' His lads either side were nodding their toadying heads off by this time.

'If we're all so keen on the truth, why did your pals here give different stories at the trial?'

Kerr and White glanced at each other and then looked poisonously at me.

DS Kerr jumped in. 'It was just a misunderstanding, so it was. That clever lassie was trying to trip us up. We didnae get a chance to explain it right.'

'Well, explain it to me then. One of you said Donovan confessed *before* you took him to the coal cellar. The other said it was after. Which was it?' I challenged.

They looked down at Silver for guidance. He shrugged. Kerr started up.

'It's simple, so it is. Donovan confessed, *then* we took him to the crime scene for corroboration. Is that no' right, Davy?'

Davy White nearly shook his head off agreeing with him. 'Aye, that's it. I just got confused with all that bloody woman's talk. You ken what women are like. Always twisting what you say.'

'Did the court look at your notebooks? You still keep notebooks, don't you? Showing times and incidents?'

Again the furtive looks between them, before Silver cut in. 'Of course the officers kept notes. They referred to them at the trial. But *you* know how it is, Brodie. Sometimes their scribbles need a bit of interpretation. They're not all as clever or educated as you.'

'You mean they hadn't bothered to collude on their notes before the trial? It was such a watertight case, you didn't think anyone would care?'

'I think we've given you enough of our time, Brodie.'

'Were the notebooks submitted as evidence?'

A cold look came over Silver's face. 'There was no need. The court accepted my officers' statements.'

'The defence didn't. Can I see the books now?'

A look of near panic flitted over DC White's face. Kerr was quicker to fight back. 'No, you fucking can't, Brodie! Who do you think you are, coming in here and questioning us! We should fling you in one of cells for a couple of days. Kick some sense into your thick skull.'

'Glad to see things haven't changed, Kerr. When in doubt,

bang 'em up and gi'e them a good hiding, eh?'

Silver seemed to be trying to suck off his moustache. 'Shut up, sergeant,' he said to Kerr. 'Time's up, Brodie.'

I sat still. 'I have a couple more questions. If I don't get answers, we'll go to the appeal judge and see if he'll do better.'

Silver lit another fag even though the last one was still polluting the air. 'Ask.'

'You found the boy's body on the Tuesday. Next morning you were round at Donovan's, mob-handed. A tip-off?'

Silver looked down at his two fags, chose one and sucked on it. 'A member of the public is all I'm prepared to say.'

'Phone call?'

Silver nodded.

'Did you know this mysterious public-minded citizen? Was he one of your grasses?'

'I've told you all I'm going to tell you, Brodie.'

'OK. Where was the boy held before his body was found?'

Kerr butted in. 'In Donovan's flat, of course. He had him hidden.'

I pounced. 'In a single-end? It would be like hiding an elephant under your hat. Can I talk to the constable who first searched the flat?'

Silver raised his hand to head off DS Kerr. 'PC Robertson. A good man. Based at the Cumberland Street shop. But I hear he's on leave. Sick leave. Convalescing down south somewhere.' The forced smile stole back round his mouth.

'That's convenient.'

'Your next question is your last.'

I could see he meant it. I decided to ginger things up a bit.

'What will you do if another child goes missing, Silver? How will you explain that to the press? While an innocent man is rotting in prison or dangling from a rope? What then?'

Frowns rolled down his minions' faces. Silver didn't blink but he started turning his fag packet over on the desk. He shook his head. 'You'll always get a copycat out there, trying to make his name. You know that, Brodie.'

My anger boiled up. 'So you'd find some other innocent fella and hang him! You'd go on hanging them one after the other till eventually it stopped!'

'If need be, Brodie. If need be. And *that's* the truth. Now will you be so good as to *fuck off*. See him out, sergeant.'

Punching his lights out wasn't an option. Not yet. The two oafs were smirking again as I walked to the door. But I turned and looked back at Silver. His expression had sagged, become introspective. I hoped – but doubted – I'd caused him a sleepless night or two. As the door closed behind me, I heard the distinctive sound of a bottle clinking against a glass. Celebration or steadying of nerves?

SEVENTEEN

I looked at my watch. Half past three. I had time for one more visit. Tobago Street runs north to south towards the river. Walking south, I crossed Canning Street with its double tram tracks and pressed on into Glasgow Green, scene of many a violent gang battle and less violent romantic encounter. Though I suspect neither activity had featured in the original design by the genteel Victorians.

I walked past the deserted bandstand and along the Clyde path to the St Andrew's Suspension Bridge. It connects with the eastern side of the Gorbals. I paused in the middle and lit up. I had two addresses in the Gorbals. One was Hugh's, the other Fiona's. I hung over the balustrade and watched the brown water rush underneath. The symbolism didn't escape me. It had been half my lifetime ago that I'd last seen her. What was she like now? Was her hair still as long and black? Had she kept her figure? Was there still an ember? I took a last drag then pinged the end into the river.

A ten-minute stroll through the regimented grid of rundown Victorian tenements and I was in Florence Street. Hugh's old close was no different from any other I'd passed. Four storeys high and one entry serving eight flats, or houses, as they called them. Outside, a group of girls in grubby frocks and bare feet were playing peevers. They'd marked out the grid on the broken paving slabs and were using an old boot polish can as their marker. For a while I watched their agile young limbs hopping round the grid. A tableau of normality to draw on, to balance things out. It's what we fought for, wasn't it? But nobody told us the price. The terror-filled nights. The three-day headaches, vomiting till your body felt like a jellyfish. The flashbacks: the landing-craft door crashing down into the water; the heavy-calibre shells ricocheting round the open tin coffin making mincemeat of your pals before they'd even got a shot off. The sound of bullets smacking into flesh. Of hard men sobbing with fear as a barrage continued for two days and nights without pause. And now this, now another image to be added to the stinking pile: a small naked body, sheet-white and gashed, abandoned like trash on a midden ...

The entry was dark and fetid, the smell from a choked toilet filling the hall and wending up the tight stone staircase. I climbed up and up, checking the view out of the broken windows to the back green at each full turn of the spiral. I got to the top and stood quietly till my breathing calmed. There were two doors. Number 8, Hugh's single-end, was straight ahead. Number 7 would be the room and kitchen of the other family, the missing family. Someone was in. I could hear a child screaming in a temper tantrum behind the door of number 7. I stepped towards it and gave it a good bash. The noise stopped and then started again. I heard footsteps and the door opened. A young woman with a hectic face stood there with a tartan shawl wrapped round her, a baby rolled inside it. A snotty lad of four or five keeked out behind her pinny. His face was red with rage and greeting.

'What has he done noo?' she asked.

'I don't know who you think I am, missus, but I'm just here to ask a couple of questions.'

'You the polis?'

'No, I'm …'

But she was already shutting the door. 'We don't want anythin' …' she was saying. I stuck my foot in the door.

'If you don't clear off, pal, I'll scream blue murder and the neighbours will fling you oot, so they will!'

'All I want is to ask you what happened to the other family, the ones before you,' I called desperately through the closing door.

Slowly the door began to open again. 'Why?'

I looked at her sharp face with its suspicious eyes. Honesty seemed best. And my old accent. 'Because they're gonna hang an auld pal of mine for something he didnae dae.'

She appraised me up and down and we both looked towards the other door, Hugh's door.

'Him?'

'Hugh Donovan.'

'I'll tell you this. We wouldnae have ta'en this hoose if we knew who was next door. Murderin' sod. You say he didnae do it? How do you ken? Have you got a fag?'

I gave her one, took one myself and lit us both. We both took a sociable drag and I told her I was working for Advocate Campbell on the appeal. That I thought it was a police set-up under pressure to find the real murderer.

'Ah'm no' surprised at anythin' the polis dae. They took ma man in and gave him a gid hiding the other week. He was a bit fu', right enough, but it was the other fella that started it.'

I smiled sympathetically. 'Is there anybody living there now?' I nodded towards number 8.

'You must be jokin'! The factor says he'll no' be able to rent it for at least a year. Who wants to sleep in there wi' a' that blood and grief? And ghosts, like enough.' She shuddered and wrapped her shawl tighter round her. Her son wiped his nose on her pinny and she cuffed him absentmindedly, raising another howl.

'Did you know the family before you?'

'Reid, they were ca'd. But we never met them.'

The boy chipped in, 'Yon wee boy came back, mither.'

She was about to clip him again but stayed her hand. 'You're right enough, Jim.' She turned to me, reluctantly. 'One of Mrs Reid's weans came by about twa months ago. They were here for their granny's funeral over at Townhead. Said his mammy had left some bits of washin' on the line, they were that much in a hurry to go.'

'Why the hurry, do you know?'

She looked around her as if the stairs had sprouted ears. 'Ah heard from the factor that they'd come into a bit of money. Something about an aunt doon the Clyde. Arran way.'

Arran? Off the west coast of Ayrshire. A perfect place to lose an inconvenient witness. It was a big island, with villages and isolated houses scattered all round its shoreline. Where would you start?

'Do you have an address on Arran?'

She shook her head. But at the same time, wee Jim tugged at her skirt and looked up at her.

'Whit is it noo, son?'

'The wee boy said he could watch the boats come in every day, so he could. Said it was amazing. So it was. Can we go doon the water at the fair, mither?'

'Maybe. If your faither's no' in the jail. And if you stop gien' me a headache. Ma lugs are fair bleedin', so they are.'

I dug in my pocket and found a threepenny bit. I held it out to the boy. 'Well done, Jim. You'll make a good detective when you grow up.'

The boy looked at my hand and then at his mum. She nodded and his hand took the coin like a striking cobra.

I turned to go. 'Apart from the factor, has anyone been in the house since Donovan left?'

She was about to shake her head, but then she said, 'Just the once. A big fella. About your height, but heftier. I heard him mucking about with the key. I came out just as he opened the door. He said he was checking the place was all locked up and tidy for the factor.'

'A big man, you say? Anything else about him?'

'He had a 'tache, a wee ginger one. But I think it was to hide the lip. A hare lip, ye ken. It looked like he was grinnin' a' the time.'

I could have hugged her but she might have called the neighbours.

'You've been a great help, missus. I really appreciate it. I think I'll take a wee look inside now.'

'How will you get in?'

'Could I borrow a safety pin? And a kirby grip? And it would really help if you had a knitting needle or a crochet hook.'

Locks had been a fascination for me since my dad found me playing with some old padlocks he kept in his shed at the allotment. She gave me a look which wasn't all admonishing and went inside. She came back with a selection of possible tools. I strode to the door of number 8. I felt Jim's eyes on me, bulging with excitement at this cavalier approach to others' property. There were two locks: a big padlock and a mortise. I chose the crochet hook and slid it into the big padlock. I soon felt it ease and open. I pulled back the hasp. I tried the kirbies then the knitting needle on the mortise and scrubbed at it till I felt the pins lock up in the mechanism. I turned the handle and pushed the door open.

It was dark and sour inside. Dust covered the bare wood floor and eddied up as I stepped in. I doubted the gas lights would work, so I stepped across to the window and drew back the torn curtain. Behind me the woman and boy stood looking in with fascination at the murderer's den. Their looks soon turned to disappointment.

There wasn't much to see in a room that was barely ten feet by twelve. There was a recessed bed with a curtain over it, a warped Formica table and one wooden chair, a sink and a tiny stove with two rings. There was no sign of who had lived here or what had happened. No splashes of gore. I don't know what I was expecting.

I pulled back the curtain concealing the bed in the wall. There was no mattress or bedclothes, just the bare boards. I assumed everything had been carted off by the police for forensics. I gazed round the tiny room and thought about Hugh Donovan spending his last months here. Lonely, sometimes drugged to the eyeballs, and perhaps always wondering if he would have been better off going down in his plane after all. I used to envy Hugh's life. There were eight of them: four boys, two girls and his parents all on top of each other in a big messy house in the next close. Quarrelling and laughing, fighting and loving, a real family. For an only child like me they made a strong case for a Catholic approach to contraception. When I called in to see if Hugh was coming out to play, I was simply swept up in the family currents – plied with jeelie pieces, regaled by some story about the neighbours, taking sides in an argument about football. I was an honorary Donovan. Apart from the hair, of course: eight blue-black heads to one ruddy brown.

Hugh's was a noisy carefree upbringing surrounded by love

and attention. He was the youngest and – though I'd never have admitted it – the bonniest. The result was that he was both spoiled and ignored in equal measure. He was one of the few pals to keep in touch with me after they all went off to jobs or apprenticeships at fourteen. It made his betrayal all the harder. And, looking around this pitiful silent box, it made this passage of his life so much more wretched. I'm sure one of his brothers or sisters would have taken him in, in England or Canada where they'd gone to roost and establish their own families. But Hugh couldn't face them, not looking like he did now. His final vanity. He'd walled himself up inside the shattered shell of himself, hanging on for his next fix, until he'd bumped into Fiona again. And Rory. There had been an upswing in Hugh's life last year, making this hovel bearable, bringing hope. Only for the God he worshipped to dash it from his burnt lips. *This isn't for you Donovan.* No wonder he didn't much care if he lived or died.

I thought of Fiona living and breathing within five minutes of here. But I'd had enough stumbling down memory lane for one day. I caught the tram on Crown Street, changed at the big interchange at Gorbals Cross and crossed the river past Central Station and all the way north to Cowcaddens. From there it was one tram to Hillhead along the Great Western Road and to Samantha Campbell's office.

I sat smoking on the top deck, taking in the city. The red sandstone grandeur was tarnished from the noxious outpour-ings of the heavy industries. *Glas gow*: the green meadow. There were few enough green meadows left, but in their place was a sense of permanence and certainty. The city fathers back in the nineteenth century had known where they were going and how to get there. The Second City of the Empire. The trouble was we no longer seemed to have much of an empire. There was even talk of handing over India. It seemed unthinkable. The pennies I'd just handed over to the conductor still said *Ind Imp*. And thousands of British lads had fought and died to fling the Japs out of South-East Asia. Queen Vickie would be rotating in her mausoleum. At least we still had our shipyards; the boom times would surely come again when we'd got over our Bavarian hangover. We had to replace all that tonnage sunk in the Atlantic and the Pacific, or lying at the bottom of the Barents Sea. According to my mother, the Ayrshire pits were working at full blast, and you only had to glance at the trailing clouds of steam from train stations I was passing to know we had the basics right. All we needed was some money to get things going again. That was the rub. We were as broke as tinkers.

EIGHTEEN

I t was just after six when I walked into Samantha Campbell's office. The reception area was empty. I called out and Sam answered.

'Come on through, Brodie.'

I pushed open her door to find a cosy scene: Sam taking tea with Father Cassidy. They were even sharing a plate of digestives. For one daft moment I felt annoyed – no, *jealous* – at Patrick Cassidy's intimacy with Samantha. Which was simply ridiculous. The man had stood by Hugh throughout this sorry tale. I resolved to like this man and not let my stupid prejudices about God-botherers blind me to his qualities. He'd been right about the pubs to look in to find Hugh's drug dealers. In short, he was useful.

Sam nodded at the tea cosy. 'There's a spare cup and the pot's still warm. I've nothing stronger,' she added with a shade too much spice.

'You have a low view of the drinking habits of newshounds, Miss Campbell. Tea is exactly what I need.'

'You can get another chair from the outer office, or ...' She indicated one of the piles of papers.

I poured myself a cup and gingerly squatted on a shaky tower of files. 'Well, isn't this nice.'

'Father Cassidy was visiting Hugh today. He came by to see how we were getting on.'

I nodded at him. 'Good of you to see him, Patrick. How is he?'

The priest put his cup down on the edge of Sam's desk. 'They've put him back on his medication. He wasn't really with us, I'm afraid. I asked the warder about it and he told me that Hugh had been in lot of pain. It was for his own good.' He shook his head. 'I don't like it. Just drifting away. A man should be *compos mentis* if his time is short.'

'So he can confess his sins?'

'Better to go with a clear conscience, surely?'

'Well, he's not dead yet.' I slurped my tea.

'You've found something?' asked Sam.

I glanced at the priest. She saw my question. 'It's all right. You can talk freely in front of the father, Brodie. He's on our side.'

I told them about my day. Sam confirmed my perspective on the trial from my morning's review of the newspapers.

'One thing that leaped out,' I said, 'was that Rory wasn't the first child to go missing. Four others had vanished before him. Never found?' I asked.

Cassidy looked pained. 'Nothing to this day. I know one of the other families. I'm not sure which is worse: to have to bury your child or never to know …'

'Do you think there's a lead there?' Sam asked.

'I find it *convenient* that the fifth abduction resulted in a body being dumped where it could be found, and that Hugh Donovan's house should be chock-a-block with evidence to hang him.'

'Are you suggesting some sort of frame-up?' asked Patrick.

'Criminals tend to work a pattern. A thief tends to have a trademark style of operating. Same with a murderer. The way they kill, when they do it, who their victims are. If Hugh was the abductor and murderer of all five children, why would he change his pattern with the last? Careless? Stupid? Drugs ... maybe. But it doesn't feel right.'

'Did you get anything from the police?' asked Sam.

I shook my head. 'They were never going to turn round and say: "By God, Brodie you're on to something. Why didn't we think of that?" But you obviously rattled them in court, Sam. They were still moaning about how this clever lassie had got them all confused and made them look stupid. But they've had time to work on their story so that it all adds up.'

'So, nothing?' asked Patrick.

'There's a couple of angles. I asked to see their notebooks. And to interview the constable that did the first search on Hugh's flat. They just laughed. Can you get them hauled in front of the Appeals Court and force them to hand over the notebooks?'

'We can try.' She jotted a couple of notes down on her pad.

'What are you looking for, Brodie?' asked the priest.

'Differences. In their stories,' said Sam. 'Muncie claimed in court that the constable on the first search was blind or stupid. If he wasn't, and there was no sign of the boy a week before they found his body, then where was he kept? And as for the other pair, I'm betting their notebooks conflict with each other over when Hugh Donovan provided intimate details of the crime scene.'

'Perhaps I'm being naïve. Won't they just conveniently *lose* the notebooks? If they haven't already burned them?' Patrick Cassidy was leaning across to me, his face creased with scepticism.

I raised my palm to him. 'Losing your notebook was a hanging offence in my day. And it would look awfully convenient to lose two. Samantha here would have an open goal in court. But you're right, Patrick. There's a lot of "ifs" about. And we're stuck if we can't prove any of this. The police can be remarkably unco-operative when they put their mind to it.'

They both sat back, letting the gloom descend again.

'There might be something else, though ...' I began. I described my visit to Hugh's house and my meeting with the neighbour and her smart kid.

Sam was the first to speak. 'You *must* go, Brodie. You *have* to go to Arran and find them!' Her face was as animated as I'd seen it. Colour suffused her pale cheeks and her eyes shone behind her specs.

'It's a big island.'

'I think I can help,' said the priest, who seemed freshly animated. 'I know the priest in Lamlash. Let me make a phone call.' He was digging into the mysterious folds of his cassock as he spoke. He retrieved a small diary and flicked through the pages. 'May I use your phone?'

Sam and I looked at each other as he dialled and got put through to his clerical pal on Arran.

'Now, that's what I call divine intervention,' I said sotto voce, and got an admonishing look over her glasses.

The Arran priest was to call us back in the morning with news. Sam and I wandered back to her house, and en route I prevailed on her to let me buy supper, no expense spared. We picked up speed on the last leg of our journey so that our newspaper-wrapped feast was still warm.

In the posh dining room of her parents' home, on the massive oak table, beneath paintings of rampant stags and highland skies, we made two paper pokes and divvied up the fish and chips. The irresistible stink of salt and vinegar perfumed the air and we licked our stained fingers like naughty kids. I don't know if it was the carefree attack on the fish suppers or the glimmer of hope I'd brought, but Samantha Campbell cast off her glum schoolmarm air and looked positively girlish.

'It must have felt strange going back to your old police station.'

'Like using H. G. Wells's time machine. Same faces, same low morals. It even smelt the same!'

Sam suddenly went quiet. 'But that's what we're up against. Same dour policemen who'd rather see an innocent man hang than admit they're wrong.'

'So you really believe he's innocent?'

'Yes. And you sound as though you're coming round?'

I sighed. 'I was just checking that *you* did. That it wasn't just lawyer's platitudes.'

'I didn't know you then. And I'm not sure I do now. Well? Do you think Hugh did it?'

'Nothing about the crime scene adds up. And where's the motive? Saying that, I believe anyone is capable of anything.'

'You don't mean that.'

I sure as hell did but I didn't want to explain. Didn't want to drag the whole aching mess out on the table. My post-war special duties. Visiting the newly liberated camps. Using my language training to interrogate SS officers and camp commandants. Getting witness statements from some of the wretches who survived. Adding to my already swollen pack of nightmares. I slammed the barriers down and turned the question back on her.

'I'm just amazed that in your line of work you haven't become as jaundiced as an ex-copper like me. How do you manage it?'

She thought for a bit, and daintily sucked the last traces of salt from her fingers. 'My parents. They were always optimistic about folk. Always ready to see the good side. Even my father.'

'Even?'

She looked embarrassed for a moment, then defiant. 'He was Procurator Fiscal in Glasgow before the war.'

I smiled. 'So this is a family business.'

'Sort of. I thought it was time the Campbells supported the other side for a change. Even things out a wee bit.'

'Do you mind my asking what happened? I mean ...'

'How I became an orphan, Mr Brodie?'

My big mouth. 'Sorry, Sam. It's none of my business. Forget it.'

She got up and left the room. I heard a tap running. I wondered how much I'd offended her. Was she off to bed? She came back, drying her hands on a towel. She flung me a warm wet flannel and a hand towel. I cleaned myself up.

She went over to the big sideboard and opened the front. She pulled out a bottle of Scotch and two cut-glass tumblers and placed them on the table. Then she went back and pulled out a drawer. She took out what looked like a family album and sat it on the table beside the whisky. She put her glasses on, opened the album towards the end and pushed it round so I could see it. There was a photo of a middle-aged couple smiling in front of a loch. They wore rough tweeds tucked into long socks, hiking boots and backpacks. The woman was simply an older version of Sam: fine white hair tied back; same intelligent eyes challenging the viewer. The man – her father, clearly – had bequeathed her his strong chin and mouth.

'They were on a walking holiday by Loch Lomond. Dad's favourite sort of holiday. Summer of '35. I was minding the fort here. The day after this photo was taken they took a boat across to Inchmurrin Island and a squall got up. They were found two days later, along with the boat owner and his nine-year-old son. All drowned. You wouldn't think you could drown in a pleasure boat on an inland loch, would you? Such a stupid waste. *So* stupid.' She took off her specs and brushed her treacherous eyes.

'I'm sorry,' I said.

She nodded. 'Me too, Brodie. Me too. A bloody waste. And I've got all this.' She waved her hand round the room. 'I'm sorry. I shouldn't have brought it up. It's none of your business.'

'Look, Sam, it's my fault—'

'Shut up, Brodie, and pour the Scotch. We've got work to do.'

NINETEEN

We managed to leave some whisky in the bottle, so morning wasn't too spiked with remorse. I followed Sam into her office to wait for news from our clerical spy across the water. I made use of my time by checking through rail and steamship timetables. Just before noon Samantha came through looking flushed.

'Looks like we're on,' she said. 'Lamlash. A new family arrived there in January. Mother and four kids. They're renting a place. The priest there will take you to them. He's been told to say nothing to them before you arrive. He's expecting you off the first ferry in the morning.'

I took the slip. 'Cassidy's come up trumps. Let's hope it's the right family. And that they can be persuaded to talk. And, finally, that they have something to talk about.'

'We're desperate, Brodie. This has to be a lead.'

I nodded, wishing I hadn't forced the optimism to retreat from her eyes.

'Look, we can speed things up a bit. I can just about catch the last ferry from Ardrossan. I'll be in Brodick by seven o'clock. I'll stay overnight and catch the bus round to Lamlash first thing. It'll gain us half a day.'

She was nodding, 'Fine, just fine. Here's some money for

expenses.' She handed me a big white fiver. 'Go on. I can put it down as trial costs.'

I took it from her reluctantly, but glad enough for the contribution to my dwindling cash supply. In preparation for the possible jaunt, I stuffed a spare pair of socks, pants and a clean collar into the pockets of my coat. My safety razor and a toothbrush were in my jacket pocket.

I stepped out into a cloudy afternoon with a rain-tinged breeze blowing from the west. I thought I could smell the sea salt in the air but it was no doubt just smoke from the ship-yards. The tram took me to Central Station and I caught the train to Ardrossan. The *Glen Sannox* was a turbine steamer, not a magical paddle steamer. But it reminded me of the *Duchess of Argyll*, which my dad took me on just after the Great War. The *Sannox*'s twin funnels and sleek prow made me every bit excited as the small boy of twenty-five years ago. I half expected to hear my dad shout out to me to hang on to the railing as we eased our way out of the harbour and into the Firth of Clyde between the Ayrshire coast and the long hump of Arran island. This boat was quick too: its turbines sent the water racing away behind us in a long furrow. We were aiming straight across the firth at Brodick, bang in the middle of the east coast of the island.

By now the rain was whipping steadily into our faces from out of the Atlantic and the waves were slapping grey and white along our bows. The boat began plunging into the swell and I decided a cup of tea and a fag were called for to steady the stomach. I sat looking out of the splashed windows. Before the war the Firth of Clyde was thick with steamers, cargo ships and the occasional liner. Schools of grey warships would ply these waters: new ones fresh out of the yards or older ones being patched up and sent back out again to face the wolf packs that infested the waters around our coast and all the way across to America. The ferries themselves were clad in heavy metal and given popguns to defend themselves and sent off to look for submarines. I shuddered to think of dying in the slate-cold sea. Was it worse to be on a surface ship with its bows staved in by a torpedo? Or in a submarine with depth charges booming in the deep and blowing in the plates that kept the sea out? Drowning was one thing, but being trapped inside a metal tomb as it slid to the bottom of the Atlantic, water gushing in through sprung rivets, was my idea of hell.

Nowadays the Clyde was quieter. The ferries that survived their wartime duties – some had Dunkirk battle honours – renewed their daily service to the isles of Cumbrae, Bute and Arran. The wartime frenzy had stilled and it would take time for the world markets to recover and raise demand for peacetime ships again. With the amount of tonnage sunk during the war, the Clyde was expecting a boom period to follow.

For a treat I had a scone and jam and a second cup of tea as I watched the island loom larger through the forward portholes. The boat wasn't full, by any means. Too early for summer trips and too late in the day for business. It suited me fine. I was glad of the brief respite and the chance to sift my thoughts. Once again I'd found an excuse for not visiting Fiona. Was this the same warrior leading his company into battle? Scared of an old flame? Probably.

I touched the healing scab on my forehead from the knife attack. It made me wonder about the thugs who'd attacked me in the bogs at Doyle's pub. What had they known? And why did they react the way they did? Was it an automatic response to any stranger wandering into their patch and asking tricky questions? A kind of 'nice to make your acquaintance, stitch that, you bastard'? Maybe. Or were they on the lookout for just such a meddling stranger? I needed to meet their boss, Dermot Slattery, and find out what he knew. If I could find this Reid family and get them to help, I could be back in Glasgow by Saturday afternoon and putting out feelers for a rendezvous with this latter-day razor king tomorrow evening. Time was running out. It was already 5 April and we had to get the appeal in by the fifteenth, ten short days.

We bumped against Brodick pier and I shuffled out with the rest of the handful of passengers on to the wet decking of the jetty. It had stopped raining. There was even a glimpse of late evening sun behind the clouds. A portent of hope? I began walking along the seawall towards the small town itself. In the far corner of the bay, veiled by drifting clouds, I could make out Brodick Castle. I recalled my father pointing it out to me on our one and only day trip here in my other life.

I breathed deep and enjoyed the tang of seaweed and salt water in my nostrils. Maybe I should come back here in the summer, go for long walks by the sea and in the hills. The exercise would be good for my leg. And I'd get some colour in my London cheeks. See if Sam had inherited her dad's love of hiking. Which was a funny unbidden thought. She was a prim lawyer mostly, but the fish-and-chip supper had shown another side. It would be a challenge to break through the ice more often.

Today the town was quiet. Few of the bed and breakfasts had boards up, saving their energies for the chip-eating, ice-cream-sucking invasion at the Glasgow Fair. Arran got the classier holidaymakers, unless they were camping or cara-vanning, of course. The neat Victorian houses and hotels that lined the seafront were magnets for the factory supervisors and the insurance company managers and their wives with hearts set on the next promotion and a three-bedroom semi in Helensburgh.

One of the tall houses that looked out across the road to the sea and to the Ayrshire coast beyond had a 'Vacancy' sign swinging nonchalantly in the wind. Take me or leave me, see if I care. I crossed over, went in and secured a bed for the night with sea views and a shared bathroom for the knock-down out-of-season price of 5/6d. Though there was no one to share it with, as it turned out. I could have breakfast – limit-less cups of tea, square slices of fried sausage and a real egg with as much toast as I could eat – for a further shilling. Perfect. I allayed the suspicion of the large-bosomed landlady at my travelling without a suitcase by patting my coat pockets and explaining I had a short meeting in Lamlash the next morning and then back to Glasgow.

There was a café open in the town centre, such as it was – a souvenir shop, a newsagent, a butcher and a fishmonger, each with desolate counters. I thought of taking some Arran rock back to Sam but it looked like it was pre-war stock. For the second night running I had fish and chips, but the company was less distracting. I missed Samantha Campbell's abrasive tongue and sharp brain, and the no-nonsense way she stuck her hair back behind her small ears. I turned in early, slept well and sought out the Lamlash bus with a stomach filled and warmed by fried sausage topped with buttered toast. The morning was warm and the steam rose from the damp roads as we chugged out of town and up the steep hill. We were heading due south now along the ragged coast to Lamlash.

We ground our way up and over, and practically free-wheeled down into the next bay. Through the dense trees that marshalled the road, I caught occasional glimpses of the crescent of Lamlash Bay and the village itself. Offshore was the big lump of rock that was Holy Island. It looked just the sort of out-of-the-way retreat to stymie prying policemen or desperate reporters.

We trundled to a halt one stop away from the centre but near the Catholic church, according to the driver. Though Lamlash Bay had sheltered the northern fleet of the Royal Navy during the war it was smaller than Brodick and less well set up for the holiday trade. Much of the village comprised small fishermen's houses arranged in a tidy row with trim gardens out front. The Protestant kirk dominated the far end of the town.

I got out and walked along the front. I paused on a bench overlooking the sandy beach, took out a fag and watched the waves lap in. I hadn't gazed mindlessly at the sea in years. I used to love walking along the dunes at Troon or running through the shallows in my bare feet. A rare calmness settled on me. It wasn't just the nicotine. I hadn't realised how weary I was. Weary of the war and its sour aftermath. Weary of London and the faceless anger of the ruined city, rationed in food and hope. I listened to the harsh gulls and wondered if I could find sanctuary here, maybe get a wee boat, catch fish, grow my own vegetables. Drop by the local pub most evenings to catch up on village gossip or attend the occasional ceilidh or darts competition.

I was suddenly aware of a shadow. I turned and saw a man framed against the sun.

'Would you be Mr Douglas Brodie, by any chance?' His voice had the hard nasal lilt of Northern Ireland.

I stood up and saw his dog collar. He wore a blue shirt underneath and a black jacket. Thin blond hair was clamped tight to his skull by Brylcreem. He looked too young for the job and vulnerable behind thick specs.

He went on, 'There aren't so many visitors here just now and I was watching for the bus. Father Connor O'Brien, Mr Brodie.' He held out his hand.

'Just Brodie is fine. Thanks for meeting me,' I said, stretching out my hand.

'And I'm Connor. I was told yesterday you'd be in later. But I had another call this morning from Father Cassidy.'

'We're in a hurry. You'll know why?'

He nodded. 'Shall we sit here? It's a rare day, so it is.'

We sat and he took a cigarette. He was maybe my age, but already losing his hair quite badly. The hair cream kept the strands carefully in place, maximising their coverage. The glasses made him look even more scholarly but there was a surprising toughness in his voice – and it wasn't just the hard brogue – that suggested a certain underlying steel.

'How did you wash up on these shores, Connor?'

'I grew up in Belfast and wanted a change, somewhere quieter. They sent me here.' He smiled.

'Too quiet?'

'Too small. Funny, with all this space ...' his wave took in the huge sky and the dancing sea '... it's just a wee bit ...'

'Claustrophobic?'

He nodded. I knew what he was saying about the closeness, the nosiness of a small community. I'd seen it in Kilmarnock. It was part of its strength but it was certainly its downside too. Put a hand on a girl's breast in a darkened close and you could hear the mass intake of breath from scandalised neighbours.

'And you, Brodie. What's your excuse for being here?'

He wasn't asking what my mission was. In the simplest

terms he knew that. He was asking a bigger question. I could have sidestepped it, saying I hadn't the time, or pretended I'd misunderstood, but there was something in his manner that I felt I could trust. Like meeting a stranger in a pub and swapping life stories over a few pints, knowing you'd never meet them again. I told him where I was born, pointing out across the water to the mainland and the beaches I'd played on as a wee boy. I told him of my army days, and how, to shore up my dwindling demob pay, I'd started on the journalistic path I should have taken after university, instead of the police. And how my plans had been scuppered when I'd been summoned to help Hugh try to escape his date with the hangman.

He was leaning forward gazing out to sea, elbows on knees, and nodding as I talked. 'I see, I see ...'

'... so it's a long shot, but we have to try everything.' I finished by describing my search for Hugh's erstwhile neighbours.

'Well, Brodie, it's not been easy getting to this point in your life, has it? But at least I can make the next wee step a simple one. The family that we're talking about call themselves Kennedy. I've no way of telling if that's their real name. But they arrived here about at the start of the year. From Glasgow, clearly, by their accent. Not of my own flock, but, as I was saying, this is a small place and new folk stand out. Get themselves talked about in the post office.'

'A mother and four kids?'

He nodded. 'Rented a wee house round the back of Lamlash on the Ross Road. Paid the first six months' rent in advance. That got them talked about, I can tell you. Kept themselves to themselves but the children were enrolled at school and in bible class at the kirk. She says – Mrs Kennedy, that is – that she lost her husband in the war. But of course the local gossips put a different tale on her.'

'I think you'll find her real name is Reid. If so, she might know something that will stop a hanging.'

TWENTY

We walked along the seafront and took the turn-off on the Ross Road that led to Sliddery, a village on the west side of the island. We were nearly running out of houses when we stopped and Connor O'Brien pointed across the narrow street at a little house set in from the road. A puff of smoke drifted from the chimney.

'I'll leave you to it, Brodie. Good luck, now.' He turned and walked away and I crossed over. A curtain flicked. I knocked on the door. I knocked again and finally I heard steps. It opened. A big woman stood there in her pinny, pretending to be in the middle of housework. Strands of grey hair escaped from her headscarf. She clutched a worn duster to her heavy bosom like a bridal bouquet. Her eyes were wide and her nostrils were flared as though she'd encountered a snake in her coal bucket.

'Whit is it?' she managed, from a tight throat.

I took my hat off. 'Mrs Kennedy, is it?'

She blinked and said, 'Yes. Yes, it's me.'

'I'm sorry, Mrs Kennedy, have I come at a bad time?' I wondered from her pallor and agitation if there was someone behind her with a gun pointed at her head. She twisted the duster as though killing a chicken.

'No. No, I'm fine, so I am. What do you want? Who are you?' she gushed.

'Am I right in saying you used to live in Glasgow? In Florence Street? House number seven? Your neighbour at number eight was Hugh Donovan.'

I thought she would collapse as I lined up the facts and fired them at her. She was shaking her head and her mouth was opening and closing like a goldfish. Her hand crept to the door as though she was about to slam it in my face. I stuck my foot over the threshold. She saw I wasn't going anywhere until I got some straight answers. A look of resignation came over her face.

'Aye. We used to live there. But I hardly knew him.'

'I thought the name in Glasgow was Reid?'

She blushed. 'Kennedy was my maiden name.'

'Which would you prefer?'

'I'm a married woman still and all. It's Mrs Reid. My man Alex Reid died four years ago. Accident at John Brown's.'

'I'm sorry. Can I come in a minute, Mrs Reid? It might be easier inside.' I glanced meaningfully around at the net curtains of her neighbours. She glanced at my foot in her doorway.

She opened the door and let me inside. I was straight into a small room with a tiny fire flickering in the grate. It made the room too snug for today's fine weather. There was a door leading into the kitchen and a staircase that I guessed led up to the bedrooms. The room was bare with nothing to suggest who lived here. No photos or ornaments, just a threadbare couch and a sagging armchair and a smell of cigarette smoke.

'My name's Douglas Brodie. I'm an old friend of Hugh's, and I had a couple of questions for you.'

'I'll make some tea.' She scuttled into the scullery and crashed around for a bit until reappearing with two cups and saucers and a teapot. She took the armchair and I perched on the couch.

'Go on,' she said, rattling her cup as she sipped at her too-hot tea.

'You'll have heard about the terrible happenings. The trial and everything?'

She nodded.

'I'm working with his lawyer to see if there's some grounds for an appeal. And to put it simply, we wondered if you could tell us what happened that night?'

'What night would that be, Mr Brodie?'

'The police came for Hugh in the morning. That's when they found all the evidence in the house. We want to know if you might have heard or seen anything the night before.' There, it was that simple.

And just as simply she said, 'No. Nothing.' She reached beside her chair and pulled up a handbag. She took out a cigarette pack and lit one. Her hands were trembling and then were stilled as she inhaled deeply and let the smoke trickle out in a slow cloud. Stupid, stupid. I was going too fast. I tried a different tack.

'Did you know Hugh had a wee problem, Mrs Reid? That he took drugs for the pain?'

'Aye, I kent fine. He was in an awfu' bad way, pair man.'

'And sometimes Hugh would come home late and maybe the worse for wear? As though he was fu'?'

'I heard him sometimes.'

'But not that night?'

'Well, maybe. You know, you don't always notice. And you don't like to stick your nose in, do you?' she said pointedly.

'In the couple of weeks before they took him away, did you hear or notice anything strange, anything unusual?'

'Whit like?'

'Like a child greeting or shouting. In Hugh's house. Anything at all?'

'No, nothing. Just normal.'

'Why did you leave, Mrs Reid?'

She got up and flung her fag end on the fire, then stirred the sorry pile of slag to coax a flame out of it. She turned, poker in hand. 'We just wanted a change, so we did. Is there anything wrong in that?' Her voice was louder, more on edge, as though she was running out of patience.

'No, of course not. It's just ... unusual, that's all. And why did you come here?'

'We fancied it. The sea air and that. For the weans.'

'Where are the weans?'

'Oot playin'.'

'And *how* are the weans, Mrs Reid?'

She raised the poker like an épée and pointed it at my chest. Her sallow skin was glowing with a fierce anxiety. 'An' whit's it to you? Whit are you askin' about my weans for?'

'It must be quite a change for them. I was just wondering how they're getting on.'

For a moment she stood there, a fat dowdy tigress ready to belt me with a poker for even thinking about her kids. Then her shoulders slumped, she put the poker down and lit up again.

'They're fine, just fine ...' Her face slowly settled and turned from anger to what I can only call despair. I hated myself but I had to push.

'Mrs Reid, there's a man in Barlinnie Prison. Your neighbour. A war hero. They're going to hang him in a few weeks for something he might not have done. If you have anything to tell me that could help us find the truth, then ... Well, that would be good of you.'

Slowly her eyes filled up and tears started running down her creased face. Her chest heaved and I wondered if she was going to have a heart attack. Finally the sobs began and she sat hunched and wheezing in her chair.

'I cannae tell you. I just cannae.'

'Was there someone else there that night? Did you hear someone else?'

Her chest settled and she looked at me through red puffed eyes. She nodded.

'Do you know who it was?'

She hesitated and then nodded.

'What happened? Just tell me in your own words.'

Her eyes pleaded with me not to ask this of her. I held her gaze.

'It was late. Well past bedtime. It woke the weans. I heard feet, two pair. Yin of them no' so steady. Then voices. Wan was shooshing the other. Then his door opened and they went inside.'

'Who did, Mrs Reid? Who went in?'

'Yin was Donovan. His voice was slurred, but I kent it fine.'

'And the other?'

'Yon priest.'

My blood stopped. 'Father Cassidy?'

'Aye, him.'

TWENTY-ONE

I took the bus back to Brodick and caught the late-afternoon ferry to the mainland. I was in luck. The *Glen Sannox* was laid up for few days with engine problems. The sleek paddle steamer *Jeanie Deans* had been diverted from its usual runs up Loch Long to Arrochar. It would dock at Craigendoran instead of Ardrossan but the rail link along the north bank of the Clyde into Glasgow was quicker. Its twin red, white and black banded funnels belched long trails of steam as we set off for the mainland. I stood on the deck hanging over the rail, watching the white water churn past. The sea was as calm as it got out here between the island and the mainland, waves rolling past rather than flinging themselves at the bow. The big paddle wheel slapped rhythmically round and round; my brain seemed to be connected to it. It made no sense. Why in – literally – God's name was Patrick Cassidy, man of the cloth, hiding this information? And why had he arranged for me to uncover it?

I was so lost in my reveries that I didn't notice the two men who joined me at the rail, one on either side. They weren't just taking the air. Their shoulders were touching mine. Their hats were pulled down over their faces. The one on my left turned to me.

'A' right there, Brodie?'

I made to stand back and found they had pinioned my arms. For a moment I thought they were police, until the one who'd spoken nodded to his pal. They bent swiftly and expertly and grabbed me behind the knees. Suddenly I was in the air, my hips rammed against the wooden railing. My hat went first. I watched it sail away and tried frantically to cling to the rail. But they'd got right under me and my weight was now beyond the point of return. A further heave and I went over the rail in a very bad piece of gymnastics.

My body sailed right over, but my hands still clung desperately to the wood. I crashed against the side, winding myself. In sheer desperation, I flung myself round and grabbed the bar below the rail with my right hand. I now clung with my face against the railing and my legs flailing on the side of the boat. I looked up into two grinning faces. One of them I recognised from my barney in the gents the other day.

'Nice day for a swim, ya fucker!' cried Fergie, pulling out a bike chain which he'd kept tucked up over his shoulder under his jacket. He lashed down at me and caught me on my head and shoulders with the sharpened links. Then he and his pal chose a hand each and stamped on it. I tried to hang on but it was useless. Before the next swing of the chain ripped my face open I pulled myself up, got one foot on the edge of the deck and swung a punch at Fergie. He stepped back and swept the chain at my head. It caught me on my left cheek, wrapped itself around my head and tore the skin off my jaw. As I jerked away I glimpsed his pal pull out a bayonet and plunge it towards my chest.

I did the only thing I could. I jumped.

I was a long time in the air, and I could see their grinning faces watching me every foot of the way. I hit the water and went under. Deep, deep into the green. The cold stopped my heart. The salt tore at my open wounds. I was blind in the mill race of the churning wake. My one piece of luck had been to stand downstream from the paddles. Otherwise I would have been fish bait by now. As it was, I was only drowning.

I kicked and struggled upwards and blasted into the air, spewing salt water like a sounding whale. I lay flapping and coughing in the chopped furrows of the ferry. White spume kept slapping my face and forcing water down my every orifice. I felt my coat dragging me back under and struggled out of it. The shoes went next and then my jacket. Already my energy was fast dissolving as the adrenalin levels dropped. With a final push I struck away at right angles from the wake and splashed and swam till I found myself in calmer waters.

I rolled on to my back and lay gasping and spluttering like a harpooned seal. I concentrated on calming down and conserving my energy. When my body had relaxed a little and I could float without too much kicking, I turned and looked round for the boat. It was a fast disappearing hulk on my horizon. No one except my deadly pals had seen me fall. No sign of a crewman calling 'Man overboard' and a nice red lifebelt floating my way. There were still waves rolling me up and down but it was the normal swell that ran down the Clyde all the way to America.

'You bastards!' I screamed, and slapped the waves in impotent fury. The thought of dying at the hands of these scum was too much to bear. I vowed to wring their dirty necks next time we met. If …

The cold water began to cool my ire. I took stock. Fergie had timed it nicely. The distance between Brodick and the mainland was about fourteen miles. I was roughly halfway between. There was no sign of any other boat and I was aware of being pulled along by a steady current towards the next bit of mainland: either Northern Ireland or Newfoundland. Such information was only going to be relevant to my bloated corpse.

On the plus side, even at this time of year, the water wasn't cold enough to kill me outright. The blessed Gulf Stream kept the waters lapping Ayrshire and the west coast at a temperature that was survivable. For a while. Not quite the Murmansk run. Or not immediately. I could last for, well, hours, until the cool Atlantic slowly sapped my strength and my body shut down bit by bit.

Though I could swim well enough, I'd never swum seven miles in my life, far less in the open sea. My trousers were tugging at me and I slipped them off as well as my shirt and socks. They weren't keeping me warm and were only making me struggle against their sodden weight. I would look like I'd gone for a dip in my vest and pants, and got carried away by the currents. Apart from the chain marks across my face.

Big Bill, my old geography teacher, was always telling me to pay more attention, that knowing how the natural world worked was essential knowledge in a man. I wish he'd told me it could be a matter of life or death. I had no idea what the tides and currents did in the Firth of Clyde. I didn't know their direction or whether they changed depending on the phases of the moon. All I recalled was that the currents were supposed to be treacherous.

At least the seas were calm, just a shallow swell and steady ripple of waves that lifted me up and down like a soggy cork. I turned on my face and, for want of a better idea, started swimming, a steady crawl towards the mainland. I gave it up after a couple minutes with no sense that I'd made any impact whatsoever on the distance. I tried backstroke, as it was more like floating, but that got me nowhere either as far as I could see. All I was doing was using up energy and therefore body heat.

I wasn't entirely alone: the odd seagull squawked and hovered over me until it decided I wasn't yet ripe for nibbling. It would keep coming back until I was. There was other debris in the water, junk from ships and from the mainland. A nice big log would do me fine, or a stray rowing boat. Flotsam and jetsam. I tried to recall the difference; I think I was technically jetsam.

I looked at my watch. It seemed to be living up to its claim of being waterproof up to a depth of twenty feet. Though if it hadn't I wasn't in much of a position to complain about it to the manufacturer. It was already five-thirty and would be dark by eight. After that? Could I go on floating till morning? At what stage would I just say sod it, and let it all go? They say drowning is easy, just fill your lungs with water and relax. But I reasoned that if evolution had removed our gills in favour of nostrils, it wouldn't be that comfortable to go into instant reverse.

Suddenly my already damaged head took another belt. I sank and spluttered around to see what had hit me. It was a crate, a packing crate, half submerged. It said 'Tea' on the side. Thank you, Lipton's. I swam to it and clung on to it. The tea chest immediately sank. I let go and it bobbed up. I felt round it. It was open on one side. I turned it and emptied it as best I could and then upended it trying to capture as much air inside as possible. On my third try it bobbed with about one third of its bulk out of the water. Gingerly I got my arms over it and my upper body part on it. It was precarious but it held me. Only my hips and legs dangled in the water. I'd seen an odd shark hanging bleeding at Ayr fishing harbour before but couldn't recall if they were the type that had a penchant for hairy legs. But in such ignorance there is hope.

I'd been in the water an hour, and from my wobbly perch there was no doubt: I was being pulled parallel along the coast and towards the south. For a while, Holy Island off Lamlash had been my nearest chunk of dry land but I was being dragged away from it into the widening bay where the last Ice Age had taken a bite out of Ayrshire. For a time I felt I was being pushed towards the coast and my hopes rose. But then the capricious tide seemed to grip again and I lost way. Another hour later, as darkness softened the seascape, I was numb and frozen, and certain I couldn't hang on till morning. It wasn't how I expected to die. I'd been attacked by tanks in the desert and blown up in Italy, and shot at all across northern France to the Rhine. But here I was, about to drown a couple of miles off the beach I used to build sand castles on. It was almost as though I'd been living on borrowed time and the big guy who kept count had finally noticed. All those months after demob when I wished I was dead came sharply into focus. I suddenly realised I very much wanted to live. Too late. I should have spent the rest of my savings on drink and wild women.

The sun finally set way to the west but, funnily, it hadn't gone completely dark. A northern light imbued the great plain of water with a sullen glow. A half-moon rose and added to the sheen on the wave tops. That's when I saw the distant lights.

TWENTY-TWO

At first I thought it was simply town lights, from Troon or Ayr or maybe Girvan by now, but then I realised they were closer and bobbing about. Maybe a mile away, though it was hard to gauge. But there was no doubt what they were: I could make out four or five craft with lights on their masts, swinging and dipping in the swell. They had sails up and were heading – well, I couldn't tell where yet. Night fishermen. I even heard a distant voice calling and getting a laugh in response.

I shouted. Or tried to. It came out like a bark. I swallowed and tried to get more saliva down my throat, and gave it another go. I kept it simple.

'Help!'

I shouted until my throat, roughened by the salt water, began to close up. I stopped and listened. Nothing. I now thought I could see them moving. Away. It was hard to tell in the shimmering gloaming.

The trouble was I was too low in the water, except when I bobbed up on the crest of swell. I needed to be standing on this crate, like an evangelist at Speaker's Corner. I let myself sink back a little into the water then with my hands on the top of the box I shot myself up on to it, as though I was getting out of a swimming pool. I felt it begin to capsize but I kept going anyway and managed to get a knee up. With a last despairing surge I got to my feet, feeling the crate tip and sink beneath me. As I began to fall into the water, I cupped my hands to my mouth and bellowed, 'Heeeelp! Help! Help!' before I tumbled into the sea.

I nearly didn't have the strength to surface again. I just let myself float up. The crate seemed to have sunk completely. I looked around and saw it just below the surface but swamped by waves. I doggy-paddled to it and grasped its rough square-ness. I didn't have the energy to right it and get an air bubble into it. I just lay there wallowing. Until I heard, from a long way off but clear enough:

'Hello!'

Their paraffin lamps triangulated on me, and their rough hands dragged me into a small fishing boat. I lay shivering and gasping in the bottom like one of their herrings. They plied me with questions and – wonder of wonders – hot tea from a flask.

They were from the tiny fishing village of Dunure, five miles south of Ayr. They interrupted their work to land me in their high-walled harbour. They were all for phoning the Ayr Constabulary in a state of righteous anger at what had been done to me. But all I wanted was a few pennies and a phone box. They left me to it and reset their trim sails and steered back out of the harbour to plunder the waiting shoals.

I stood shivering in a borrowed plaid as the operator connected me. When I heard her voice I slammed the money in.

'Sam, it's me, Brodie. Sorry to—'

'Oh, thank God! Where are you? What happened?'

I was touched at the concern in her voice. Apart from my mother, no one much bothers if I live or die. In fact, lately, rather more seem to want me dead.

'I'm in Dunure, down past Ayr, and I'm in a bit of bother.' I gave her a short sketch of why I was standing semi-naked and dripping in a phone booth at nearly midnight. She told me to wait.

It was nearly two o'clock in the morning and I was sitting on the harbour wall, gazing out on the silver-lit sea. My thoughts kept turning to what I was going to do to Fergie and his pal when I caught up with them. I'd seen men live for hours in excruciating pain from a bayonet in the guts. Everything about this wretched business was making me seethe. I'd been hauled away from a new life in London on a hopeless mission. I'd been duped by a duplicitous priest. And two low-life scum had tried to dispose of me like fish bait.

I suddenly stopped the self-pity. What about Sam? What had they planned for her? I wasn't a praying man these days, but I was fervent in my hope that she was well on her way and that she'd checked the brakes on her car.

I lit another fag. As well as the plaid – which I had promised to drop off at the harbourmaster's office – the fishermen had left me some fish-paste sandwiches and a pack of Woodbine.

I was steadily working my way though the last of the ciggies when I heard the sound of a big car coming down the hill to the village. The headlights flashed on and off as it swung round the curves and finally blazed down the little street that bordered the quay. I stumbled towards it in my bare feet, like a refugee from the Highland Clearances.

She was standing waiting for me with the rear doors open.

As I got close I could see it was a Riley, a Kestrel Sprite by the looks of the big headlamps and the three panels of glass down the side. A nice twin-cam 1.5-litre engine and wire-spoke wheels. Was there no end to the surprises from Miss Samantha Campbell?

'God, Sam, you're a sight for sore eyes.'

'I can't say the same for you, Highland Laddie. Look at your poor wee face.' Her eyes were full and she only just stopped herself touching my torn cheek and chin. I hate women weeping over me. It usually means I'm in deeper trouble than I think.

'I can assure you it wasn't the fishes.'

She turned and dug into the back seat. 'Here, try these. My dad's.'

She held out a pair of Harris Tweed trousers and a thick cotton shirt. I slid my now shaking legs in and found the slacks were an inch or so too long and too wide at the waist. But a pair of braces did the trick and this beggar wasn't feeling choosy. The shirt went on, and with it some real warmth. She dipped back into the car and held out a pair of shoes and a fancy pair of argyle socks.

The socks were luxury and the shoes – solid, well worn and polished so much they shone in the moonlight like fish scales – were only a size too big. Tightened laces soon did the trick, and I stood there, a new man, comprehensively baptised and reborn. Hallelujah. She'd watched as I went through my transformation. She sized me up and nodded.

She started up the Riley. The neat but powerful engine thrummed comfortingly in the night. As we drove, I worked backwards with my story. I told her about the ferry incident, then my meeting with Mrs Reid. I watched her jaw muscles work in anger and then open in incredulity.

'Father Cassidy! She must be wrong. She's confused. It's not possible!'

'Aye, maybe. But how do you explain my burial at sea?'

'How do you mean?'

'Who except you and Cassidy knew where I was going? And I assume you're on my side.'

She was silent for a while then she hit the wheel. 'This can't be right. It's just too stupid for words.'

I let her concentrate on a negotiating a tight bend near Greenock. In the moonlight, the big cranes stalked the landscape down to the Clyde. I made a mental note to look up Firth of Clyde currents and tides when I was next in a library. Then I turned to her. She was staring intently ahead, every so often pushing her glasses more firmly up her nose. A good profile, but too many worry lines.

'Unless I was being followed, only you, Father O'Brien and Father Patrick Cassidy knew where I was going. O'Brien seems an unlikely mastermind and has no obvious motive. And I'm as certain as I can be that I wasn't followed. I'm trained to spot them, especially a couple of ogres from Dermot Slattery's gang.'

'Are you really saying that Father Cassidy set you up, was in league with Slattery, and ...' She stumbled for words.

'And arranged to have me killed. It looks like it.'

'But why would Cassidy give us the contact in Arran? Why make it easy for you?'

'I wasn't supposed to meet Mrs Reid.'

'Oh ... You were supposed to catch the *morning* ferry, not one the night before.'

'And Fergie and his pal would have thrown me to the fishes on the way out. They couldn't change their plans in time.'

'But *I* knew where you were going. Even if you'd ... disappeared. I would have been able to follow things up. Wouldn't I?'

'If they'd let you.'

Her jaw tightened again. We sped on in silence.

'You realise what this would mean for our appeal?'

'If we can make it stick. Mrs Reid is scared to death of something or someone. I think they've threatened her kids. They may even have them now. That's why I don't want to get the police involved just yet.'

'How do we prove it, then?'

'Let's drop in on the good father when the sun's up, and see how many "Hail Marys" he's doing for having me murdered. I don't know how they do their sums, but I reckon he should be on his knees till Christmas.'

We garaged the car behind the house. She made me have a bath. Then she gave me a slab of Dundee cake and insisted I wash it down with a glass of her finest malt. I did as I was told. All she had to do was tuck me up in bed to finish the job, but whether she did or not, I don't know. I fell asleep as if I'd been felled.

I woke flailing from the embrace of seaweed, my arms encrusted and stiff with barnacles. As I gasped to the surface, I found the bedclothes wrapped round me like winding sheets, and even when liberated, my limbs felt like I'd wrestled with the Loch Ness monster itself.

I eased my way to the bathroom and stood staring at my ruined face. The cut on my forehead from my fight in the pub toilet had opened again. But the worst was the livid horizontal weal that ran from the back of my head round under my ear and across the chin. Part of it was just bruising, but two-thirds was lifted raw skin. It wasn't bleeding or oozing, though – the salt water had been a good antiseptic. Fergie was going to pay.

'Brodie! There's breakfast on the table if you can face it!' she called from the hallway outside my door.

'I can face it. But can it face me?'

I found a heavy tartan dressing gown hanging behind the door. I slipped it on over my pyjamas. I smelt again the same old man's smell that came with the tweed trousers: a lifetime of tobacco smoke and humanity. I presented myself at the kitchen door. She couldn't help put her hand to her mouth. Her eyes were wide. I guessed it wasn't just her father's dressing gown.

'You poor wee soul, you.' She gathered her wits and busied herself. 'Sit here. Start with the tea, and breakfast will be in front of you in no time.'

I sat down, picked up my teacup and raised it high. 'To Lipton's.'

That got a laugh from her, and then she was as good as her word. A great plateful of powdered-egg omelette, black pudding and tattie scones was served up with a flourish. She must have used up her ration coupons for a week. She sat there sipping her own tea, elbows on the table, watching me proprietorially as I devoured the lot. Toast was grilled and buttered for me. All I had to do was wash it down with the steady flow of life-giving tea.

Then came the iodine for the wounds. We couldn't work out any sensible way of bandaging the jawline without my looking like a bad advert for tooth decay. So we let the wound be. It was healing fast after the tender ministrations of the Atlantic.

I had another bath to ease the aches, and dressed for our Sunday outing. There was a jacket that matched the trousers.

A good fit, if a bit dated. And with the plain brown tweed tie I looked as if I'd strolled off the heather after an encounter with a stag, said stag having won the first round.

'You'll do,' she said, eyeing me at the door.

'I hope the holy father doesn't decide to put up a fight,' I said, wincing as I tried to free up the strained muscles in my arms and shoulders. 'You'll have to wrestle him to the ground. Then these fine brogues of your dad's will come into their own.' I pointed down at the slabs of leather that would certainly outlive their present temporary owner, as well as their last.

'There's one other thing,' she said, walking over to the sideboard and picking up a cloth-covered lump in two hands. She placed it on the table in front of me. It clunked.

I walked over and unwrapped it. It was a big brutal Webley Mark VI revolver, standard officer issue in the Great War. Its cylinder took six bone-crushing .455 shells; its 6-inch barrel gave it an effective range of about 50 yards. Accurate with each shot if you could hold the damn thing down each time. It kicked back in the hand like a mule.

'Your dad's again?'

She nodded. 'He brought it back from France in 1918. Kept it for hunting. The *coup de grâce*. Don't, and I really mean this, Brodie, don't use it unless you have to. I don't want you turning Glasgow into the Scottish Wild West.'

I hefted it, broke it open and examined the barrel. It was a nice, simple weapon. Double action, so no need to cock it each time you fired. Ideal for bringing down a villain and keeping him down. A hit from one of these bullets would leave a huge exit wound and a lot of internal damage, no matter where it struck. I opened the tweed jacket, and found a pocket that seemed to have been strengthened and tailored to take it. It

143

bulged the front of the jacket a little but otherwise sat neatly enough, as though it had found its way home.

She went back to the sideboard and brought me a pack of shells. They had to be at least ten years old but looked as if they'd do the trick. I broke the revolver again and filled the chambers. I made sure the safety was on and stored it in the sideboard under the cloth, ready for my next confrontation with the Slatterys. I didn't think I needed a gun for Sunday mass.

TWENTY-THREE

We drove round to the square chapel in the Gorbals. Sam explained on the way that she'd nearly sold the magnificent Kestrel after her parents' death, but had simply never got around to it. I was grateful for her tardiness. We pulled up outside. There were some folk milling about. Chapel-goers in their Sunday black.

'Are you sure we shouldn't call the police?' she asked for the third time.

'And tell them what? A well-regarded priest of a prominent chapel is in cahoots with a drugs baron and arranged to have me murdered? And the very same pillar of the community was there the night before Hugh Donovan was found drowning in enough evidence to hang him twice over? How do you think they'd take it?'

She raised her hands, palms up, over the steering wheel. 'So we just pop in for a wee chat? Maybe beard him in the confessional and hope he'll do the talking?'

'I want to see his face. When he sees mine. We'll take it from there. OK?'

'OK.'

We got out and walked up the short path to where people were standing and talking to each other.

A wee white-haired woman looked up at me. 'Yer wasting yer time, so ye are. It's no' open.'

'What do you mean it's not open?' I asked, knowing as I said it that I'd just given the perfect opening for a Glasgow response.

'Because it's shut,' said the wee monster.

'How often does this happen?'

'Never been known, so it hasnae,' she said triumphantly.

'Is there a back door?'

She looked at me as though she'd only just realised she was talking to a heretic condemned to eternal damnation.

'That's the priest's private door. That's his robing room. Ye cannae just walk up there and chap on his door.' Her head was indicating the way, so Sam and I took it, despite the evil eye that followed us round the back of the chapel.

Here the regular sandstone lines were broken up by a small brick building leaning against the rectangle of the church itself. A door was set into the side. It was locked. I really needed to get a proper set of burgling tools made.

'Do you have any kirby grips or a nail file in that bag of yours?' I asked Sam.

'You're not … Surely you're not going to …'

'He tried to have me killed.'

Without another word she delved in her bag and laid a neatly rolled wax-cloth tube in my hand. I undid it and found three screwdrivers, an adjustable spanner, a small pair of pliers and two sparkplugs in my hand.

'My father insisted I learn the basics,' she defiantly.

I inspected the locks and set to work with the screwdrivers. It took me less than a minute till the door clicked open. I pushed it ajar and stepped in. It was dark inside and I waited till my eyes had adjusted before finding the curtains and letting light flood in. There was a sink and two gas rings by one wall.

A carpet and an old armchair and bookcase were the only furnishings. I crossed the small room and opened the door in the far wall.

It led to a short hallway in the body of the chapel itself. At the end was a curtain framed by light. I pulled it open and stepped into the chapel proper, just under the pulpit and facing the empty rows. We edged forward till we were standing in front of the altar and could take in the whole view. Sam was right behind me, so that she was only a second later than me to meet Father Patrick Cassidy. We stood staring at the latest, real-life addition to the body of tragic art that surrounded us.

Directly behind the altar and about twenty feet up stood the gleaming tubes of organ pipes. The rope was secured at one end to the heavy leg of the altar. It rose up, taut as iron, and looped round the back of four of the pipes. It then dropped a few feet and ended in a noose about ten feet off the floor.

Suspended from the noose was Father Patrick Cassidy, his purple face contorted in the terror-filled realisation that the 'Hail Mary's hadn't been enough. He had met his Maker and been found wanting. His long scrawny body dangled naked and unadorned save for the crucifix of his office round his stretched neck. The hair on his chest and groin were white as snow. His fingers were wrapped tightly round the noose, suggesting he'd had second thoughts after kicking away the ladder that lay at his feet. A stink rose from beneath him where his bowels had emptied.

I heard a soft sigh, turned and caught Samantha Campbell as she began to crumple. I half carried, half steered her to a front-row pew and made her put her head between her knees. She was breathing like a fat lad on an assault course. When I was sure she was past the point of fainting, I walked back over to examine the scene.

Tragic, and bloody inconvenient. It wasn't conclusive, but the case against Hugh was looking more like a colander by the day. But Cassidy's demise fairly messed up our case unless we could convince the courts that he'd taken his life in remorse for his guilt. Hard to prove unless we could get a phone down into the flames of hell. Or he'd left a suicide note explaining everything.

I stood by the altar, scanning the area carefully. His cassock lay folded across the altar. His vest, pants, shoes and socks were scattered underneath. A rosary lay piled on top of the robes. The ladder was a big one, two equal sides of steps. It lay twisted and useless where it had fallen.

I got up close to the dangling body. The stink was overwhelming. Watching where I stepped, I walked round the rigid corpse. His lower limbs were darkened by pooling blood. His upper body was blanched. Only his face and his trapped fingers showed colour. Soon they would turn black. His feet were level with my head. Big yellow toenails and hard heels, and something more interesting: darkening rings round his ankles, not complete, just on the outside, as though they'd been held together. I looked up at his hands; there seemed to be a similar pattern emerging round his wrists.

I began to widen my search. I walked back to his little room at the back. In a cupboard hung his best raiments: the white surplice and heavy chasuble. In a drawer by the sink were a few bits of cutlery, including a sharp knife. I examined the sink. The plughole had fibres clogging it, the sort of fibres you might get if you'd cut up a rope. I kept searching and soon found what I was looking for by the side of the old armchair: a short piece of the simple cord he used to cinch his surplice. It was cut roughly at one end. I didn't touch it.

When I got back to the hall Sam was sitting upright and breathing easier. Her face was starched and sweaty, but she gave me a weak smile, all the time averting her eyes from the dangling priest.

'Sorry, Brodie. I just ...'

'I nearly passed out myself. Shall we summon the boys in blue?'

Just then I heard voices coming down the passage from the back room. Then the wee woman who'd been so helpful outside burst through the curtain closely followed by two of her pals. They were all in black coats and clutching black handbags in front of them.

'Stop!' I shouted, but they had too much momentum. They piled up a few feet from us and demanded:

'Whit's going on here? Whit right have you to come into oor church?'

And then her pals saw it. Saw him.

'Oh, dear God, Mary mother of Jesus ...'

'Oh, my God, Lizzie!'

Then their words just turned into shrieks and I shepherded them back to the corridor in a mêlée of accusations and calls to their Maker. I kept ushering them through the back room and outside. Then I stopped and tried to get their ashen attention.

'Don't go back in there. And don't let anyone else get in. Can one of you go to the nearest phone box and call the police?' The three wee dears were gibbering still. 'Ladies! We need you to help. Can you go and get the polis, please.'

They broke away from me as though I'd had time to nip in, capture their priest, strip him naked, throw a rope round the organ pipes and string him up myself. In a stumbling, clutching group they vanished round the corner, sounding like a seal colony under attack from skuas.

I went back in. Sam was in the anteroom now. She looked up; colour was returning to her face in livid splashes.

'What now?'

'We wait and we don't touch anything.'

She looked puzzled. 'He hanged himself. Is there anything more to look for?'

'In the nude? He was murdered, Sam. His ankles and wrists were tied before they strung him up. There might be marks round his mouth. I imagine they gagged him before taking the ropes and the gag away after he was dead.'

The colour seemed to be leaving her face again, but she was made of tough stuff. She straightened. 'Will the police see that?'

'That's why I'm staying here. It's going to be a long day.'

TWENTY-FOUR

t was. A local constable came running in within ten minutes. I pointed him towards the hall. He came back slowly, his cap off and mopping his white forehead.

'Take some air, officer.' Outside I could hear the rumble of voices. Cassidy's parishioners here to pay their respects. Or lynch me, depending on what the wee women had reported.

'I don't know who you are, sir, but you have to leave here immediately.'

We shrugged and walked out into a barrage of questions and accusing looks. Sam and I stood to one side and shared a cigarette. Soon I could hear the bell of a squad car. It stopped at the front of the chapel and, shortly after, two familiar faces shot round the corner.

Detective Sergeant Kerr skidded to a stop. 'Well, well. If there's trouble you're never far away from it, Brodie. What happened to your face?'

'I got hit. What's your excuse, sergeant? I think you have bigger questions to deal with.'

He flushed, looked me up and down, clearly wishing there wasn't a bunch of witnesses around, and then followed the young uniformed constable into the building. DC White gave me a strange look, as though something puzzled him about me.

Then he went in too. They came out within the time it took to finish my half-smoked fag.

Kerr stood at the door. 'Brodie, Miss Campbell, will you kindly step this way.' He indicated the door. We walked back in and stood in the now crowded kitchen.

Kerr started up. 'Did *you* find the ...?'

'Body? Yes. Nothing's been touched. Unless any of you gentlemen have been fingering the evidence?'

'What were you doing here?' asked White.

'Visiting Father Cassidy. He, as you know, is ... was ... Hugh Donovan's priest. He's been helping us.'

'How did you get in? The front door is locked. Was the back open?'

'Not exactly.'

'You broke in!' exclaimed DS Kerr, thinking of the charges mounting against me: breaking and entering; permitting a woman to see a priest in his birthday suit; cheeking a police officer; upsetting their boss; being a smug bastard.

'The question is, DS Kerr, who murdered Father Cassidy?'

'Don't be stupid, Brodie! It's as clear a case of suicide as I've seen!'

I explained what *I'd* seen. The detectives looked at each other and vanished into the corridor. A while later they came back.

'It doesn't prove a thing. We'll need a proper forensic report,' Kerr blustered. I nodded. 'And what's more, Brodie, I think you'd better come down the station with us. If – and I do mean if – this is murder, you are my prime suspect,' he said with what could only be classed as glee.

'Don't be ridiculous. We found the body and reported it.'

'But you broke in! Up to no good, you were. Who's to say what else you got up to?'

'Does your finger of suspicion point at Miss Campbell, Advocate, too?'

Kerr's face screwed up as his lightning brain engaged. 'We'll have to see, won't we?'

'Fine. We'll follow you down in Miss Campbell's car. Unless you have grounds for our arrest?'

We left through the muttering crowd. White and Kerr posted the constable at the door with orders to keep everyone out.

They separated us and took our statements. Then both of them grilled me for an hour until they were joined by Detective Chief Inspector Willie Silver, his red nose glowing in irritation.

'This is pish, Brodie! Total pish!' said Silver as I repeated Mrs Reid's assertion that Father Cassidy had carried Hugh Donovan home the night before he was arrested.

'No, I'll tell you what's pish, Chief Inspector! It's you lot standing around, grilling me, while poor Mrs Reid and her kids are sitting in their house in Arran waiting for someone to pop in and cut their throats!'

'You don't know that! There's no connection between these … events!'

'No? Tell me, then, who was the mysterious caller who phoned the police and told them to raid Hugh's house?' I asked.

White and Kerr exchanged guilty glances. Silver looked even more riled. 'That's none of your bloody business, Brodie!'

'Well, it is my bloody business if someone *tried* to murder *me*! And succeeded in murdering the one man that could save Hugh Donovan from the gallows! Don't you think so, Silver?'

'We've only your word for the attempt on you, Brodie.'

'I have the names and addresses of a dozen fishermen at Dunure who'll gladly tell you what you want to know.'

'And there's no proof yet that we're dealing with anything other than a tragic suicide.'

'In that case, it's time you let me go. Or do I need to call my lawyer? I think you'll find she's quite easy to get hold of.'

Silver was gripping the table as though he wanted to throw it at me. He turned to his minions. 'Out.' They all left.

DC White came back in about five minutes later, looking as if he'd pulled the short straw. 'You can go, Brodie. But you're not to leave Glasgow.'

'I have no intention of leaving Glasgow until Hugh Donovan is proved innocent. What are you doing about Mrs Reid? Are you giving her protection?'

White shifted from foot to foot and pulled at his collar. He waved his hand at me as though trying to swat me off. He turned and walked out of the room, leaving the door open.

Sam was waiting for me and passing the time haranguing the desk sergeant, any passing member of Silver's team, and now Silver himself with threats of legal action unless she and I were released within very short order indeed. When he saw the bitter look on my face, Silver nodded to his sergeant and sidled off to his office to check the level in his bottle.

Twilight was falling on a perfect spring day as she drove us back. We were quiet with each other at first, hardly knowing where to start with our pent-up anger and frustration. I didn't know whom I wanted to manhandle more: my former colleagues or the Slatterys. Finally I broke the silence.

'I need to get back to Arran.'

She nodded, then: 'We used to take a house at Lochranza. Great views. Bloody midges.'

'Midges indeed. I need to be on the first ferry in the morning. Could I take the car? It would save time. We may be too late as it is.' I patted the wooden fascia in front of me.

There was a long silence and a couple of sidelong glances between us.

She said very quietly, 'Do you really think they'll try to kill her?'

'After what they did to a priest?'

'I'm coming with you. I might as well. I've nothing to build my appeal on if we lose our only witness.'

We were quiet again. 'Have we enough Scotch?' I asked.

'There's an off-licence on my corner.' The side of her mouth lifted in just the hint of a smile.

TWENTY-FIVE

First thing Monday I called the newsdesk at the *Bugle* and left a message for my boss telling him I was following up a murder inquiry. I didn't say it was nearly my own. He sounded sceptical and long-suffering. Who could blame him?

The *Glen Sannox* was back in action. We drove the Riley on board the eight-thirty to Brodick. Its twin funnels were soon belching streams of smoke as we hurried through the waves.

'Shall we take a stroll on deck or would that worry you too much?' she asked with a fine balance of seriousness and amusement.

'I'm safe now. They already think I'm dead.'

We took the air as though we were on a day trip for the fun of it. As we passed the midpoint between the mainland and the island, I stared out into the choppy dark waters and thought how improbable it was that I'd survived. After my unlikely escape from St Valery in '40 I found I'd acquired a fatalistic shell. Even as I was stretchered off the battlefield in Sicily I wasn't surprised that the shrapnel hadn't taken my head off. It wasn't that I felt I was being saved for some more dramatic end, or that someone was watching over me. I just stopped worrying about it. Some of the other blokes understood. I guess it was how the brain adjusted to daily exposure to the randomness of dying. It was only when I got back to Blighty that the dam seemed to burst and all my pent-up fears and terrors spewed out. Was that how it was for the others? Maybe I should get in touch with the regiment, compare notes?

As for this latest attempt at shortening my life, I felt no after-shocks other than the physical. Had I donned my protective shell again? So easily? Had a sense of danger been cauterised from my mind? Though it was only two days ago, the whole thing seemed like a bad dream. And I knew all about bad dreams. I touched my cheek. No dream. It must have shown. Sam laid a slim hand on my arm and raised an eyebrow. I smiled to reassure her. A cold dip was nothing to worry about.

'I could murder a cup of tea and a bacon roll.'

'You certainly know how to spoil a girl, Brodie.'

We trundled off the ferry and turned south out of the town. The journey up and over from Brodick Bay to Lamlash took us half the time of the bus. Sam nurtured the pre-select gearbox and pedals like a Le Mans driver as we took the gradient. As we crested the top, the sun came out and how I wished we were indeed on a holiday jaunt. But my heart didn't stay light for long.

We drove down and into the village, found the Ross Road and pulled up outside Mrs Reid's house. The curtains were drawn and there was no smoke from the chimney. Not necessarily anything to worry about, but I made Sam stay in the car and walked up to the front door. I knocked and waited, knocked and waited. I could see nothing from the window; the curtains were tightly closed.

'She's no' in,' came a voice behind me.

I turned round. A small woman was standing by the gate. She was in her slippers and sporting a hairnet over pink rollers. A cigarette dangled from her mouth.

'Is she shopping? Or at the school?'

'Ah wouldnae think so.' She shook her head. 'You're not the first wi' your big cars.'

Samantha had wound down her window. 'What's happening?'

I walked up to the neighbour so that Sam could hear her response. 'You say a big car came? When?'

'Just yesterday.'

'And took her away?'

'Aye. Twa men, big men. Took her and the weans.'

'Took them? You mean forced her?' Sam asked.

'Weel, Mrs Kennedy didnae look that comfortable, ken. But she was watching for her weans. Ah was inside, ye ken. So Ah didnae hear anythin'. Just keeked the look on her face. She wisnae happy, neither she was.'

'Had you seen the men before?' I asked.

'Oh aye, they were the ones that brung them here, a' they months back. Right big hard men, ye ken. Scars and everything. Nae offence,' she said, eyeing my face.

'You'd seen the car before?'

'You don't see mony big cars like thon. No' here.'

'So it wasn't a local car?'

'Nup.'

We drove to the seafront and got out. We sat on the same bench I'd used two days ago. We gazed across at the mainland. I took out my pack and offered her one.

'They didn't lose much time,' she said.

'While *we* were being questioned by Silver's idiots!'

'Would they keep her on the island?' Sam asked.

'Depends.'

'On what?'

'Whether she's alive or dead.'

We finished our cigarettes and flicked the butts into the sea, watching the trail of sparks sail through the air and land with a swift hiss.

'We could look for the car,' she suggested.

'We could. But let's think about this. If it's on the island, it's likely to be in a garage or on a drive somewhere. We could search for days. If it came from the mainland, it went back there. We might get something from the manifest of yesterday's ferry.'

'Well, it's better than just sitting here watching the waves come in,' she said.

I looked out at the gentle surf and let my eyes fill with the sight of the green hills of Holy Island.

'I'm not so sure.' I sighed and got to my feet. 'But duty calls. And before we go, there's one thing I should have asked wee Mrs Busybody.'

We slipped back to the Reid-Kennedy house and I knocked on the neighbour's door. She opened it fast, as though she'd been waiting behind it, eye pressed to the net curtain over the glass panel.

'I don't suppose you saw the number plate, missus?'

She shook her curler-clad head. 'Nup.'

'OK, thanks.' I turned to walk back to the car. She waited till I was at the gate.

'But oor Alec did.'

I walked back. Nosy wee boys seemed to pop up just when you needed them. Alec was produced. Standard-issue urchin. Shorts hanging off his skinny hips, a vest under a sleeveless jumper and a runny nose. But wee Alec was also clutching a scrap of a notebook.

'He collects nummers,' his mother said. 'Nae trains here, so he collects car nummers.'

'See, in the summer, a' thae folk come ower here for the fair an' I get their nummers,' piped Alec.

'Don't taigle the man, son, just tell him the nummer o' the big car frae yesterday.'

Alec flicked through his little pad of childish scrawl and with his filthy finger tracing across the last page he proudly declaimed: 'An Austin 10. SD 319. That's a Glesga nummer, mister.'

'So it is, Alec. So it is,' I replied, only just forbearing to bend down and kiss his nitty head.

We stopped at Brodick harbour and enquired at the ticket office. They kept no record of cars using the ferry unless it had been booked in advance. Most people just rolled up, as we had. The only bookings they took was for sheep, especially in the months after the lambing season.

We tried again on the ferry itself as it battled back to Ardrossan. Same story from the purser, but he suggested we have a word with the deckhands who guided the cars on and off. We found a pair of crewmen lurking by the stern on the car deck, grabbing a fag.

'Ah mind it fine,' said the short one. 'A big black Austin wi' twa men in black suits. Looked like they were undertakers.'

'Mair like folk that kept the undertakers in business, Bobby.'

'Is that why you recall them?' I asked.

'No' just that. Ah've seen yon car before. An' this time they kept in it a' the way to Brodick. Just sat there. Ah telt them they could go upstairs, ha'e a tea and that. But they wurnae interested. Rolled up their window, so they did.'

Lofty wasn't about to be upstaged. 'They didnae go back neither.'

'How do you know that?'

'Sunday service. We were the only boat coming back in the afternoon.'

We thanked our sharp-eyed sailors and retreated to the passenger deck. Keeping my back to the rail and a roving eye out for thugs with evil intent, I heard myself sounding optimistic to Sam, like with my men just before battle.

'First, they're still on the island. And it sounds like they have a base there if they come and go. But it's a big island. Second, if we trace the car, we trace Mrs Reid's kidnappers. And I bet we'll also know who killed Cassidy. That in turn will give us a connection to Rory and maybe the other four missing boys. SD is a Glasgow plate. We can go round to the Glasgow Council offices in the morning and find out who's the proud owner. Maybe there's an Arran address? Then, bingo!'

Sam looked less cheery. 'You make it sound dead simple, Brodie. But Mrs Reid could be dead, and the appeal hearing starts in a week. All I have at this stage is circumstantial.'

'A dead priest isn't circumstantial.'

'He is if we can't prove he was murdered and can't link him to your attempted murder.'

'But you will use it? You will try to make a case out of it?'

'Of course! God, it's something! More than I hoped. But I need to prove these allegations or the Appeals Court judges will just smile and ignore them.'

'But without our witness – Mrs Reid – we can't link anything?'

'Exactly.'

TWENTY-SIX

I was at the counter of the council offices at nine o'clock the next morning. They were helpful in that chatty-I'll-no'-be-a-minute way that forces you to take a seat and wait till you've properly acknowledged the onerous nature of your demand before they hand over the information. Just when I'd reached the last stage of hopelessness and was contemplating throwing my chair over the counter, the clerk came back with the information I'd asked for. But it wasn't what I'd wanted. The car was owned by a privately held company: Ireland Scotland Shippers. The clerk went the extra distance – it seemed like Edinburgh and back – and found out for me that it was an export/import company headquartered in Glasgow and owned in turn by another unlisted company owned by a certain Miss Elizabeth Reilly.

'She's the wife of one of Gerrit Slattery's henchmen,' said Sam, putting the phone down in her crammed office. She'd phoned the organisation that registered private and public companies in Scotland. 'There are no accounts or other company information because it's not a publicly listed company.'

'And if I recall, Gerrit Slattery is—'

'The brother of Dermot, yes.'

'What else do you know about these characters? I heard of them when I was in Tobago Street nick, but never came across them directly. Just some of their underlings. It was a running joke that if we couldn't solve a particular crime then we blamed the Slatterys.'

'Well, you know they're Irish. Lived in Glasgow for years. They shared a huge house with Dermot's wife up in Bearsden. But not such a happy family, apparently. Mother dead long since, and they say Dermot, the elder brother, did time in Belfast for killing his father. Some sort of drunken fight, I imagine. When he got out, the brothers came here and used their muscle to set up a thriving drugs trade with sidelines in extortion and business insurance – with menaces.'

'Well, at least we've made a connection with the missing Mrs Reid.' I looked at her arching eyebrows. 'I know, I know. It's tenuous and doesn't prove anything. But we know we're on the right track.'

Sam ran her hands through her short blonde hair and then thrust them out at me as though pushing me away. Which she was.

'Brodie, I need to prepare this case or we're going into court next Monday equipped with only a charming smile and a silent prayer. It's over to you on the follow-up front. What's your next step?'

'Maybe it's high time I visited the brothers Karamazov? Oh, and checked with our local sleuths how far they've got with the murder of Patrick Cassidy. Lastly …' I paused at this. The prospect wasn't something that made me glad and happy. 'I'll try to have a word with Fiona McAuslan.'

Sam looked quizzically at me over her glasses. 'I assume you mean Hutchinson? Is that wise? What will you get from her?'

The question made me feel guilty. Which was ridiculous. 'I haven't the faintest idea. But no stone unturned, eh?'

As I walked out into the hard daylight of a cold Glasgow morning I was replaying Sam's question. I hadn't told her about my boyhood romance. I assumed Hugh hadn't mentioned it either, otherwise Sam would have been even more inquisitive. Questioning my motivation. Like me. I mean, what the hell was I up to talking to Fiona? Was this some faint echo of our teenage fling? That I had to see her one more time to get her out of my system? God knows, the world had changed since those torrid but simple love affairs at the local dance hall. She'd lost her husband in the war, and then lost her wee boy to a maniac, who might or might not have been my former best pal. She'd found Hugh again but he was the X-rated version of the boy she'd jilted me for. Was it prurient curiosity to see if Fiona still looked the same or had turned into some haggard old bird that I was glad not to be tied to? Or, daftest of all, did I secretly nurture a hope of starting something again now that all the competition was out of the way?

Idiot.

I ducked the whole thorny question by heading first to Tobago Street nick. I marched up to the front desk. The automatic smile of the desk sergeant froze when he saw who it was.

'It's yoursel', Brodie,' said Sergeant Alec Jamieson.

'It is, Alec. How's it going?'

'Aye, fine. What can I do you for?'

'I want to talk to one of your detective pals. White or Kerr. Silver even. I want to hear how they're getting on with the murder of Father Cassidy.'

Alec's bland face screwed up to show he was thinking. 'Murder, you say? That's no' what I hear. Killed himself, poor bastard. Seems he was a bit doolally, you ken.'

*

I left a short while later, with the supercilious grin of DS Kerr following me like the Cheshire Cat. As far as they were concerned there was no evidence of foul play and that was what they would be recommending to the coroner. Tragic way to go and all that, God rest his soul, but case closed. And as for the missing Mrs Reid and family, there could be a dozen different reasons for them not being in when we called. Glasgow police had no need to interview them anyway. The verdict was in. Bring on the hanging.

Every opening was turning into a dead end. Every time I had my hands on something, it slipped away like an eel. I decided I was in a sufficiently pessimistic frame of mind to confront some of my old demons. I headed down towards the Clyde and over the Alexandria Bridge into the Gorbals. Within twenty minutes I was standing outside Fiona's close looking up at the blank windows and praying she was out. Praying she'd flitted with no forwarding address. The street was patched and holed. The pavement ripped up and the stone doorway into the entry was covered with scratched territory markers of the Beehive Boys. The hall stank of pish. This was no place for her. Her family hadn't been well off in Kilmarnock but they'd never lived in such squalor. How has she fallen this far? How had she survived? How had all that grace and promise led to this?

I climbed the spiral staircase, my feet slapping on the bare stone, and stood, heart hammering, outside her door. It wasn't just the climb that had set my pulse racing. I took a deep breath and clacked the knocker on her door. Nothing. I breathed out, tapped again and heard the silence echo away down the stairs. Half disappointed, half relieved, I turned to head down. I'd put my foot on the first step when I heard the door open and a voice call, 'Who is it? Who's there?'

Her voice tore back the years and squeezed my heart. I turned and walked back. I took my hat off so she could see my face.

'Hello, Fiona.'

Her hand went up to her mouth. Her eyes, her dark eyes, widened as though I'd hit her. For a confused second I thought I'd got it wrong and that this was her mother. It had been seventeen years.

'God almighty, Douglas, is it you? Is it really you?'

I nodded and stood like a child in front of his torn dreams. Her long river of black hair had been chopped at the neck by a pair of blunt scissors. A fringe sliced across the pale skin of her wrinkled brow. Her black eyes were framed by sad shadows and crow's feet. It was as if a bad fairy had cursed her and sprinkled ageing dust over her. The fire and challenge in her eyes had been replaced with all the cares in the world. And who was I to say she didn't own them? Her slim frame in her cardigan and loose skirt looked thin, pinched. Was this the lithe body I'd once held? Did she once wrap those dancer's limbs around me? Her heat enough to scorch my defenceless skin?

In that defining instant, all the anger and longing dissolved and I was left with nothing but pity for this stranger who'd stolen some of the features of a girl I used to know. She was shaking her head and putting her hand out in front of her like a blind woman feeling her way. Her huge eyes were filling and the dark pools underneath each one became more pronounced.

'It's too much. It's a' too much. I cannae … I just cannae …'

I went to her and pulled her to me, and felt her thin breasts press against me, and wept inside for what had happened to her and for what might have been.

'Fiona, whisht, it's OK. It's just me. Just Douglas. Can we talk? For a wee while?'

She shuddered and pulled away. She took a hankie out of her sleeve and dabbed her eyes. She straightened. 'Sorry. There's been that much. I never thought I'd see *you*. Not here. Not now. I'm such a mess, look at me. Look, you'd better come in.' She smoothed her skirt and blew her nose and held the door open.

It was a typical two-roomed house. Kitchen-cum-living room and good room beyond. The curtain was pulled across the bed in the wall in the living room. We sat at a tiny wooden table with a blue and white checked waxcloth covering. The place was heavy with smoke. She bustled around and made us tea, all the time with a cigarette going. While we waited for the tea to mask, we began our dance.

'How have you been, Douglas. What happened to your face?'

'I've been fine. The face? A sort of fishing accident. And you? How are you keeping …?'

And so on, until we came to the heart of the matter, the unquiet heart.

'I can't tell you how sorry I was to hear about Rory. It was just terrible.'

Her eyes filled and she shook her head, too charged to speak.

'Look, I'd better tell you why I'm up here. Hugh got hold of me. He phoned me—'

She waved at me to stop. 'I ken, I ken. I heard you were helping that lawyer woman.'

'I'm sorry, Fiona—'

'It's OK, so it is. It's OK, Douglas. You're doing the right thing.'

I looked at her. I'd been expecting her to turn into a wild woman, accusing me of helping her son's killer. But she was calm and gazing at me steadily.

'Am I?'

She nodded. 'That pair man. What happened to his lovely face.' She forced a teary smile on her face. 'You and Hugh were that handsome. The pair of you could have had ony lassie at the dance. *You* still could.'

'I only wanted you.' I regretted it instantly.

She shook her head. 'Douglas Brodie, if I had a pound for every time I wished I could have turned back the years, why, I'd be sitting in Culzean Castle the now.'

I smiled, remembering our youthful fantasies of the high life. 'With butlers bringing high tea. Fancy cakes and hot scones.'

'And cream and strawberry jam.'

We gazed at each other in a smiling thoughtful way for long seconds. I wondered what she meant. Had she just said she wished we'd never parted? I'd never understood. Never asked her why. Was she saying it had been a mistake? That I should have fought for her instead of walking away? That would be too cruel all round. I blinked.

'About Hugh ...' I began.

She waved me quiet. 'He didnae do it, Douglas. I know that.' She sat upright in her certainty, and dared me to argue. How could I? For a brief moment her eyes flashed with the nerve and defiance of the girl who'd speared my open heart on the dance floor.

'How do you know?'

'It's no' in him. No' Hugh.'

'He might have changed.'

She shook her head. 'Folk don't change. No' really.'

'It's not much to build a defence on.'

She gazed at me for a while. 'He told me never to say this ...'

'What?'

'It doesnae matter now.'

'Tell me, Fiona. We need anything and everything we can.'

She studied her teacup, and then looked up at me. 'Have you seen a photo of Rory?' She got up and walked to the mantelpiece. She took down a cardboard-framed photo and placed it on the table in front of me. I held the black and white in both hands. A young boy with a big cheeky grin and dark hair.

The boy I used to play soldiers with.

TWENTY-SEVEN

At last I spoke. 'Did Hugh know? I mean before you left him? I mean …'

She sat down. 'Hugh and I were always having rows. Half of them were about you, Douglas Brodie, if you must know. He was drinking a lot. All that free stuff from the cooperage. We finally broke up and I met another fella, an older fella, Jimmy Hutchinson. His wife had died. I didn't know I was pregnant. Jim and me got married. He was a good man. I always think he knew about Rory.'

I took out my cigarettes and we both took one. 'Did you tell Hugh?'

She blew smoke into the air. 'No. Sleeping dogs and all that. Then the bloody war came. The bloody Nazis took my Jim and they … well, you saw what they did to Hugh.'

'When he came back, when you saw him again, did you tell him then?'

She scoffed. 'There was nae need. The first time he saw Rory, he knew.' She pointed at the photo.

I took my time working out how to ask her the next question. There was no easy way.

'You don't think, even though he knew he was Rory's dad, that …?'

She said calmly, 'That he did it to spite me? That it was some horrible, revenge thing? You should have seen them together, Douglas. And after, when Rory went missing, he was like a wild man. Worse than me, even.'

'But why didn't this come out at the trial, for God's sake? It could have changed everything!'

'You think so? You never saw those polis. They were going to get him no matter what. Besides ...'

'Besides what?'

She sighed. 'Hugh didnae want it brought up. Said it wouldnae help and might look even worse for him. A father doing that to his own son. And how the Procurator Fiscal would spin the story, just like you were suggesting. And any road ...'

'And?'

'He said I'd had enough. That I didn't need bad things being said about me. And Rory shouldn't have his name linked to his, if things went really bad. As if it mattered.' Her eyes were filling again. 'As if it bloody mattered!'

I let her dry her face. 'What about the drugs? You knew about the heroin?'

'Oh, aye. But he was coming off that muck. It didnae really affect him. No' like when he used to be fu', for example. He just went calm and easy after he'd taken some stuff.'

'So there was no time you were worried about leaving Rory with ...'

'With a *junkie*? Is that what you mean? No. It wisnae like that. Never.'

'Fiona, did you ever know who gave him the stuff? Who was the dealer?'

'Oh, aye. Everybody kent that.'

I knew the answer, of course.

'Gerrit Slattery.'

*

I left the tenement and began walking back to Sam's place. I left behind a great big pile of 'if onlys'. But that way madness lies. Once we take certain turnings, once we make certain choices, there's no way back to a time or a place or a person. We start down diverging paths and become changed in the process. Distance lends objectivity, but distorts perception. And then it's gone. No turning back. The seventeen-year-old part of me would never be over the young Fiona. But the woman of thirty-four held no answer for me.

But would anyone? I know I wasn't alone in this sense of dislocation. The war had ripped a great big hole in the continuity of all our lives. We look back with incomprehension at the time before. Like England viewed from France. Men were coming home to strangers, frightening children they'd never met. Five years of fighting alters a man's perspective, hardens him or turns him to mush. Coming back to wives and lovers, how would they explain the night terrors and the daytime despair? How could they talk about it? The vocabulary was different and there were no translators. I was glad not to have anyone to burden.

Was I therefore being unfair to Fiona? Unfair to us? There had barely been a glimpse of the girl I had known, but in her way she'd been through worse wars than many a squaddie. Who was I to judge anyone who could still function, still hold her head up, living in a slum, with all that she'd loved torn or distorted? We owed each other some kindness for what we'd been. Maybe once all this had passed I'd take her out for fancy cakes and hot scones on her day off at Miss Cranston's.

The other revelation was that all roads led to the Slatterys. But how the hell was I to get at them? I could just walk up to their big house at Bearsden and beat the door down, but I assumed they'd have boiling oil perched on the battlements to fend off intruders. Or even if they let me in, they were hardly likely to open up their black hearts to me and confess their sins. They knew they'd get no absolution from me.

I could do my pub crawl again and wait till I ran into the pair of blackguards that had thrown me to the fishes. That was certainly tempting. I had a score or two to settle. And with Samantha Campbell's gun in my pocket, the sides were more evenly balanced. However, apart from the personal satisfaction of breaking the bastards' heads open, it wouldn't provide me with evidence of a stitch-up for Hugh's appeal.

'Can we use it?' I asked a disconcerted Sam later.

'Being the father neither proves nor disproves Hugh's guilt. But if I'd known that the boy was his during the trial, I could have used it. Now, even if they believed her statement, it doesn't basically alter the case against him.'

'Surely they'd believe Fiona? Why on earth would she make that up?'

'But why bring it up now?'

'To save the father of her son from a hanging!'

'It's not a proof of anything.'

'Don't be so ... so lawyerly! Wouldn't they consider it impossible that a father could do that to his own son?'

Sam shook her head resignedly. 'You've led a sheltered life, Douglas Brodie, if you think it's too far-fetched for a father to abuse his child. The cases I've seen ...'

In truth, I knew it too. As a copper I heard whispers in the street about certain families. You tried not to believe it. But in these overcrowded stinking dens, where three generations lived piled on top of each other, things happened that would turn your stomach. With his wife always pregnant, a goatish father with a drink in him is too easily distracted by a promising daughter. They operated like primitive tribes on the very fringe of civilisation, amoral and driven by bestial yearnings. No one wanted to believe it, and there was a silent conspiracy to keep it hushed up, as though the shame on our fair city was too much to contemplate.

But sometimes the cases were so bad they seeped into court. There the tragedies were brought steaming to the surface by a distraught daughter or a tortured son. They found it no use to cite scripture; the stories of Lot and his daughters, or Abraham and his wife-sister Sarah offered no precedent in the eyes of the Kirk or the law. The red-eyed abusers were given hard labour by the courts and rougher justice by their fellow inmates. Even criminals had standards.

I mulled over what the Appeal Court judges would make of the revelation about Hugh and Rory. If Sam was representative of the sceptical judicial mind, they would have seen and heard everything in their time and wouldn't be seduced by emotional appeals. I'd seen judges in action. They dealt with interpreting the law. It was nothing to do with justice, a term only layfolk believed in, like kids and the tooth fairy. My meeting with Fiona had edged me closer to being convinced of Hugh's innocence, but the Appeal Court hadn't danced all night with her at the Attic.

TWENTY-EIGHT

I watched Defence Counsel Samantha Campbell turn in on herself, give up the Scotch and work on the appeal till her eyes grew red-rimmed and dark-lined. I went with her on two visits to Barlinnie and sat beside her as she ran through her approach with Hugh. Hugh himself seemed past caring, or maybe it was the medication. Though he came to life when I told him about the Arran trips and my unintended dip.

'Christ, Dougie! You have to stop! I don't want you killed to save my neck. It's no' worth it.'

'It's no longer just about your neck, old pal. This is personal. Someone's out to kill me and I've got some payback for them when I catch them up.' I rubbed my livid cheek scar for emphasis.

'What about Father Cassidy?' asked Sam.

He shook his head. 'I don't believe it. I just don't believe it. He was always that good to me.'

She went on: 'That night, the night before they found all the evidence at your flat? Do you remember him helping you to bed? Do you recall anyone helping you home?'

He rubbed his tortured face. 'I don't remember. I just don't remember a thing. It's a' a blur.'

I waited till he settled. 'I saw Fiona, Hugh.'

His head shot up. 'Oh, aye. How's she keeping?'

'Not bad. She was asking for you.'

'She doesnae come to see me. I told her no' to. It's no' fair.'

I gave it a beat. 'I saw Rory's photo.'

He sprang to his feet. 'That's no' for the trial! I won't have it, you hear? She shouldnae have told you.'

The warder came over and made him sit. He started rubbing his hands together and twisting the fingers as if trying to screw them off.

'Hugh, listen to me. It could help you, man!'

'It'll no'! It'll just hurt her. I don't want her being dragged into court. Her name in a' the papers again. Ye hear me?'

Sam and I looked at each other. She shrugged. 'We hear you, Hugh. We won't pursue this line in court.'

I took another tack. 'She said your contact, the man with the drugs, was Gerrit Slattery and his pals. Is that right?'

He just nodded.

'How do I find him?'

'He finds *you*, Dougie. He finds *you*.'

'Look, that's not good enough. This is important. He must have some hangouts?'

Hugh looked at me speculatively. 'You'll no' be stopped, will you? Just as bull-heided as ever.'

I said nothing.

'There's a bar in the West End. Where they hang oot. The Tappit Hen. But, Dougie, it's a thieves' kitchen. Even the polis won't go in. It's no' the sort of place that you can just casually wander into and ask for a wee chat with the local razor king, you know. At least, no' without getting a hatchet in the head.'

'I like pubs with character.'

'Talk sense, Dougie. They'll murder you.'

'They think they already did.'

Hugh looked at me as if I was daft.

176

*

It *was* daft. But the events of the last few days hadn't left me feeling too rational. I was being treated like a puppet. I don't respond well to other folk yanking my strings, especially vermin. It's a failing of mine, but not something I'm working on.

I slipped the big Webley inside my borrowed jacket. I left Sam to her pile of papers on the dining-room table and headed out into the warm Saturday night. I got off the tram at the Byers Road and walked down a couple of side streets, noting the alleyways all round me. I found the pub. It was seven o'clock and the Tappit Hen was already buzzing. I could see the silhouettes chatting and laughing through the stained-glass windows of this poor man's cathedral.

I was very conscious of my outfit; a tweed suit would stand out like a tart in a convent in this neck of the woods. But its soft shape and hidden pocket disguised the line of the revolver. I had topped the ensemble with her dad's flat cap, having removed the beautifully constructed fly from its brim. I was a gamekeeper hunting poachers in their own back yard. If the Slattery clan was behind all this, then I should just walk in and shoot them like rats. Six bullets; six bad guys the world would never miss. I turned down my anger to a simmer, pulled the cap over my eyes, shoved the door open and entered the warm fug.

Instantly I felt eyes on me. Conversation paused and mates nudged each other at tables filled with glasses. I walked stiffly straight towards the bar. The barman looked me up and down, his mouth twisted in a grin.

'Ah think you've got your dates wrong, pal. The fancy dress do's the morn's night.'

It brought a gale of laughter from the lads at the bar.

I laughed myself. 'Ah, well, seeing I'm here, I'll have a half and a half.'

I felt the conversation pick up the normal rhythms again, and supped at my beer as I recce'd the room. I was standing at the apex of the horseshoe bar. To my right were tables with men playing cards and talking their heads off. Fringe men, not inner core, just voyeurs of the lowlife. I'd give them something to watch.

To my left was the real action. There were two tables with men huddled over them, one with three at it, the other four. From under the brim of my cap I studied the four-man table: Fergie and his sailor pal made two, and his backstabbing buddy, whose throat I'd staved in, made three. The fourth man was new to me but of the same stamp. Three of them were tucking into pints of ale. The one with the throat problem was sucking at his through a straw. The centre of the table was filled with empty bottles and a smouldering ashtray.

At the other table were three men, two of them clearly older than their entourage at the other. These three had marked out their territory with pints of black stout. The oldest was a man in his mid-fifties, I'd say, thin grey hair and the bland, sandy features resulting from the generations of intercourse between the West of Scotland and Northern Ireland. Like mixing children's coloured clay; after a while it just goes grey. Dermot Slattery, I presumed.

A younger version sat beside him, unmistakably of the same stock but with a little more hair and a ginger 'tache that he kept stroking. As if it were alive. Gerrit Slattery. Though it was too far to confirm the hare lip, the description fitted the man who'd been seen going into Hugh's old house by his new neighbour. Doubtless on a tidy-up operation, making sure there was no evidence. The third man had his back to me but wore his dark hair long and curly. By the width of his neck and the set of his shoulders he wasn't a man to tangle with in a fair fight.

I sunk my large Scotch and felt the fire eat all the way down my throat. I slipped my hand into the inside jacket pocket. The butt of the gun felt reassuringly cool and hard. I clicked the safety off.

I motioned to the barman. 'Have you got Jameson's?' He nodded at the bottle behind the bar. I placed two half crowns on the top. 'Two doubles, and send them over to the Slattery table. Keep the change.'

He involuntarily looked over to the table with three men at it. 'Who will I say?'

'Just say the ferryman.'

He looked doubtful, but took the money and filled the glasses. He lifted the bar up at the side and walked over. He placed the two glasses in front of the two brothers and indicated where they'd come from. As their heads came up to inspect me, I was already walking round to them, smiling, with my hands in my trouser pockets. As casual as you like.

'Evening, boys, mind if I join you?' I stood above the table next to the curly-haired bruiser and faced the bog Irishmen. Curly, the bruiser, was quick to his feet, but ginger moustache signalled him to sit. He did so reluctantly. His face showed disappointment through the old scars and broken bones of the lifetime bodyguard. Ginger lifted his glass, sniffed it and sank it in a oner. I now noticed that the moustache was trying to cover the harelip.

'Cheers, and who the fuck are *you*?' he said.

The older Slattery said nothing, did nothing, took one look at the whiskey and then gazed at me through hard eyes. He waited. The other table had gone quiet and their heads had turned. Comprehension slid across Fergie's face like a slow car crash. He shot to his feet, spilling his beer. He stuck his finger out at me.

'Jesus fuck! It's Brodie! You're fucking drowned, ya' bastard!'

This set off Curly again and he was back on his feet, with fists clenched. He wasn't sure what was happening but he thought he was going to enjoy it. The rest of the pub had gone quiet and expectant. The old man spoke quietly out of the corner of his mouth.

'Tell them to sit down and shut up, Gerrit.' His voice still carried the thick nasal tones of his youth.

Gerrit Slattery gave a signal. Curly moved back to the bar and leaned against it within jumping distance of me. Fergie and his pals at the other table lowered themselves into their seats. Fergie kept wiping his mouth with the back of his hand, wondering how I'd been reincarnated as a ghillie. Dermot Slattery looked me up and down.

'Sit down, Brodie.'

I pulled a chair slightly back from the table so that I had free movement of legs and gun hand. I sat.

'You're quite the swimmer, then, Brodie,' said Dermot, his bitter little eyes carrying a glint of hard humour.

'And how would you know about my swimming talents, Slattery?'

'Cut through the shite, Brodie. What do you want?'

'Fergie's balls on a plate.'

Dermot Slattery sized me up and down. Without turning his head, 'Ye hear that, Fergie? Should I let him have a go?'

I half expected Fergie to beat his chest or pound the sawdust with his hoof. Near enough. He was back out of his chair and poking his finger at me again.

'Just let him try, Dermot! Any time!' To prove how tough he was he stuck his hand inside his jacket and pulled out his sharpened chain. 'I'll mark the other side of his heid and see how he goes without his fockin' ears!'

'I've told you about your language,' Dermot said softly. Fergie sat back and glowered at me, playing with his chain and waiting to be slipped from his leash.

Slattery turned back to me. 'If you can take him, you can have him. Now, what do you *really* want, Brodie?'

I gazed at him and his brother who was fingering his ginger lip. 'Mrs Reid and her weans. And don't insult my intelligence by asking: Who?'

He cocked his head to one side. 'You've a rare nerve, Brodie, I'll give you that. And say we knew who this lassie was, and indeed *where* she was, why would we hand her over to you?'

'Does the car registration SD 319 mean anything to you? On a black Austin 10? It should. You own it. And I have witnesses that will testify that two of your muscle-brains here abducted her and took her to Arran four months ago. Last Sunday they came for her again. Turn her and her kids over to me or I turn the details over to the police.'

Dermot Slattery studied me for a bit, then he looked at his brother. Then he turned back to me and began to laugh, a slow cackling laugh that cut through the pub noise. It started them all off. They hadn't heard anything as funny since Chamberlain's 'peace in our time' speech. Curly at the bar was doubled up with mirth.

I got to my feet, pulled out the gun, cocked it and shot Curly in the foot.

TWENTY-NINE

For a long second, the only noise seemed to be the echoing crash of the gun. It was a relief to find the ten-year-old shells still worked. Then Curly began screaming.

'He shot me! He fucking shot me!' he advised us all, superfluously.

He fell over clutching his foot, squealing like a kid. At the two tables, every man jack of them was on his feet. Chairs crashed to the floor, pint mugs went flying, and the whole pack reared back a couple of feet from this madman in tweed. Before any of them decided to play the hero and rush me, I aimed my gun directly at Dermot Slattery's head.

'Shut up!' I shouted. Peace fell on the pub except for Curly's whimpers.

'Shut up, for Christ's sake,' said Gerrit, his pale face now blotched red with what I hoped was fear. Curly stifled his moans and lay breathing heavily with blood staining his shoe and leaking into the sawdust. There was a two-inch hole in the wood floor where his foot had been, so it must have hurt.

I heard a movement from the other side of the bar and saw the swing door open and some of the hangers-on flee into the night. It wouldn't be long before they summoned the coppers. I had to move fast while I still held the initiative provided by a smoking gun. I stepped forward quickly and jammed the barrel into Dermot's gut. At last I got a different look in his sardonic eyes. Fear and uncertainty.

'Turn round. Fast!' I shouted at him.

He turned to face his gang and I rammed my fingers down the neck of his soft-necked shirt so that I was throttling him with his buttoned collar and tie. I had a good grip of him with my left hand. I rammed the gun barrel into the side of his head.

'Anyone tries anything and the next bullet will blow his head off. Understand? I said: Understand?' I got nods from the five faces in front of me.

'What do you want us to do, Dermot?' shouted Fergie.

He choked out, 'Do nuthin', you eejit. Nuthin'!'

I whispered in his ear. 'Smart, Dermot. Keep being smart and you might not end up dead this night. OK?' He nodded as best a man could while being garrotted with his own shirt collar.

'Right! I want all of you to walk round to the other side of the bar, where I can see you. Move it!'

They unfroze and began to mill round to the far side. Gerrit stood still facing me.

'If you so much as ...'

'Save your puff, Gerrit. Get round there with the rest.' I pressed harder on Dermot's skull with the gun.

'Do it, for Christ's sake,' croaked Dermot.

Gerrit and the others clustered round the bar and I began to walk Slattery to the door. I kicked it open and pushed him through, keeping tight grip of his neck. I stood in the open doorway and looked back at the pack. They were already creeping forward.

'I'll shoot the first man that walks through this door. And then I'll shoot your boss here. Got that? I said: Got that?' Grudging nods. It would give me about twenty seconds. I pushed Dermot on to the pavement, tightened my grip on his collar and began to run him ahead of me down the darkened side alley. He wasn't fit, couldn't breathe easily and was soon puffing like a broken steam engine. I propelled him on, encouraging him by jabbing my gun into his neck from time to time.

'Jesus, Jesus, I can't ... Jesus ...' He was well into his second time round the rosary when I hauled him down a cobbled alley that ran parallel to the pub. Halfway along I threw him into the dark gap of a garage entrance. I rammed him against the wall and let him slide to the ground. I put the pistol to his head. The anger was thudding away in a tight place inside my head.

'Shut up, Slattery. Just shut the fuck up.' I squeezed the words out through gritted teeth.

He gasped and spluttered and then threw up his stout. The sour stink tainted the air. But at least he wasn't calling for his Maker any more. Behind us, I could hear shouts and clattering feet on the pavements and cobbles.

'Don't – kill – me – Brodie,' he gasped. 'I can pay you. Anything you want.'

I wanted to kick him, badly.

'I want Mrs Reid and her kids. I want the life of my pal, Hugh Donovan.'

'OK, we can talk. We can help.' He kneeled in front of me in supplication. I brought the cold snout of the gun against his temple.

'Can we, Dermot? Can we? Can I trust you?'

He shook his head up and down like a puppy. The hard man was gone.

'As God's my judge.'

'I'm pretty sure he is, Slattery.'

It was a dizzying moment. I caught a glimpse of one of his futures: a shrunken body sprawled on the cobbles, with half his face missing and a dark pool forming under his head. I rubbed my face and focused on the present. The moonlight reflected white on his pinched face. Sweat dripped from his brow and breath panted in his throat. I'd taken life in battle but not like this, not a cold execution of a tired, middle-aged man. For all his foul deeds, including ordering my death, an unexpected pang of shame shot through me. I pulled my gun away and stepped back.

I listened to the shouts and the running feet. There was confusion, with the search party splitting up. At the end of the alley, backlit by the orange glow of the streetlamp, two men had stopped and were staring into the blackness. They were wondering whether they should take the chance and venture in or look somewhere brighter, less threatening. I leaned in close and told Slattery in a voice only he could hear.

'I want you to pick Mrs Reid and all four weans from wherever you're hiding them on Arran. You've got Sunday to pick them up and get them back here. You will deliver them to the public library at Townhead, Monday morning. Ten o'clock. Got that?'

He nodded.

'If they're not there, Slattery, I will come after you and your kin and I will shoot you down like rats. Do you understand?'

I peered at him in the moonlight. His small eyes glittered with hope and some of the old cunning.

'It's a deal, Brodie.'

I looked at him. I doubted it. But it was worth a try. The prospect of Slattery handing over a witness capable of putting him and his crew on the scaffold had as much chance as a three-legged donkey of winning the Derby. But I had stirred up the nest. There would be action resulting from it. Some of it might play my way. On the other hand, I could just get badly stung. To death.

'Get up. Start walking towards your pals. Don't run. Don't shout out, or I will put a bullet in your back.'

He stood up and backed away, still facing me, trying to gauge my mood and intention. A spark of triumph? Contempt? flitted across his face. Then he turned and began to walk towards the entry, his back stiffened in anticipation. I turned and ran. My leather soles slapped on the cobbles. That was enough for Slattery. I heard him break into a run in the opposite direction.

'Here, you fuckers! I'm here!' he shouted.

I stopped, turned and fired. Into the air. The bang reverberated among the tall buildings. Slattery flung himself to the ground and the two figures at the alley end dived to the side. I broke into a sprint, erupting from the alley and off down the quiet streets. I twisted and turned and slowed to a walk and found my way back on to the Byers Road. The sweat was pouring down my body under my good tweed suit. I pulled my cap off and rubbed my face dry on its rough surface. I wondered what I'd done.

THIRTY

'You did what? Are you absolutely stark, staring, raving bloody mad?' Samantha Campbell was stomping up and down the dining room, pirouetting and waving her arms.

'I take it you're not impressed?'

I was in my shirtsleeves at the table, nursing a whisky and soaking up my punishment. I let her splutter to a halt. She stood facing me with her arms crossed like an irate wife who'd been waiting for her man to come home fu' and hadn't been disappointed. With hindsight it was a daft thing to do. The sort of thing that earns you the military cross. Posthumously. Sometimes I wondered if I could have been a role model for Stevenson's Dr Jekyll, with whisky as my transfiguring potion.

'Sam, we're stuck. You're in the middle of an appeal case without any hard proof. I had to try something.'

'And what did you do to help my *legal* action? You *shot* a man!'

'In his foot.'

'You *shot* him. Then you dragged Glasgow's biggest gangster out by the scruff of his neck, at gunpoint! And made him beg for his life! The whole pack of criminals, murderers, drug pushers and God knows what else are out there right now, hunting for you! They want to skin you alive and put your head on a pole at the Trongate!'

I shrugged and smiled in as chastened a way as possible. Sam reached for her glass and took a big swig. She wiped her forehead with a trembling hand and stared at me. She grew calmer. She found her normal voice.

'Monday's too late. Even if they produced the Reids. The appeal starts then.'

'I know, I know. Assuming they're on Arran it's going to take Sunday for Slattery's crew to get over there and bring them back. And I wanted this done publicly with loads of people around. You'll just have to stall, Sam. If they hand them over first thing Monday, and Mrs Reid will talk, you can spring the surprise Tuesday.'

She shook her head. 'You're a madman, Brodie.' She took another mouthful and regarded me for a long minute. A smile broke to the surface of her lips. 'I wish I'd been there. To see Dermot Slattery's hard wee face.' Her mouth tightened and thinned again. 'But we're still in trouble!'

'Not *we*, Sam. You're fine. They don't know I'm here. In fact, I'd better leave. Find digs somewhere.'

'You're going nowhere. Stay in. Read some books.'

I shook my head. 'I don't expect Slattery will deliver Mrs Reid on Monday, but I need to follow it through. I'll go to the meeting point and see. You never know.'

We lay low on Sunday, gathering our strength, pretending to read the papers. Sam made some last changes to her case and I heard her do some practice runs up in her library. I couldn't make out the words but I liked the passion. I made a start on some of her leather-bound books. Sir Walter Scott always worked for me.

Come the morning, Sam piled her papers into a battered old briefcase and packed her robes and curly wig into a small suitcase. She looked every inch the professional. She would need to be. A car picked her up at nine and whisked her to the Appeal Court. I closed *Ivanhoe* and headed out into the warm streets.

At a quarter to ten I was lounging by the street corner within view of the Townhead Library. There was no sign of Slattery and his crew, far less Mrs Reid. I chain-smoked and changed my position. I walked past the library and stood looking up and down the road checking for cars or unusual movements. By a quarter past, I had given up. I gave it till half past and wandered back to the library. I threw my butt into the gutter, and turned to walk home when I heard the clang of a police car.

It shot past me and shrieked to a halt in front of the library. Four men jumped out, two in uniform, two in plain clothes. The plain-clothes men ran into the library and the two uniforms took up position by the doors. A few moments later, people started flooding out. They looked distressed. A woman was crying. My stomach knotted and I walked back towards the front doors and up to the nearest copper. He was young, barely of shaving age.

'What's happening, officer?'

'Can't tell you, sir. You cannae go in. Bit of a problem inside.'

'What sort of problem? Fire? An accident?'

'Cannae tell you, sir.'

'Look, constable, I'm a friend of Willie Silver. I was a detective sergeant before the war. Tobago Street.'

He looked me up and down, then he looked round to check his pal wasn't within hearing. He was young enough and inexperienced enough to be bursting to tell someone. 'Seems there's somebody dead in the library. A woman.'

'Why didn't they call for an ambulance?'

His young face took on the thrill of encountering horror. 'She seems to have been *murdered*.'

*

I walked away and kept walking till I was by the Clyde. By instinct I kept a lookout in case I was being followed, but otherwise I was numb. I stood staring at the turbid waters and tried to make sense of the nonsense that my life had become since Hugh Donovan phoned me just two short weeks ago. I thought he was guilty then but the murder of poor Mrs Reid finally pitched me over on to his side. My copper's training said we were still short of incontestable proof, by some way. But I didn't need an ounce more hard evidence to shift my gut belief that Hugh didn't kill Rory, or either of the other missing kids. War had taught me to trust my instincts.

There was no doubt in my mind that the dead woman was Mrs Reid. Slattery's revenge for his humiliation. I should have shot him when I had the chance. Instead, my moment of madness, my need for action, had resulted in the murder of an innocent woman. I felt revulsion well up in me. Revulsion for Slattery. Revulsion for me for provoking this, for being so egotistical, so stupid. No good blaming Mr Hyde – I had wanted to hit back at them, show them they weren't winning. That Douglas Brodie wasn't easily taken out of the picture. There was never any chance of them complying with my demands. The price of my vanity was a woman's life.

The evening papers were full of it. Woman slaughtered in public library. Body found in the toilets. Stabbed several times and propped up in a cubicle. Her blood had pooled under the door. No one saw anything or anyone. The woman's identity was not known, but she was thought to be mid-thirties, dark curly hair and of medium height. The public were asked to contact the police if they were aware of a missing person that matched the description.

I was staring out of the window, with the paper in front of me on the table, when Sam came in. She looked drained. Before I could open my mouth, she said, 'I've heard.'

She flung her wig and briefcase on the table and pulled the paper to her. She read it and pushed it back to me.

'It's my fault, Sam. You were right. I pushed them too far.'

She looked me up and down, then shook her head. 'Scum like that don't need much provocation. Even by their base standards, this plumbs the depths. Have you been to the police?'

'If I had, do you think I'd be sitting here now? This being the second murder I've been associated with in a week? They would have been interrogating me for a fortnight.'

'But they need to know who she is.' Then she added quietly, 'And what about her children?'

'It's what worries me most. Look, I phoned the police. From a call box. Didn't leave my name. I gave them her name, her last address and her address on Arran. I said there were four kids.'

She nodded and sat down. She rubbed her face with both hands. Her eyes were dark-ringed.

'How did the appeal go?'

'Oh, they were very indulgent. "What an interesting line of attack, Miss Campbell. We compliment you on your impassioned argument."'

'But?'

'"But where's the proof, Miss Campbell? Where's the proof?" Patronising old buffoons.'

'How long can you keep this up? I mean, is there a deadline for putting your case?'

'This Friday, the nineteenth. Then next week they sit by themselves and mull. Probably over a good Amontillado. They have to come to judgment by the twenty-sixth if they intend to carry out the sentence by month's end. Unless I can get a stay that allows us to gather more evidence.'

'Chances?'

'Between nil and zero.'

The next day Sam went off to battle against the old buffoons and I did something similar.

'Morning, Brodie,' said Sergeant Jamieson. 'They're expecting you. This way.' He held up the desk flap and I walked through and into the back offices of Tobago Street nick.

'Why are they expecting me, Alec?'

'About that woman. Yesterday. In the library. It was the one you were telling them about. The woman on Arran, wasn't it?'

'Could be, Alec. Could be.'

'Wait a bit, Brodie. I'll just go in and tell them you're here.' He knocked, went into the smoke-wreathed room, and was out in a second. He held the door open.

'Come in, Brodie,' said Silver from behind his desk. His book-ends – Kerr and White – stood either side of him, but the air of arrogance and surliness had gone. These men were worried. I sat down without an invite and took out a cigarette to add to the communal pall.

'Is it Mrs Reid?'

Silver nodded.

'How?'

'We think she was taken in – alive, so far as we know – to the toilets by at least one person. There's a back way in, so nobody saw anything at the front desk. The forensic boys say there was a strong smell of chloroform on her. So it suggests she was drugged to make her pliant. She was pushed into a cubicle and then stabbed to death. They got her doped enough for her not to mind what they did to her. There's also the possibility of drugs. We're waiting for the full autopsy. Seven knife wounds on her body. One through the heart.'

'Seven! So, boys, do you suspect foul play?'

'It's hardly funny, Brodie!'

The rage tore at my throat. 'No, it bloody isn't! I warned you that this woman was in danger! That she and her kids had been abducted! I told you she had specific knowledge about what went on in Hugh Donovan's room the night before you arrested him. What did you do about it? Bugger all!' I was half out of my seat, leaning over the desk at him, and as close to punching him as I'd ever been.

Silver saw it in my face and pushed his chair back. The other pair took a step back to demonstrate their loyalty. Kerr was about to say something in their defence but Silver lifted his hand to still him. He sucked at his moustache.

'Steady on, Brodie. There's no proof of anything here.'

I gathered my wits and sat down. 'Really? You say Mrs Reid had *seven* knife wounds. Sheer coincidence that Rory Hutchinson was stabbed seven times?' I raised my eyebrows.

Silver tugged at his tie. Even they'd seen it. 'OK, OK, I admit there may be a connection. But we can't rule anything out. My main concern is the woman's children. Do you have any ideas?'

I could see that asking my opinion was costing Silver blood, but this was no time to twist the knife. 'I wish I did, Silver. All I can tell you is what I told you before. The house on Arran, the kids supposedly out playing, the local priest. And Mrs Reid telling me about the late-night visitor that turned out to be the now murdered Father Patrick Cassidy.'

Kerr couldn't help himself. 'It was suicide!'

'Don't be so bloody infantile!' I shot back.

Kerr reddened. Silver again raised his hand for silence behind him.

'There's one other thing, Silver. I know who did it.'

'Did what?'

'Killed Mrs Reid.'

'Oh, aye, Dick Tracy. And who would that be?' Silver's nose was heating up.

I told them of Sam's and my trip back to the island and the neighbour's description of the car. I told them I'd traced the number plate.

'Who, Brodie. Just tell us who.'

'The Slatterys.'

They looked at each other as though I'd just stubbed my fag out on Silver's pristine desk.

I pressed on. 'If you want to see those weans alive, I suggest you get the squad cars out and hit every hidey hole you know for Dermot and Gerrit Slattery. Of course you won't find anything. They'll be expecting me to give you this lead.'

Silver was red in the face now and his nose close to exploding. 'So what's the bloody point, then? Of telling us all this ... this ... story.'

'You can put pressure on them. Force them to make a mistake. Drive them out of cover. Hell, I don't have to tell you how to lean on gangsters, do I, Chief Inspector? You worked for Sillitoe before the war.'

I couldn't help the mocking tone in my mouth, or my bitterness and frustration with their slow-wittedness. By their looks and flushed faces I was making my sarcasm felt.

I eventually left them to it, still squabbling over what to do next but slowly edging towards a courtesy call on the brothers Slattery. I had nothing else to do except head back to Sam's and wait for her return. It was her second day for making her case to the Appeals Panel judges. Then it would the Procurator

Fiscal's turn to demolish her arguments. The judges would then retire to consider their verdict. I didn't think it would take them long.

THIRTY-ONE

For me, the rest of that week and the next drifted by in a limbo of reading and walking through Kelvingrove Park and round to the Botanical Gardens. I would sit for an hour in the hothouse in silent communion with the greenery around me, drinking in the scents, letting the humidity soak into my pores. Everywhere I went I kept a lookout for men with razors. Slattery had made it plain he wasn't going to take his humiliation lightly and was unlikely to stop at one killing. But having silenced my only witness, maybe he could afford to bide his time. I felt his hard, mocking eyes on me wherever I went. I even wondered about heading back to Arran to see what I could see, talk to the priest again. But the island was probably hoaching with armed policemen. I didn't want to get in their way. Unless their marksmanship had been honed during the war, it was best to keep clear.

Instead I took the train down to Kilmarnock and visited my mother. I walked my boyhood routes round the parks and through the rough of the municipal golf courses. And all the time I racked my brains to see if there was something I'd missed, something I hadn't done. I felt useless and ineffectual. Apart from listening to Sam's courtroom battles each night and keeping her fortified with fags and fish suppers, I couldn't help. She was still off the Scotch to make sure she applied every particle of her being to the appeal. And I went on the wagon to support her.

Even in the second week, when the judges were considering the appeal and we were left in limbo, we forsook the booze. Perhaps it was in respect for a man's life being at stake. We visited Hugh a couple of times but we had nothing much to say to each other. Hugh seemed in better heart than we were. Maybe his doctor could prescribe us some of his drugs. Sam took to coming with me on my walks. She sat with me watching the vines grow in the Botanic Gardens. We took the train down to the seaside and walked the deserted sand dunes of Barassie Beach between Troon and Irvine. I put my mac down on a damp sand dune and we sat gazing out at the hulk of Arran.

'My dad and I used to come down here and walk for miles. A lot of the miners did. For the contrast.' I pointed up at the huge herringbone sky marching over us. 'We always talked about having a dog.'

'When did he die?'

'Back in '30. My first year at Glasgow.'

'An accident? I mean, he wasn't very old, was he?'

'Just turned fifty. No accident. Unless you count getting accidentally gassed during the war. Then accidentally going down with black lung when he went back down the pit.'

'I'm sorry. How did you manage? I mean, university and all?'

'On a coal miner's wages? Bursaries. I would have left in my first year if he hadn't made me promise to see it through.'

We were quiet for a while listening to peewits calling and watching the gulls soar and pitch out at sea.

'You didn't have much choice either, I suppose?'

'You mean the law?' she laughed. 'My father didn't badger me. In fact, he tried to talk me out of it. Said they weren't ready for women yet. He was right.'

'Regrets?'

She gazed away from me. 'You mean husband, kids, all that domestic bliss kind of regret?'

'Sorry.'

'No, it's all right. Sometimes. Yes. There was a man. A lawyer too, but also a sailor. His first commission was convoy protection on the Murmansk run. No one was protecting him, though. Torpedoed. I waited a long time. They still don't know for sure. I have a secret hope that he was picked up by some fat Russian lady who won't let him go until he's sired a new Red Army.'

I came close to taking her to see my mother, but both of them would have read too much into it. And maybe I was ashamed of the room and kitchen by comparison to her palace. I hoped not. I was long over that.

Come the Friday we dreaded, the day of Hugh's judgment, I joined her in court, or at least I took a seat in the crowded public gallery. Hugh had been brought down from Barlinnie to hear his fate. There was an indrawing of breath when he was brought into the court. He was wearing a shapeless suit and a shirt without a tie. They did nothing to make him look normal. Someone called out, 'There's the beast! Hang him!' The usher called for silence and a large policeman made his presence felt by walking down the gallery steps and standing smacking his truncheon in his hand.

It didn't take long. Some fatuous praise for the defence lawyer's arguments, but it was a veneer. These three wigs were direct descendants of Judge Jeffreys. They would have needed sworn testimony and photographic proof from Jesus Christ himself before they would even think of overturning the original sentence. It was in their eyes, their well-fed cheeks, their couth tongues. Before them was a pitiful creature who'd done vile things to wee boys. He even looked like a creature from hell. How could he not be guilty – of something? The fact that he'd acquired his melted face in heroic endeavours on their behalf gave rise to some token words of sympathy. But in the same breath they speculated that his harrowing burns had not only given him monstrous features but monstrous propensities. A sad business but society needed protection.

It was no surprise then to hear the lead judge – Lord Justice James Edgar Stewart – pronounce that the appeal had not been upheld and that the original sentence would be carried out forthwith. Forthwith meant in four days' time. Next Tuesday.

This time neither the usher nor the judge himself could quieten the crowd; the smell of sulphur was in their nostrils. Hugh was led out, head bowed, leaving Samantha Campbell staring after him. The Procurator Fiscal's man came up to her and muttered something platitudinous. She smiled grimly at him and took off her glasses and her wig. Her blonde hair was kirby-gripped to her scalp and damp with perspiration. She pulled out a few pins and ruffled her hair to release the pressure. She put her papers together and waited till the court had emptied before leaving the now echoing room. I waved down at her and she caught the movement and looked up at me with eyes so despairing I nearly jumped over the rail to join her and hold her. We met outside. Her eyes were red from rubbing.

'Justice was done, wouldn't you say? Take me home, Brodie.'

We went to see Hugh on Monday, the day before the deadline – was there ever a more apt word? He was calm, too calm. It was clear the prison authorities were topping him up with morphine to make the whole thing easier – for them, I suspected.

It wasn't much of a conversation. He was back in his prison drabs and shackled at wrist and ankle. Just in case he made a run for it. Sam and I muttered some apologies for our failure to get him off. Hugh was magnanimous in his exoneration.

'You did your best. Both of you. More than onybody could. Forbae, it disnae matter, Dougie pal. I'm past it. I should have died in that bomber. This is all borrowed time.'

The phrase shook me. It's how I'd initially felt lolling in the waves off Arran. All the bullets and bombs that had missed me during my campaigns across Africa and Europe were surely storing up the certainty of a violent death. But the survival instinct runs deep. I didn't care about such fatalistic claptrap. I wanted to live. I couldn't accept Hugh's stoicism.

'Bollocks, Shug! You might as well say you shouldn't have been born.'

'Even better, old pal.'

Suddenly a guard came over and whispered to Sam. She turned to me and Hugh. 'Hugh's got another visitor. We need to go.'

For a moment I wondered, then I knew who this was. I got up and, regardless of the guard's admonishment, reached out for Hugh's hands. I gripped his claws. He tried a smile.

'Well, we'll soon ken who was right, ya Proddie sod.' He raised his eyes to the ceiling.

'I hope it's you, Shug.'

'Naw, you don't. Where would that leave a' you unshriven Orangemen, come the day?'

It was a brave face. We both knew he'd be buried by the wall outside D Hall in unconsecrated ground. The thought of not getting a proper Catholic burial and what that might mean in the afterlife must have been unbearable to him. That and knowing that his own priest wouldn't be around to guide him over. And probably wouldn't be there to welcome him on the other side, if there was any justice in heaven. I hoped they would double his morphine tonight.

Sam and I left him sitting there. He waved as we got to the door. I gave him a thumbs-up. In the waiting room outside stood Fiona. She'd made an effort. Her hair was better cut and shining, held back by an Alice band. She'd put on make-up and good red lipstick. The coat looked new but too big. Borrowed? She clutched a black purse. Her eyes were bright with fought-back tears. She raised her head, ready for another challenge. She looked smashing.

'Hello, Fiona.'

'Hello, Douglas. How is he?'

'Better than us. And he'll be better for seeing you, Fiona.'

She nodded. 'I had to come.'

Sam said, 'Mrs Hutchinson? We're here in a car. We can wait. Give you a lift.'

Fiona shook her head. 'No. I'm fine. Thanks. Just go.'

She squared her shoulders and fixed a smile on her lips. The guard opened the door for her. As she stepped through Hugh spotted her. He began to struggle to his feet. The door closed.

Sam asked me to drive us back to her home.

'Will you stay till tomorrow, Douglas?'

Douglas? I hadn't thought about it. Hadn't wanted to. To do so was to accept we'd lost and Hugh would hang. I hadn't drawn that line yet.

'Of course. But then I suppose I need to get back. See if I have still have a job.' I joked, but in truth it was no joke. I'd been away a month and it would be a struggle to pick up the pieces. My long-suffering editor had stopped taking my calls. There was no chance of a full-time position now. I'd lost all momentum.

*

That evening became a bit last-supperish. In this case, Sam had had enough of my steaming newspapers filled with salt and vinegar and fat and cooked some stringy chicken and vegetables. We tried to eat it but it was more about pushing the food around the plate than getting it into our mouths. After her days of abstinence, Sam joined me in a glass or three of single malt. Glenlivet, smooth and soft on the tongue like molten heather. It was a taste I couldn't afford to acquire, and it would be back to Red Label in London. Back to my old habits. My mouth went dry. Would the dark days and long nights start again? Would I fall back into the pit? Though it had ended badly, this quest had forced me to think outside myself. I couldn't see what would replace it, where I would find a purpose compelling enough to keep the black dog at bay.

By unspoken agreement we talked about anything and everything except the trial and the impending hanging. At least we tried; it always crept back in.

'Would you ever come back here and live?'

'Some day, maybe. It depends on my mother. How she is. But I have to say it's warmer down south.'

'Getting soft.'

'I had a taste of the real south. I'd like to see what Sicily's like without someone shooting at me.'

'You haven't mentioned it before. Is that what gives you the nightmares?'

'Christ! You heard me? I thought I'd been better.'

'It was just the first week or two. I didn't want to say anything. Do you want to talk about it?'

'What is there to say? It's not unusual. I was a soldier. You see a lot of things. Best forgotten.'

'My dad was the same. Never a word. But sometimes you have the same look.'

I poured another glass. 'What about you, Sam? What's next? You'll have made a name for yourself. The judges were impressed, even I could tell.'

'I might take a wee holiday. Go up north, spend time in the Highlands. My folks loved Skye. I might rent a cottage in Portree for a few weeks. Blow the cobwebs away.'

Suddenly that seemed a highly attractive thing to do. I almost said so. We drifted though dinner, on into desultory conversation in the library and called it a night as the clock struck eleven.

I had been lying in the dark, tossing and turning for an hour or more, smoking, wondering if Hugh was getting any sleep in the condemned cell in D Hall. Did he know that the scaffold was just a short walk across the landing? I heard a faint knock on the door.

'Come in.'

The door opened and Sam stood in her dressing gown, uncertain and silhouetted against the moonlight streaming on to the landing.

'I couldn't sleep,' she said.

'Me neither.'

'Douglas, this doesn't mean anything ...'

'Come here.'

She shuffled over and sat on the edge of the bed. She sat staring out of the window, her hands clasped in her lap, her bare legs showing beneath the dressing gown. She was shaking.

'Are you cold?'

She nodded. I pulled the covers back and edged over. She took her dressing gown off to reveal a nightdress. She slipped into bed, with her back to me. Her thin shoulders trembled. I pulled the covers over her. She pushed back towards me and I lifted my arm and put it round her. We pulled closer till she was spooned and shivering against me.

'It doesn't mean anything ...'

'Shush. It's OK.'

Later, when the shaking stopped, she turned towards me. Our faces were inches apart. There was enough light to see each other's expressions. She looked grave and thoughtful. We didn't recognise each other. But her kiss wasn't a stranger's. Her body wasn't unfamiliar.

She didn't make love like a lawyer. There was no cool calculation, no steady build-up and smooth exposition of her case. This was criminal stuff, pent-up and violent, wondrous bodily harm. We committed crimes on each other's bodies, pummelling, biting, pounding in sweet assault and battery.

We slept and woke together in the dark middle of the night. This time we were gentle, easy with each other. Sliding and sensual, careful of each other's needs, pretending to be lovers.

THIRTY-TWO

We woke with a start at nine o'clock, guilty as sin. Not for our deeds, but for sleeping past eight o'clock. Dozing in sensual comfort while a man's life was snuffed out. Sam slipped on her nightdress and dressing gown and went downstairs. I heard her on the phone. She came back up to the bedroom and stood in the doorway. I was sitting on the edge of the bed smoking and looking out the window.

'It's done,' she said.

I nodded.

'I'm getting dressed,' she said, and went off to her room. I heard the bath run. The trees outside were lush from the frequent drenchings of Scottish rain. *Look thy last on all things lovely every hour.* Wordsworth, I think. Or was it de la Mare? An hour ago while we slept Hugh would have seen only blank prison walls and prison bars. Then they would have come to him with the black bag and the leather strap to bind his arms before his last short walk. Who'd heard his last confession now Cassidy had *gone on ahead*, as Hugh would put it? Did he have any doubts at the end? I hope what was left of his faith carried him through and that there was a big guy in blinding white waiting on the other side saying, *Everything's all right now. Don't worry. Here, see. Your son's waiting for you.* But I didn't think it worked like that. But however you looked at it, with faith or without, it was a bitter final chapter to a wretched adult life ...

I thought back to our boyhood and the mad days running wild across the back greens. It was as well we had no idea of our future. I think Hugh would have thrown himself under a train if he could have seen this end. I might have joined him. I reran the past month in my mind and harangued myself for not doing enough, not being smart enough. I castigated myself for wallowing in self-pity in London since last November. I should have come back to Kilmarnock right away and not dallied down south with a bottle stuck to my mouth. Maybe then I'd have heard about Hugh. Maybe done more. But would I? Wouldn't I have gone on nursing my anger against him for stealing Fiona from me? As though my boyhood love was more precious or significant than any other teenage passion? I had let it define too much of my life. Their betrayal – how melodramatic that sounds now – had probably been the clincher in making me knuckle down to my exams and drive me on to Glasgow university. Just to put distance between us. I thought of her going to him yesterday. I hoped they were kind to each other. I hoped they spoke without regret of their son and their brief days together. I hoped they found some of their old love.

I veered between anger and emptiness. It was over. I could get out of here and back to London. I would put aside last night's maudlin thoughts and get on with my life. I had a good degree. I had risen to major by being tested on the battlefield and not found wanting. I could now hold my head up alongside any of my old pals who'd followed their fathers down the mines. I had no right to squander these achievements. I thought of my old CO, General Tom Rennie, who led the 51st across the Rhine. We were within days of the German surrender when Tom was

killed by a shell. Like me he'd been at St Valery with the BEF.
He was captured but escaped to lead us through north Africa,
Italy, Normandy and finally into Germany itself. It was Tom
who gave me field promotion to major when Davy Sinclair took
a bullet. I remember his words: *This company's now yours,
Major Brodie. Their very lives are in your hands. And for God's
sake, Brodie, smile! The men hate a gloomy bugger!*

I washed and shaved and we met at the breakfast table. Our
consciences didn't get in the way of sliced sausage and tattie
scones. Something had wakened all our appetites at once. Inti-
mations of mortality? After mopping up the juices with our
bread, we faced each other over cups of tea to discuss beginnings and endings.

'You're off south, then?'

'Time I earned some money. If I still have a job, that is.'

'About last night—'

I waved my hand. 'It's OK, Sam. It was just one of those
things. You don't have to—'

'No! I mean I don't feel bad about it. Do you?'

'It was lovely.' I smiled at her, remembering her surprising
curves and her sharp teeth.

She toyed with her cup for a bit. 'And I go north. Ever been
up there?'

'To Skye?'

She shrugged. 'Just a thought.'

'It's a great thought.' It was. But what then? It would be a
strange foundation for a love affair. Was there anything other
than guilt to build on?

'But? Forget it, Brodie. It's time you went back.'

She got up and clattered dishes in the sink. I went over and
put my arms round her and held her to me. She resisted at first

but then slumped and I realised she was crying. I turned her round and held her sobbing body to me till she was still.

'I'm sorry, sorry ...' she began.

'So am I, Sam. But you know it wouldn't work. Not ...'

She pushed me away. 'What are you talking about? It's not about you!'

'Oh, right. I mean, what ...?'

'He's dead and I couldn't save him.'

'You did everything possible.'

'Not enough. I wasn't good enough. They shouldn't have appointed me. I shouldn't have taken the case on. I didn't have the experience.' Her face was blinded by tears again, this time with anger.

'How do you think I feel? My blundering around got Mrs Reid killed. Her four weans are missing! I probably got the bloody priest murdered! If anyone's to blame it's me. I used to be a detective! I couldn't detect a currant bun in a tea house.' Suddenly we were shouting at each other.

She waved her arms. 'Listen to us! *Mea culpa*, and that's it? We both just let it go at that? This time next year we'll drink a toast to absent friends, shed a tear of remorse and carry on? That's bloody it?'

'What else *can* we do? We can't bring him back!' Even as I spat it out, I knew what else. So did she.

We stood, chests heaving, staring at each other. Her challenge had caught me out. I'd judged victory or defeat solely in the context of saving Hugh's neck. He'd died. We'd lost. Time to move on. Revenge was surely a tawdry objective. But what about justice? I was a sceptic. Everything I'd seen in the last month had reinforced my view that it was as rare as hen's teeth. And if it did exist, who would deliver it? The legal brains and the law enforcers had let Hugh down. If Sam and I left the field now, who would pick up the banner? I faced her probing stare.

I smiled. 'You just don't like drinking alone.'

'Oh, I don't mind. I'm good at it.'

'What, then?'

'Five wee boys vanished. We found one, dead. This is a habit. If Hugh didn't do it, who did? It will happen again.'

'You want us to play detective?'

'I want Slattery's head on a plate.'

'OK, Salome, nothing would make me happier.'

She inspected my face for irony. 'Are you serious? If you are, I am.'

I sighed. 'Sure. Why not? I've got enough bones to pick with him.'

She sat down facing me, rubbing her face dry with the dish towel. 'All right. Where do we start?

I realised I was already prepared for that question. 'At the beginning. When you got involved. You told me before that *you* shouldn't have been given the job. It didn't add up. Maybe we've been looking in the wrong direction. Talk me through the process. I mean, tell me how you were appointed.'

She stared at me for a bit longer then nodded her head. 'I'll make tea.'

'It's all about contacts,' she said. 'First, you need to be a member of the Faculty of Advocates, headed by the Dean. We all work as independents but we belong to one of twelve groups or stables. The most senior are King's Counsel. Normally, KCs get the toughest roles but it's not mandatory. Though I'm not yet a KC, I've been around. I've served often enough as junior counsel. It's not unusual in itself that I was given this work.'

'Who decides?'

'Strictly speaking, you get instructions from a solicitor. In this case my old firm were given the case, as a *pro bono*.'

'So it was normal to come to you, an old girl of the firm?'

'Partly, but it's not clear why they were chosen as Hugh's solicitors in the first place. And they could easily have picked someone more senior and experienced.'

'So how does an advocate get selected?'

'It's not that formal. You have to serve your time, of course, and senior advocates and judges are always keeping an eye on you. Most of it gets done in the corridors of the Advocates' Library in Parliament House. Or over a glass of Scotch in the Glasgow and Edinburgh clubs.'

'*That's* why you practise.' I nodded at the whisky glasses on the sideboard.

'That's for my own sanity. They don't let women in *those* clubs. I stand more chance of making Pope. It's just a wonder they thought of me at all, far less assigned me to lead on a capital case.'

'Your father's reputation?'

'That's all I can think of. I'm not such a high flyer, you know.'

'I rather think you are, but you need more than talent to succeed in this game. Still and all, it's not exactly a favour to drop this one on you. So, there are two possibilities. Either someone thought that no one would blame you if you didn't get Hugh off, given the sheer weight of evidence. And that you'd come out looking plucky and smart but not having lost anything. A kind of salute to your father.'

'Or?'

'Or someone didn't want to take any risk that Hugh would get off.'

Her face flushed. 'By giving it to someone incompetent!'

'No! And I'm not going to butter you up any more than I

already have by saying how wonderful you are. You know you are. You're not a bad lawyer either.' I smiled.

She threw her tea towel at me. 'Sod!'

'Sam, can you find out who put your name up? Because maybe if we knew that, we'd know why.'

She stared into her cup, looking for her future. 'I should have done this before, shouldn't I? I didn't want to find out, Brodie. I just wanted to believe I was good enough. That my father would have been proud. Do you understand?'

'Only too well.'

'I'll make some calls. It's time I did some more socialising. What will *you* do?'

'Go to the bank. I need cash.' My heart sank at the prospect, not just because I would be dipping into my meagre savings but because of the sheer amount of bureaucratic effort involved in cashing a cheque at a bank other than my own in far-off South London.

'I can help. You can still be on the case. They pay from public funds.'

'You've been more than generous. But I think that *that* case is over. This is personal. But if you'd let me stay on a week or two?'

Her cheeks went pink. 'Of course, Brodie. Your old room's yours for as long as it takes.' If I read that right she was saying that the old arrangements – prior to last night – would hold good too.

'Could I borrow some paper?'

She delved in her briefcase, which sat on the sideboard, and plonked a lined foolscap pad in front of me. She retrieved a propelling pencil and rubber and handed them to me.

I drew five circles on the pad and started to write names into each. I pointed to each one in turn.

'I'm going to find out what links the late Father Cassidy, Hugh Donovan, Glasgow's Finest, Mrs Reid and the Slatterys.'

'You think the police are bound up in this?'

'I know they're incompetent. They're also arrogant and pig-headed and would rather do time in Barlinnie than admit they're wrong. Some of them are surely taking back-handers to turn a blind eye to drug-dealing in the city. But it doesn't explain their sheer monumental cussedness over the murders of Father Cassidy and Mrs Reid. Nor why they should be so ready to see Hugh Donovan swing for a murder he didn't commit.'

I drew a sixth circle. I put a question mark in the centre.

'This is for you to fill in. Someone in the judiciary picked you. We need to know who and why.'

She nodded. She leaned over the table and pointed at the pad, at the two circles embracing Mrs Reid and the Slatterys.

'We're pretty sure they killed her. We're also pretty sure it was to stop her testifying about what she heard and *who* she heard the night before Hugh's arrest. But what's the link between these two?' She pointed at the Slatterys and Father Cassidy. 'Why would they kill him?'

'He must have been a risk to them. If Cassidy was the mystery man that brought Hugh home that night, he probably knew something about the real murderer. Presumably one of the Slattery clan. Did the good Father Cassidy learn something in the confessional? Or was he actively involved with these thieves and murderers? What possible service could a Catholic priest be giving to a bunch of gangsters? And if so, why would they want to kill him now?'

'Do you really think he told them about your Arran trip?'

'Who else? No one else knew. One day he arranges for me to be tossed off a boat, the next he's found hanging naked in his own chapel. What happened? I'm certain it wasn't suicide. Was he going to turn King's evidence against the Slatterys? And if so, why? A pointing finger from the Virgin Mary or a sudden glimpse of the fires of hell?'

'But how did he get involved in this mess?'

'If we knew that …'

'How are we going to find out?'

'I wish I knew.'

THIRTY-THREE

ometimes you need a bit of luck. Mostly it appears out of the blue, looking like a ten-bob note when what you needed was a fiver. But sometimes luck flings itself at you like a long-lost love. Propitiously, it came the next day, May Day, summer's harbinger, in the form of an early-morning knock on the door. Sam and I were up and about, having risen from our chaste beds. I wondered if she'd lain awake waiting for footsteps on the landing as long as I had?

Sam took the door. I heard a man's voice and Sam ushering someone into the library. She called out to me to join her. I came in from the kitchen. Sam was standing with her arms folded. A man stood fidgeting in front of her, turning his hat round and round in his hands. You would never normally confuse him with Lady Luck. Anger swept through me.

'You've got a bloody nerve! What have you come to arrest us for this time? Or are you just here to gloat?'

Detective Constable Davy White had the decency to flush, whether from anger or embarrassment or a mixture. Either way, I savoured his discomfiture.

'If you must know, Brodie, I'm here to help.'

'A bit bloody late for that, White! How could *you* possibly help?'

'It's this Donovan business. And Mrs Reid.'

'And Father Cassidy? And the missing Reid weans? It's a stinking business, White!'

He was nodding and fingering his too-tight collar. 'Ah ken, Ah ken. It's why I'm here. I cannae thole it any longer, neither I can.' His face screwed up. For a horrible minute I thought the wretch was going to break down and cry in front of us.

'I'll make tea,' said Sam.

'I think you should be here for this,' I said.

'Well, talk about football or something till I get back. What do you think of that new winger for Rangers, Detective White? I think he's got the speed but his passing is rubbish.'

She walked out, leaving us in wondering silence. We sat, him on the edge of an armchair, me sunk back on the couch, studying my man. Sam returned wheeling a trolley like an office tea-girl. She did the honours and we turned expectantly to DS White, who seemed to be having trouble keeping his brew in his cup.

'OK, White, the floor's yours. This had better be good!'

The man was visibly sweating now and pulling at his tie. Finally he undid it. 'Do you mind if I smoke?'

'You can turn cartwheels for all I care, Detective. Just tell us why you're here,' said Sam with heat.

White lit up. 'This hanging business. I cannae sleep. It wasnae what I joined for.'

I was getting exasperated. 'Spit it out, man.'

'Ah don't think Donovan did it.'

Sam and I looked at each other. 'Neither do we. But it's a bit bloody late for you lot to come to that conclusion!'

'Ah ken, Ah ken. Look, there's something you should see.'

'Show us.'

White stood up and fumbled in his crumpled inside jacket

GORDON FERRIS

pocket. He pulled out a small black notebook, familiar in shape
and colour. I used to have one myself.

'Here,' he said. 'It's marked at the place.'

I was on my feet facing him now. I knew what this was. I
guessed what he was telling us. Hugh's ruined face swam into
my mind, his eyes beseeching as they pulled the hood down
over his scarred head. If only this little book had surfaced a
month ago. I wondered whether, in the circumstances, if I strangled this so called detective the courts would let me off.

'What does it show, White?' I asked quietly. I made no move
to reach for it.

His eyes spoke before he did. 'That Donovan confessed *after*
we took him to the coal cellar.' He held the notebook out to me.
I stepped forward, took it with my left hand and brought my
right round and up in one movement that Les himself would
have applauded back in his sparring ring in the Old Kent Road.
My fist took White on the point of the jaw. It lifted his head up
and back. It may even have lifted his whole flabby body up off
the floor. He went back in an arc and crashed to the wood floor
in a flailing pile of arms and smashed teacups. He lay still for
a long second or two and then started groaning.

'Sorry about the china, Sam.' I rubbed my knuckles.

'You don't think I gave him the best?' said Sam, picking up
his smouldering fag and stubbing it in the ashtray. 'Shall we
see?' She held out her hand. I passed her the notebook. The
elastic band round its middle had been set at a point well into
the notebook. She opened it at the place and read quickly
through the next few pages. She looked up, her face drawn and
resigned. She turned and marched over to the supine detective. 'You bastard!' Then, very thoughtfully and with great
precision, she kicked him in the side. White yelped and rolled
away. Sam spun on her heel and waved the notebook at me.

'This could have saved him, Brodie! Or at least thrown enough doubt on the facts as to give me a real crack at the appeal. I could have saved Hugh!' She swivelled again as if to go back and kick him again.

'Sam! Don't. Leave some for me. What's it telling?'

She turned back, her face mottled with fury. 'It shows this pair lied in court! Perjured themselves! Hugh *didn't* tell them where to find the body. He *hadn't* confessed before he was taken to the coal cellar. He gave *no* information about the body, the number of stab wounds, even that the boy was naked. It says here: "Tuesday, 3 December 1945. Report of boy's body found in coal cellar behind Carol Street tenements."'

'That's just two streets away from Hugh's place in Florence Street,' I said.

She went on:

'Tuesday 3 December 1945. Time: 15.35 hours. Accused taken to crime scene. Accused wept at sight of body. Accused said, "No, no, no," several times. Covered his face with hands. DS Kerr and I took him back to the station where he was questioned again about his knowledge of the crime scene. He refused to talk. He lay on floor. Accused left in his cell.

'Wednesday, 4 December 1945. DS Kerr and myself returned to the cell. Found the accused calm but staring at the wall. DS Kerr made him sit at table. He was questioned again about involvement in the murder. Finally accused said, "All right, for God's sake, all right. I did it. I killed him. I might as well have. Let's get this over with." At this point, DS Kerr brought the accused pen and paper and made him write out his confession.'

'And in this confession he describes all the details of the coal cellar and the state of the body?' I asked. She nodded.

White was sitting up now and nursing his jaw. He had a hankie to his mouth. It was bloody. He got on to all fours then eased himself erect using the armchair.

'Assaulting a police officer, Brodie. You shouldnae have done that.' He clutched his side.

'And I'm minded to assault you again, you little shit! So don't tempt me! Because of your lies in court, they hanged an innocent man!'

Sam interjected. 'I saw your chair tip and you fell and hit your mouth on the table, *officer.*'

He stood swaying slightly, looking at the pair of us, and then he nodded. 'Ah don't blame you, Brodie. It's what Ah deserve. Let me just say Ah was telt what to do by Silver and Kerr.' He paused and I thought he had finished, but then, miserably, with a shake of his head: 'It wisnae what I joined up for.'

'I know another bunch of blokes in uniform who claim they were only following orders. The Nuremberg judges don't seem to think that's much of a defence. My betting is they'll be hanged for acting like sheep! Isn't that's what you deserve, White?'

'Brodie! Let's hear him out.' She seemed to have got herself under control.

I took a deep breath and walked back to my seat.

Sam switched to her courtroom voice. 'Tell me what happened, Detective White. In your own words.' Her calm authority brought White's head up and he began his account.

'We'd been trying for hours to get him to admit it. But he just kept saying he knew nothing about a' the evidence we found in his hoose. And he claimed he knew nothing about where the boy might be. Nor onything about the other missing lads. And a' the time, he was like he was hungover. No a' there, if you like. In a dwam. I suppose it was the heroin.'

'And when you took him to the crime scene, did he know where he was going?'

'He didnae seem to. As I said, he was in a bit of a dwam.'

'Did he change when you showed him the body?'

'Oh, aye, and how. It was like he woke up. And then he started greetin'. Like a big wean. He said ...'

'Go on.'

'He said ...' White seemed to lose control again for a minute. 'He said, "My boy, my boy, what have they done to you? My wee boy." Something like that.'

I thought of the photo of Rory in Fiona's house. Vivacious dark eyes glinting out at us. Sam and I couldn't look at each other. Her voice went softer without losing any of its authority. 'Why didn't you record *that* in your notebook?'

'Kerr said I shouldn't. He said it wisnae important. It was irrelevant.'

'And Silver himself told you to hide your notes?' she asked.

'Aye, and he was telt by Muncie himself. So he said.'

I asked softly, 'Did you beat him, White? Did you knock a confession out of him?'

He wriggled in his seat. 'No' much. I mean we didnae gi'e him a pasting. It was more a slap or two.'

'Did you ever leave him alone with Kerr or Silver?'

He looked up at Sam beseechingly. She raised her brows and waited.

'Aye. A couple of times that night.'

'Did they do him over, White?'

'Aye. They did. No' on his face. Just the body.'

'And after that he confessed?

'Yes and no. I don't think we made him confess. He didnae seem to care what we did. I think he just finally got kinda bored with it a'. Like he wanted to be left alone.'

'And the details? How did they get into the confession?'

'Sergeant Kerr. He kinda dictated it. Though he couldnae get Donovan to say onything about the other four kids.'

I could see Hugh now, chest heaving and eyes blinded with tears after another round of punches to the kidneys or kicks to the balls. Rolling in physical agony from the relentless punishment and accusations. But almost welcoming the torture for the brief respite it gave him from the searing images of his dead son. Through it all, just wanting time and space to grieve. Wanting these sadistic clowns out of his face. He saw no future for himself. His brief link with normality, the time with his son and with his former lover, had been wrenched away from him. There was nothing left for him, even if he got off. Back to the heroin fixes and the squalid tenement flat? Alone again more finally than even he could have imagined. In that mood, ready to say or do anything if these thugs would just let him rest, let him mourn. And not caring that by signing the confession he'd as good as set a date for the gallows. For Hugh, at that moment, death couldn't come quickly enough. Sam broke my reverie.

'Are you willing to testify to all this in a court of law?'

'Oh, Christ. Could you no' just use the notebook? Would I have to stand there?'

'Your choice, White. The witness box or the defendant's box,' Sam stated. There was a heavy pause, and his shoulders rose and lowered. 'Aye. It's a' one, now.'

There were some last questions from me, though I could hardly bring myself to look at him.

'Did you plant the evidence in Hugh's flat?'

'No! Not at a'! We wouldnae go *that* far!'

'No? After what you did it's only one more wee step. And before you know it you're personally putting the rope round an innocent man's neck!'

'Ah didnae! So help me!'

I gazed at his pathetic face. He seemed genuine enough. One of his buddies could have done it and just kept White in the dark.

'Who made the phone call that led you to Hugh's flat? Who was the mystery caller?'

He sighed. 'Cassidy. Father Cassidy.'

'And yet you sods refused to believe what Mrs Reid told me? Didn't you make the connection? Cassidy was the last man to see Hugh that night! And the next morning he phones you to have him arrested!'

'We were in too far. We couldnae back oot. We'd have looked like eejits.'

'You mean you'd rather string up an innocent man than look stupid?'

White was wringing his hands. 'You don't understand. We had all the bloody press after us. Muncie told Silver we had to do something. Get them aff our backs.'

'Including framing someone?'

He lifted his hands, palms up, in resignation. Then something struck me, like an icicle driven into my stomach. Surely not?

'Wait a minute. Why are you doing this now, White? Why did you wait till Hugh Donovan was barely cold in his unmarked grave?'

He said something that I didn't catch. 'What?'

He lifted his head. His eyes were glassy. 'They've found the weans. The Reid weans.'

THIRTY-FOUR

They'd received a phone call yesterday from the police station at Largs. Four bodies had been found on the beach. Children who'd fitted the description of the missing Reid brood. They were washed up within twenty yards of each other. Three wee boys and a girl. Drowned without a moment's remorse, like you'd drown a batch of surplus kittens. The Largs police, knowing the currents, reckoned they'd been dumped into the sea from a boat out in the bay. From the state of the bodies, they'd been in the water about a day. My too vivid imagination churned through images of how the killers had gone about their filthy deed.

They were unlikely to have thrown them from a ferry. Too public, too noticeable. So some sort of private boat. Had they ushered the kids on board with promises of a trip around the bay? Rothesay rock? Were they laughing and joking with them right up to the time when they threw them overboard? Taking bets on how long they'd thrash around in the water knowing they lacked my grown-up strength? But sticking around until they went under, not taking any chances of a Brodie-like resurrection? Had the kids been bound? Were they all thrown in together or made to watch as one by one the bastards chucked them over? Did they try to cling to each other as they went down?

I stood looking at White, my rage white hot, wanting to hurt him until he screamed for the mercy that was denied to four children. But then I saw in his eyes that a personal punishment had begun. It would go with him to the grave. He was part of the team of so-called professionals that had allowed this vileness to happen. Sam had her hands to her mouth, her face racked with horror and grief. Tears coursed down her white cheeks.

I found a voice. 'What's Silver doing? And Kerr. What are they saying and doing?'

'They're a' kind of in shock. No' saying much, you know? But telling each other it couldnae be helped. No way of knowing. No ransom note. Nothing to warn us.'

'Except *me*! Except *me*! I told the lot of you she was in danger. And after *she* was murdered, I told you the kids were next! What did you do?' I was shaking and could feel tears burning my own eyes, tears of outrage and frustration and bitterness. 'Bugger all!'

White stood, pale head hanging, like a chastened school kid. I turned and faced Sam.

'What now? What do we do with this confession? How do we get Slattery and clan inside?'

Sam wiped her face and struggled for control. 'There's nothing here that adds up to a case against Slattery, and it's a bit damn late for Hugh Donovan and the other innocents that got in the way. But we can start a case against the police for, let's see … perversion of justice, dereliction of duty, conspiracy, perjury …'

'OK, hen, that's enough,' gasped White. He looked as if he'd collapse, and we didn't want our prime witness to be carted off to an early grave. Not before he'd helped put the rest of his cronies behind bars.

'You ...' she began, and now her horror had turned to a cold burning anger. 'You might just get off with a light sentence by turning King's evidence. But only if you tell us everything. The rest of your cronies will never see daylight again, if I have my way. Understood?'

He nodded, abjectly.

She turned to me. 'I'll phone the Procurator Fiscal's office. We'll get them to take this ... this *officer's* ... confession.'

'I'd like to pay a call on his pals. Just to see Silver's face. But we'd best leave my little bout of schadenfreude until you've got White's confession in the bag.'

I stormed up and down the kitchen long after Sam had summoned a taxi and whisked White off to the office of the Procurator Fiscal. One day too late! That was all. The difference between life and death for Hugh was one rotting stinking day. It was too cruel to take. I felt the bleakness break over me. I grabbed a glass and the whisky bottle and sat at the kitchen table. I wondered how long it would take to reach oblivion. I stared at the bottle for a while, feeling my heart race and thinking through my conversation with Sam yesterday. We vowed to go after the truth. Wasn't this the breakthrough we needed? Too late for too many people, but a breakthrough. I pushed the bottle away, lit a cigarette and drew deep on the smoke, and deep on my soldiering. The difference between winning a battle and losing it was all in the heart. Taking the fight forward, not cowering behind a tree. I had to keep the momentum going.

I put the bottle back in the sideboard. While I was there I pulled out the package. I put today's *Gazette* on the table, placed the package on it and uncovered the massive Webley. I hefted it. The cold weight felt good. I took off the safety, cocked the hammer and aimed it at Slattery's head. All the circumstantial evidence pointed in his direction. But the question I kept coming back to was: Why? Why had they embarked on this murder spree? It didn't fit with the antics of the typical Glasgow gang. They would be in to dope-running and burglary – off-licences a speciality. They'd be doing extortion, providing 'insurance' for local businesses against acts of theft and violence – by their own men. Murders tended to be incidental, even accidental, in the course of their everyday scummy business.

How did this particular mob evolve differently? What led them down this gory path? It had to be something big, something violent, something that knocked them out of the ordinary run-of-the-mill petty criminality. This was a massive cover-up operation, rubbing out the evidence of some much bigger crime. What was bigger than murder? I needed to know more about their background, where they branched off, how they came to this point.

I nudged the newspaper with the barrel, staring at the headlines. Tomorrow's edition would be sensational. I put the gun down, got up, holding the paper, and headed to the phone in the hall. If Justice was blind, she'd never notice if I loaded the scales.

I met him at lunchtime in the Scotia Bar between St Enoch's and the river. It was a typical lair for his kind. My kind. Cubbyholes, and low ceilings, with light spilling through the stained-glass windows and separators. A rack of mutton pies seethed and dripped behind the counter. It smelt of beer, hot fat, fresh sawdust, and the fags of ages. Its cosy intimacy was a magnet that drew the drinkers in from the clusters of offices all round the city centre.

I was good and early and took a corner seat in one of the small lounges at the back. I nursed a pint and pretended to read the paper. I was nervous. The man I was waiting for had long been a hero of mine, a legend. I'd got through two fags and the crossword before I became aware of a shadow lowering above me.

'You Brodie?' He was skinny and sallow and old, the threads of his remaining grey hair carefully plastered across his scalp in a parting that defied the evidence of his mirror. He wore a shiny suit with a missing front button. The tie was more like a piece of string and likely remained knotted every night, to be slid on and tightened after his cursory shave and brief wipe with a damp face flannel. But his eyes were searching and cynical, weary and incredulous, the eyes of an ace reporter. He already held a pint in one hand and a sagging mutton pie in the other. Was this my future? I nodded; he sat.

'I'm McAllister. The *Gazette*. Fire away, pal.' He took a bite of pie and a swallow of beer, and waited. He'd seen everything, heard everything. For him this was a waste of good drinking time. I wondered if I'd made the right decision.

'I told you I had a story.'

'Yeah. The Donovan hanging. You said. But it's old news.'

'Not if they hanged an innocent man.'

He shook his head and lit a fag. 'You related? Sometimes you just have to get on with your life, you know?'

'This morning, one of the police officers who handled the arrest confessed they'd set up Donovan. As we speak, he's spilling his guts to the Procurator Fiscal.'

'Jesus!' He stubbed out his fag in the remnants of his mutton pie and dug out a soiled hankie to wipe his hands. From inside his jacket he produced a slim notepad and pencil. 'Talk.'

'I'll talk. But first I need some information from you.'

'Oh, aye?' His eyes slitted.

'You've been a columnist on the *Gazette* for years. I remember reading you before the war when I was on the force here.' I didn't tell him that his tight, vivid prose had probably contributed to my post-war shift into the inky arts.

'You were polis?'

'Detective sergeant. Tobago Street.' That had him interested again. I went on: 'You've followed the Slattery boys over the years?'

'They've often been my bread and butter. Is this about them?'

'Could be. But not the story I'm gonna give you. Not quite. When did Dermot and Gerrit come on the scene? Can you recall?'

'I thought you said you were in the force before the war?'

'I was. From '33 up until I enlisted. We all knew about the Slatterys but they were pretty quiet then. We had other fish to fry. Other gangs to bust that were a bit more, shall we say, blatant. The Billy Boys, the Norman Conks, the Calton Entry, the …

He shook his head in fond reflection. 'Glory days, sure enough.'

I went on. 'The Slatterys had things sewn up by that stage. Everything under control. Out and out villains but never causing rammies in the street. No banners or marching bands for them. Staunch Catholics but never to be seen throwing cobbles at Orange parades or taking hatchets to the Derry Boys. I'm trying to understand how they got going, how they became … untouchable.'

His lined cheeks creased in memory. 'One of my first stories for the *Gazette*. Back in … '24, it would be. I'd only just joined the *Gazette* from the *Record*.'

His eyes glowed with the memory. It was touching to think he'd kept the tie as a memento.

'Aye, they hit the scene like a hurricane. Gerrit in his twenties and his big brother Dermot early thirties, I'd say. Fresh off the boat and straight into one of the biggest rammies the Gorbals had seen. They took on one of the razor kings. It was a turf fight. They got the Catholics out behind them and just slaughtered the razor king's gang. And I mean slaughtered. Glasgow Infirmary was like a butcher's shop. They never looked back.'

'What was their trade?'

'The usual. Bookmaking, drugs, protection rackets, the odd bank, even, as they got more confident. They branched out into street girls, even had a few flats. They installed the lassies there and charged the punters at the close entry. It was quite the wee empire.' He sounded impressed.

'Was?'

'Still is, but it's changed. As they got more well off they decided to pull back from the mucky stuff. Bought a big house out in Bearsden, installed Dermot's wife from the old country and started wearing better suits. But they were still running the drugs racket for half of Glasgow. And from what I hear, they went upmarket with the birds for hire. Top-quality totty, apparently,' he said wistfully.

'I know they were picked up a few times but we never managed to make it stick. How come, do you reckon?'

'Oh, they were in court more often than a judge. Particularly Gerrit – he was a total bampot. Big brother Dermot was always bailing him out, literally. Old Campbell, the Procurator Fiscal, never gave up. But they always had the best lawyer. Kept getting them off even when it seemed impossible. There were stories that they'd nobbled some heid yins. Never proven, mind.'

'Did you say Campbell?'

'The very man. Hard as nails. At times it seemed personal, you know, between him and the Slatterys. Then things calmed down and the war started. And here we are, business as usual for the Slatterys, but all the time trying to change their image. Get respectable. Now, what about this story of yours?' He licked his lips.

I tucked away the connection between old Campbell and the Slatterys and told McAllister how Hugh Donovan had been set up by the police. He jotted notes down in what seemed to be personalised shorthand, only occasionally interrupting to ask questions.

'So, Advocate Campbell? The daughter of old Campbell. How wheels turn, eh?'

And: 'If Donovan didnae do it, who did? Is this you blaming the Slatterys? Do you have any proof?'

I decided to hold on to the little I knew. I painted a picture of a policeman overcome with remorse after they'd concocted a confession and saw to the hanging of an innocent man. I didn't tell him about the links with Father Cassidy's murder or Mrs Reid, far less the four dead weans, a story that would break in the coming days, once Silver and co. had worked out what to say. I wanted one main story released at a time, otherwise it was all going to become indigestible. I also wanted the Slatterys to feel the heat without panicking them into more wild deeds or simply vanishing.

'There's no solid proof yet, and I'd avoid any speculation if I were you. I think you have enough to make a story with what I've given you?'

'Front page, Brodie. Front page. Another pint?' He eyed his empty glass thirstily. 'It's on expenses.'

THIRTY-FIVE

By the time the story hit the evening edition, Muncie was already facing the press and announcing the suspension of the entire team involved in the Donovan case. Sam and I sat opposite each other in the kitchen. She was pointing at the lurid headlines

'Is your speciality kicking over hornets' nests, Brodie?'

'I'd rather smoke them out.'

'So this was you in subtle mode? "Corrupt police get innocent man hanged."'

'It proves Advocate Samantha Campbell was on the right lines.'

'But too late. I should have pressed Muncie harder about the notebook in court.'

'It would have conveniently disappeared, Sam. I'm amazed White hung on to it.'

'Insurance?'

'You think he was smart enough to see it like that?'

'Conscience, then?'

'Habit, more like. It's drummed into us at police college. *Write it up or forget it.*'

We both fell silent.

'Well, it's done. Now what?' she asked.

'Now we wait. And keep our heads down. There's going to be

a lot of flak over the next few days. You're seeing your legal colleague tomorrow?'

'Dinner with Judge Thompson. An old lech but talkative. Should I go ahead?'

'More than ever. As well as finding out who suggested you for the defence role, I want you to ask him some questions about your father's time in office.'

'My father? Why?'

'It sounds like he was a scourge of the Slatterys. I'd like to know whatever you can find out about those cases and how they got off.'

She looked quizzical but didn't argue. Just as well. I had no real line of inquiry. It was just about stirring up the mud and seeing what crept out.

What crept out next night was a lizard. Sam got home well after ten o'clock, slightly the worse for a skinful of red wine or maybe it was the brandy chasers. With her blonde hair released from her kirby grips, full make-up and a flushed, flirty expression on her face, Samantha Campbell was the saucy alter ego of the hard-faced professional I'd first met. She looked ten years younger with a grin on her face. I nearly took her in my arms but it would have been cheating.

'C'n you believe he tried to put his hand up my skirt?'

'During the dinner?'

'No, silly. When we were coming out of the hotel. He grabbed me and told me he'd always fancied me. Old goat!'

'What did you do?'

'I wish I'd kneed him in the balls!'

'But?'

'I giggled. And slapped him playfully. Isn't that what we're supposed to do? We little women? It's all we're good for, isn't it?'

'Sam, if you're looking for a fight over the rights of women, you're picking the wrong time and the wrong bloke. I met women agents who'd landed in France before D Day with as much guts as a highland regiment. I'm on your side.'

''S just as well, Mr Douglas Brodie.'

'*I'll* make tea.'

An hour later, after she'd thrown up and was sitting ashen-faced across from me, nursing a foaming Alka-Seltzer, we got down to business.

'It was Lord Justice Craig Allardyce himself, it appears. He put my name forward. Told everyone – except me – it was a wee favour for my dad, helping his lassie up the ladder.'

'Kind of him.'

'No, it bloody wasn't! If my father had known who'd done this he'd be back to haunt him. Dad hated Allardyce. Said he was a wee shit, if I recall right. Trouble was they had to work together. Allardyce was number two to my dad, Deputy Procurator Fiscal.'

'And he became a judge?'

'Later. The wee shit got my dad's job.'

We sat quietly with the thoughts between us.

'Anything about the Slatterys? Did your old lech know much about the cases brought to court under your father?'

She nodded. 'They were big deals at the time. Late twenties, early thirties. Just before your time. A lot of press coverage, especially when they walked free wearing big smiles and proclaiming their innocence.'

'Was it both brothers?'

'Judge Lech said it was usually Gerrit in the dock or some of his henchmen, wild men they'd bring over from Belfast or the backwoods of Ulster.'

'With Dermot pulling the strings?'

'Apparently. Dermot likes a low profile.'

'What were the charges?'

'Nothing out of the ordinary except once: 1932.'

'And?'

'Gun-running. Suspected membership of the IRA. Shipping arms to the Republic.'

I sighed. 'Perfect. Gangsters *and* revolutionaries. Killers with a cause.'

It suddenly added up. Why else would they go to such lengths to silence witnesses and bury evidence? It could certainly account for the involvement of an Irish Catholic priest like Cassidy. But why *murder* him? And how had Hugh got ensnared? And why now? Caught once but not jailed, the Slatterys went quiet for over a decade. Did it mean they were active again? That there was some big event in the offing? Had Cassidy tried to stop them? Finally, and not the least of these stomach-churning questions, what, in the name of all that's merciful, had all this to do with the abuse and murder of an innocent wee boy?

THIRTY-SIX

Sam crept off to bed and I sat and wondered why McAllister hadn't mentioned this little peccadillo of the Slatterys. I slept on it and phoned him in the morning.

'Cracking headlines, Brodie! I owe you one.'

'Good. So tell me why you didn't mention the IRA connection with the Slatterys?'

'An old chestnut. It was never proven. Every Irishman who kicked with his left foot was thought to be plotting the next Easter Rebellion. But they never made the charges stick.'

'Didn't they have evidence to start off with? I mean, there must have been something to put them in the frame?'

'Aye, you're right. I think they found guns. But we're talking back in the early thirties. When the polis were responsible for more frame-ups than Rembrandt. Maybe before your time, Brodie. But things haven't changed much, as far as I can see.'

'Why do you think I left?' I asked dryly.

'Just wondering, Brodie. Just wondering whose side you were on. If you were on nobody's payroll except the Crown's, you were the exception, laddie.'

I thought for a minute. 'I think you'll find there's another breaking story, McAllister.'

'I'm all ears.'

I could picture him wiping his grubby hands and digging out his pad.

'It's about the four missing Reid weans ...'

I put the phone down. Even the hardened old crime reporter had been shocked. Not shocked enough to stop him heading off to interview Chief Superintendent George Muncie, though.

By the time an ashen-faced Samantha Campbell was ready to face her first cup of tea I was shaved, washed, fed and ready for the off.

'Brodie, if you think this is an IRA thing, shouldn't you ...? I mean, isn't it getting just a bit too risky?'

She was right, of course, but that wasn't enough to dull the glowing coals of anger that seemed to live in my guts these days.

'I'm just going to look around.'

'What? Where?'

'Bearsden. Stroll those leafy lanes and admire the big houses. See if there's one I fancy.'

'Will you take the gun?'

'For Bearsden?'

She looked at me. 'You're daft. Be careful.'

I had their address but I wasn't sure what I'd do when I found the house. I just needed to be moving, doing something. I took trams and buses out to the north-west of Glasgow, only about four miles, but it felt like forty. Bearsden is a place apart. A separate community out in the countryside, and settled by folk with loads of money and a preference for big sandstone villas. Sam's house was pretty fabulous by my standards but it was terraced. Many of the big villas in Bearsden were detached with gardens front and back, and approached down quiet, tree-lined streets.

I felt conspicuous, like a door-to-door salesman on the prowl, except I'd forgotten my bag of brushes and chammy cloths. I asked my way of a genteel woman outside the row of pretty shops in the main street. She was politeness itself, despite her clear suspicions that I was 'trade' at best, and an axe murderer at worst. They could spot strangers here a mile off. Maybe it was the remnants of the scarring along my jaw. Maybe my accent. Her polished vowels made mine sound like a butcher's mincing machine.

It was a perfect morning in an idyllic setting. Warm sun and fluffy clouds. I was glad I'd left my coat behind. I was tempted to carry my hat, loosen my tie and sling my jacket over my shoulder, but I would have stood out even more amidst the prim privets and laurel bushes.

I followed the twists and turns up the gentle hills until I was walking along a beautiful street, filled with beautiful villas, nestling in their own grounds. Blue hydrangeas burst out of every garden. There was no traffic, in fact no people. It felt like a Sunday. It would always be Sunday here. I was counting out the numbers where I could; often enough the houses simply had names, like Lochinvar or something inappropriately Gaelic. I was keeping to the even side of the street as Slattery castle was an odd number.

Suddenly I could see which it was. About fifty yards ahead. Unlike the other leafy-fronted houses, this one had a high wall with railings and a gate. I did some counting and confirmed it was chateau Slattery. I slowed down, but it wasn't the sort of street you could dawdle on innocently. Not the sort of place to stand leaning against a lamppost with a fag without someone coming out and demanding to know who you were. That's if they hadn't just called the police to arrest you for walking around without a hat.

Suddenly, from ahead, from Slattery's, came the sound of clanking chains. The big metal gate swung back and a woman came out. She held the chain in her hand, and carefully threaded it through the bars and locked it with a massive padlock. There was another lock built into the gate itself and she put a big key in it and turned. She began to walk towards me. I crossed over.

'Good morning,' I said as she came closer. She was about fifty, I'd guess, plainly dressed, not at all like the owner of a big pile like this.

'Morning,' she replied warily. I took the chance.

'I wonder if you can help me. I'm looking for Mr Slattery's place. I was supposed to meet him. He had a job for me.' I smiled. She looked suspicious. I had really blown it if this was Dermot's wife.

'Och, they're away. You've missed them. I suppose he didnae have time to get in touch. Are you on the phone?'

'No. Gone, you say? That was short notice.'

She softened up. 'Aye. Packed up and left last night, so they did. Left me a message to clean up the place and lock it up weel. Never a thought about paying me. And no telling how long they'll be away. See, they're awfu' good to work for but at times—'

I cut in. 'Do you know where they've gone?'

'Back hame. The auld country as they call it.'

'Ireland?'

'Aye. I hear it's awfu' wet there.'

I watched her plod off and thought that only a West Coast Scot could picture somewhere wetter than here. I looked again at the drawn curtains and big locked gates and cursed myself. It seemed like the rock I'd thrown in the pool had made too big a splash. All the pond life had fled. I turned and ran after the woman.

'Missus? Oh, missus? Sorry to bother you again. You don't happen to have an address for Mr Slattery in Ireland? I could send him a wee note.'

She eyed me up and down. 'You're no' the polis, are you?' She paid particular attention to my scarred face.

'Do I look like the polis?'

'Ah'm no' supposed to do this, but if you just want to write a letter …' She was digging in her string bag, then in her purse. She brought out a scrap of envelope and unfolded it. 'Here. Have you got a pencil?'

I jotted down the address and handed the slip back. I hoped I hadn't stored up trouble for her. But now what? I gazed at the address. Planner Farm, Lisnaskea. It was a place I'd never heard of, presumably a village. But it was in County Fermanagh, Northern Ireland. Bandit country.

THIRTY-SEVEN

I got myself back to central Glasgow and went to the library. I trawled through some gazetteers till I found some references to Lisnaskea. It claimed to be one of the major villages near Enniskillen in Fermanagh. Which put it in the middle of nowhere. It was the former family seat of the Maguire kings, the ruling family in the area for generations, until good king James VI of Scotland and I of England decided to supplant the local Catholic top dogs with loyal Scottish Protestants. The Plantation.

Locally, this was badly received, and to this day, the population in this wildest and most westerly of the six counties of Ulster was still mainly pissed-off Catholics, and therefore a stronghold of nationalism and the Irish Republican Army. A Scottish Protestant strolling into such a village intent on making a citizen's arrest of one of their distinguished old boys – as I assumed would be the case with the well-off Slatterys – would find it easier to stick his head into a bear's cave, bang on a drum and ask how the hibernation was going.

Even I knew when I was beaten. The British Army were given a hard enough time of it over the last three hundred years. Why would one man fare any better?

*

When I got back to the house there was no sign of Sam. She'd left a note in her elegant copperplate on the kitchen table:

Brodie,

Had a phone call from Craig Allardyce. Lord Chief Justice himself! Said he wanted to chat about my career! Can you believe it? Judge Lech must have put in a word.

What's to lose? I can ask him face to face about the Donovan case and why he picked me. Meeting him at 11 for coffee at the Royal Crown.

I can be a sleuth too!

Sam

Good for you, Sam. Things were really beginning to happen, it seemed. I picked up the *Gazette* and read McAllister's latest piece of invective against the police. He'd be piling on the sorrows in tomorrow's edition by breaking the news about the Reid kids.

It made me think about Arran again and Father Connor O'Brien. He'd been conspicuous by his silence. Though Arran was an island they still got daily papers and news of his old pal Father Cassidy's demise must have got through to him. Surely the news of Mrs Reid would have set tongues wagging and heads shaking in sympathy in that little community of Lamlash?

But O'Brien hadn't tried to call me. I wondered why. Given how recently we'd met and our reason for meeting, it would have been perfectly natural for him to have phoned me as the bodies piled up to find out what the hell was happening. But nothing. Suspicious bloke that I am, I also wondered how much of a coincidence it was that after my visit to O'Brien's island, I'd nearly met a watery end. At the time I'd dismissed his involvement out of hand. Now I wasn't so sure. His silence was compounding my everyday religious paranoia. I picked up Sam's phone and asked the operator to connect me. It rang for a while, then: 'Father O'Brien. How can I help?'

'Hello, Connor. This is Douglas Brodie. You remember?'

There was a silence, then, 'Of course, Brodie. How are you?'

'Surprisingly well, actually. Unlike your colleague. I'm sorry, Connor.'

Silence again. 'Brodie, I won't lie to you. I was shocked to my bones. I owe a great deal to Father Cassidy. He was my study guide when I was taking orders at Trinity.'

'I didn't know that, Connor. Neither of you mentioned it before.'

'It never came up. But it's of no importance.'

It was if you were paranoiac like me, but I let it pass.

'The official view is that it was suicide. Does that square with your knowledge of him?'

'I have prayed night and day for understanding. It's not what I would have expected of the man.'

'You know it was me that found him?'

'I saw your name in the papers.'

'And you know *how* I found him?'

'If you don't mind, I'd rather you spared me the details.'

'Well, Connor, I don't think I can spare you from knowing that in my opinion, my professional opinion, Father Cassidy was murdered.'

'But the police ...?' There was just about the right level of shock in his voice.

'The police are covering it up. It's linked to the Hugh Donovan case. If you've been getting the papers over the past few days, or listened to the wireless, you'll know they framed Hugh for the murder of the boy. And in case you haven't heard about Mrs Reid – you knew her as Kennedy – she was found dead in a library in Glasgow.'

'Merciful Father.'

'God's mercy seems to be a bit strained these days. Just three days ago her four wee weans were washed up on Largs beach.'

'Dear God in heaven ...'

I felt as if I was punching this man with every new bloody fact. And if he'd been within striking distance, I might well have bent his dog-collar. This priest knew something and was holding back. I was certain of it.

'My God, my God ...'

I waited for him to finish the quote: '... why hast thou forsaken me?' But all I heard was something like a sob, then silence for several seconds.

'Father O'Brien, why would someone want to murder Patrick Cassidy?'

'I don't know, I don't know.' The anguish sounded real enough.

'I think you know *something*. Is there a link between Cassidy and the Slattery gang here in Glasgow?'

There was a sigh. This felt like a confessional but with roles reversed. But there would be no absolution from me if this priest had bloody hands.

'Belfast. A long time ago. The Slattery boys were placed with the Church.'

'Placed?'

'They were sent to the Nazareth House in Belfast. As children.'

'And Cassidy was there?'

'He was the visiting priest at the time. Their paths will have crossed.'

'Will have? You're not sure?'

'Right enough, they did cross. Francis told me they were ... shall we say, troubled children?'

'Troubled in what way?'

'I understand that their father sent them there. After his wife died. That's all I know.'

'I'm assuming Father Cassidy came to Glasgow first. Was he upset when the Slatterys showed up?'

'Surprised, I believe. They came to his chapel. It was a difficult time for Francis.'

'Why should it be? What happened between them in Belfast?'

'I know nothing else, Brodie. I think I've told you all I know.'

'Tell me, Connor, was Father Cassidy involved, in any way, with the IRA?'

'Why do you ask that?'

'Just fishing. It was something the Slattery boys were accused of. Before the war. Nothing proved, mind.'

His voice was shaken. 'No more than any of us in the North, I'm sure. The Republicans were mainly Catholic, of course. But that doesn't make every priest an IRA man.'

'Especially with the IRA being allies of the Nazis, eh, Father?'

The silence ran on until he cleared his throat.

'What will you do now?'

'Find the Slatterys. I think they murdered Patrick Cassidy. I think that's one of the keys to this whole wretched business.'

'I wish you well, Brodie.'

I wondered if he did. We hung up and I made myself some tea to help me digest what he'd told me, and what he hadn't.

By five o'clock, there was still no sign of Sam, so I went off and had a pie supper at our local Italian chippy. I ate it, piping hot, at the table, washed down by a glass of Tizer. I walked round to her garage and found the car gone. By 7 p.m. I was pacing up and down with worry. I had no means of contacting her and unless she'd called me while I was out, she'd not been in touch. If the note had been left some time before eleven o'clock, it meant Sam had been gone for at least eight hours, far too long for a simple meeting. Finally I did what I should have done hours ago and took a tram into the centre. The Royal Crown is a majestic sandstone building off Sauchiehall Street. As I walked towards it I kept glancing around at the few parked cars. I found hers with ease.

I strolled up to it. There was no doubt it was her Riley, all locked up. The bonnet was cold. No sign of Sam. I walked into the hotel and looked around. A big welcoming lobby with plenty of deep-pile carpet and big flower arrangements. To the left was a seating area with stuffed leather armchairs and low tables. No Sam. I walked up to the receptionist.

'Hello, sir. Can I help you?'

'I'm looking for a friend of mine. Miss Samantha Campbell.'

'Is she a guest, sir?'

'No. She was meeting someone here. Lord Chief Justice Allardyce.'

'Oh, yes. Justice Allardyce is a guest. He reserved a suite for today. Him and his manservant. I don't know if he had a guest or not. Let me ask Stanley, our doorman.' She struck the bell by her side. A middle-aged man appeared. He wore his uniform tight round his thin chest. His hair was greased flat and parted in the middle.

'Yessir?'

I explained.

His eyes brightened. 'Oh, I remember her, sir. The lawyer lady. It was a legal conference with the Chief Justice, I understand.' He winked at me to show how important this hotel was and, by association, he was too, if these important folk were having important meetings here.

He jabbered on. 'Smart lady with blonde hair. I took her up to Room 301. One of our nicest. Big lounge area and nice and quiet at the back of the hotel, sir. Good for sensitive meetings, sir.'

'This Allardcye. Did you know him? I mean, have you seen him before?'

'Not *as* such, sir.'

'So how do you know it was him?'

The receptionist looked at me as though I was daft. 'That was the name he gave us.'

'So you have no proof it really was the Chief Justice?'

The doorman and the receptionist were beginning to look askance at each other. The doorman chimed up.

'Is she better, sir?'

'What? What do you mean, "better"?'

'It seems the lawyer lady took a bit funny. She came down in the lift a wee while after I'd taken her up to 301. Maybe twenty minutes. She was being helped by Justice Allardyce's manservant. He got her outside. I offered to hail a cab, sir.'

'When was this?'

'Oh, about twelve of the clock, sir.'

'Did Allardyce go with them?'

'No, sir. He stayed in his room.'

'The manservant. Did he come back?'

'Not that I know of, sir. Said he'd look after her. Didn't need a cab. That he'd escort her home. Went off in the car.'

'What car?'

'I assume it was the Chief Justice's personal car. An Austin, I think.'

'Was it just waiting?'

'It had been there a wee while. I think.'

'You let a strange man take an ill woman off in a strange car?'

He nodded, fear flitting suddenly across his face. Within spitting distance of retirement and Stan realised he was heading into big trouble.

'This manservant. Did he have a name?'

The receptionist was now looking as desperate as Stan. 'No, sir. 'Fraid not.'

Stan piped up. 'But I'd ken him in future.'

'How come?'

'The ginger moustache. Looked like he'd killed the cat for it.'

It was as though Slattery himself had squeezed my heart.

THIRTY-EIGHT

'Room 301, you said? Have you got a spare key?' I asked the receptionist.

'Yes, sir.'

'Get the manager.'

The duty manager, a slick Englishman doing penance in the North, and I arrived on the third floor and strode to 301. The door had a 'Do not disturb' sign up.

'Open it,' I demanded of the manager.

'We can't simply barge into a private room with that sign up, sir. A senior judge and all that.'

Through clenched teeth I said, 'A woman has been abducted from your hotel. Her life is in danger. Open the door before I break it down.'

The manager fumbled through his keys, knocked a couple of times on the door and then, seeing me on the point of combustion and portal destruction, unlocked the door. I dashed inside and found myself in the lounge. It looked unused.

But there was a strange smell back in the hall. I looked around and noticed a white hankie lying by the door. I picked it up. The stink assailed my nostrils and made my head buzz. Dental chairs and hospitals. Chloroform. On the floor partially tucked under a sideboard was a folder. Sam's folder. I reached down and grabbed it.

I heard a gasp from the doorway to the bedroom beyond. The manager was standing looking in. I pushed him to one side.

A man lay flat on his back, face bulging and blackening, with a cord round his neck. At least he was fully clothed. If this was Lord Chief Justice Craig Allardyce, he'd found out the hard way how it felt to have one of his ultimate sentences carried out.

I dropped the chloroform wad back on the floor but took her folder. The manager had gone into full 'how do we protect our reputation' mode while at the same time summoning the police. It was time I got out of there, before I got snared. It was nine o'clock at night and the trail was already cold.

I had the spare keys for the car on my key ring. I drove back to the house oblivious to the rest of the traffic. I left it sitting outside instead of garaging it. I ran up the stairs and barged inside, calling her name like an idiot. My voice echoed and rolled around the big old house. No one replied. I hadn't really expected them to.

As darkness settled, I sat quietly in the kitchen, doodling on my pad. I seemed unable to break out of my circular thoughts. What I kept writing on the pad was *Why?*

Did they take her to shut her up? Was she a hostage to shut *me* up? Would they make demands? Or would they kill her as casually as they had slaughtered the others, including a Lord Chief Justice of Scotland? Would they even now be pushing her broken body off the Stranraer ferry to Belfast, her torso weighed down with stones? I clung to the thought that they'd wanted her alive, at least for the moment. They could simply have left her strangled body alongside Allardyce. And how had a Lord Chief Justice got mixed up in this escalating slaughter anyway? What unholy alliance existed between a bunch of

Glasgow gangsters with IRA affiliations and one of the top men in the Scottish legal system?

I had one large Scotch, drunk too fast and with too little water. I wanted the fire and pain to break me loose from my meanderings. I coughed and wiped my eyes and then I stoppered the bottle. I needed a clear head for the long drive and what I had to do in the morning. I was amazed that the street outside wasn't yet filled with clanging squad cars. Wouldn't this house be their first stop? Maybe it had all been too much for the police top brass. Maybe they were all sitting paralysed with empty bottles at their feet, wondering what new catastrophe would be in the papers in the morning. Maybe they were all in jail.

I began with her room, feeling like a burglar. It was neat and clean and surprisingly frilly. Her scent was everywhere. I leaned forward and sniffed her pillow, then I pressed my face into it. My senses thrilled to the memory of the other night when she'd joined me. But this wasn't what I'd come for. Feeling mildly ashamed of myself, I checked her drawers and found what I was looking for. I took the big bunch of keys and left her room. I'd never been to the top floor of the house. The layout was like the second floor where our bedrooms were. A toilet, a bathroom and two larger rooms.

I tried one and found it laid out as a bedroom. It had similar colours and tastes to Sam's and I assumed it had been her mother's. Opposite was the room I was looking for. It was dark until I got a fresh bulb for the overhead light. Very much a man's room. Solid woods and plain curtains. Hairbrushes sitting neat on a dresser. A wardrobe full of men's suits and perfectly polished shoes. The room felt like a shrine. There was another cupboard on the far wall, locked and padlocked. This looked like it. If Sam's hunting father had a hand gun, it was likely he had other weapons.

I tried several keys before giving up and breaking into it. Inside on hooks was a pair of magnificent 12-bores. The metal gleamed dully and seemed to flow into the hardwood stock as though wood and metal had chemically fused. I lifted one of them out, savouring the weight and balance. Then as my hand smoothed its way down the barrel from the trigger guard I noticed the unique round action and knew instantly I held a Dickson, a product of Scotland's finest gunsmiths.

My father had never owned a shotgun but we fished, and we'd spent hours in the fishing and shooting shop in Kilmarnock buying fly-making materials and surreptitiously admiring the arrays of guns. Like any young boy I was entranced by these weapons and the shopkeeper was happy to indulge my endless questions. He even let me hold some. Maybe it was why I joined up.

It must have been well over twenty years ago that he called me over to the gun counter and put a long polished wood box in front of me. It was a special order for one of the factory owners at the big metal works. Inside was a pair of Dicksons with their trademark round action so visibly different from the square action of the English Purdeys or Holland & Hollands.

He told me that it was more than just cosmetic, delightful though it was to the look and touch. The opening action was smooth as silk and the spent cartridges were automatically ejected when the gun was broken, saving time on reloading.

I hefted this Dickson, feeling it settle snugly into the shoulder and the barrel come up and hold steady as a rock. I checked the levers and the barrel. Still well oiled and smooth action. I broke it open and closed it again, feeling the springs tug and give properly. I pulled the triggers, one after the other. They clicked neatly and loudly.

The shelves were full of boxes: cartridges for the Dicksons

and shells for the Webley I'd already tested on one of the Slattery gang. I took down a leather pouch and filled it full of ammunition. I checked the remaining drawer and discovered a fine-edged gutting knife in its leather sheath. I slipped it into my pouch. There was an old army water bottle in webbing. I slung it round my shoulder. I relocked the remaining gun in its cupboard and left the room. I packed a couple of overnight items, locked the house and loaded the car. It was midnight. I could chance getting some sleep here and being wakened by heavy knocks on the door, or I could start out after Sam.

By twelve-thirty I was steering the big car back down the coast road through the douce towns of Troon and Ayr. My headlights swept the quiet roads ahead and only once clashed with the beams from another car. Well into the middle of the night the sign to Culzean Castle flashed up in my lamps. This was where General Eisenhower was about to take residence. A grateful British nation had offered Ike a suite in the castle in perpetuity in thanks for his leadership during the war. Or at least from the time the Yanks finally showed up.

By 3 a.m. I was pulling into the tiny village of Maidens far down the coast and rolling on to the sandy grass at the seafront. I eased down the window a bit, got into the back seat and fell asleep to the swish of waves on the beach.

By first light I was awake and walking on the shore in my shirtsleeves, swinging my arms to free my stiff limbs. For breakfast I had a cigarette sitting on a sand dune, watching Ailsa Craig define itself in the morning light. I didn't think much about the messy business ahead or whether I'd come out of it with my skin. The slaughter so far had all been one-sided. It was time to even things up. It was that simple. My boiling anger seemed to have evaporated like sea mist. In its place was a cool certainty about my next steps.

The first time I had this feeling was when the old 51st was surrounded at St Valery en Caux and forced to surrender, stuck as we were in the middle of a French army who'd already waved the white flag. I slipped away with four of my men and hightailed it along the cliffs until we found a fisherman's boat and sailed it back to England. It was the same feeling on the morning of our counter-attack against Rommel outside Tobruk. The sun swept aside the cool desert air and brought with it clarity and a tingling readiness. I ushered my platoon to their positions and prepared for the off as if we were on a training romp at Aldershot. I came to see it as a gift that I could draw on when the die had been cast, when the time for planning was done. My mind was working as smoothly and efficiently as the action in the beautiful Dickson lying in the boot. And with equal deadly purpose. The months of vacillation and gloom in London were swept aside. This was what I was trained for. It's what I'm good at.

By six I was back in the car and pressing south along the coast. On any other day I would have been grinning with the sheer pleasure of the trip, the big car feeling tight and powerful in my hands as we swept round bends and down green hills. The sea on my right lay flat and calm like a pewter dish. As the road swung round to the west the whale shape of Arran swam into view to the north. South again and the symmetrical granite stump of Ailsa Craig appeared and disappeared in the sea mists. These two islands had floated through the days of my youth, markers of long dreamy picnics among the dunes, backdrops to mad games in the shallow pools. Now, I didn't know if they were omens or endings, signifying the full circle of my life.

On down the rocky coast and through Girvan, until the signs pointed me towards Stranraer and the ferry to Ireland. I was in luck. I made the eight-o'clock boat and was soon tucking into a bracing Ulster Fry of tattie farls, sliced black pudding, streaky bacon and mushrooms. Other than the fry-up it was a three-and-a-half-hour uneventful crossing. No one tried to throw me overboard.

I stood on the top deck leaning over the rail, watching for the first line of Irish coast to come over the horizon. The grey line took on definition and formed itself into green hills and a township with an open harbour. Soon I was flicking my last cigarette into the briny and going down to collect the car as we eased into Larne. My stomach was churning, either in protest at the greasy breakfast or the prospect of facing Slattery and his men on their home turf. The ferrymen saluted me as I powered up the engine and drove the Riley out on to the ramp.

I had a rough idea where I was going but I needed fuel and a proper map. I stopped at the first garage and tore off the last of my blue coupons and one of my rapidly disappearing pound notes to fill the tank. I bought a map and got directions from the attendant, and drove off towards the west.

By my reckoning it was about 120 miles from Larne to my destination, through Antrim on the A6 and then on lesser roads round to Enniskillen. The final stretch would be on the B514 to Lisnaskea.

I had no grand plan but was relying on figuring something out once I'd seen the lie of the land. The address I'd got from the cleaning woman suggested some sort of farm on the outskirts of Lisnaskea. Was it in open fields or woodland? Was it by a stream or tucked behind high hedges? Were they waiting for me or not? Had they abducted Samantha Campbell and staked her out as a goat to capture this tiger? All I knew was that they were almost a day ahead of me, and every hour that passed added more peril to Sam's situation. If she was still alive.

By early evening I was starving, mouth-dry and weary. I drove through a town, Fintona, up the long incline of Main Street, and looked at my watch. It was six o'clock and I reckoned I was an hour's drive from Lisnaskea. I had thought to press on to Enniskillen tonight and down to Lisnaskea to do a first recce, but that was daft. I'd had two fitful hours' sleep. I'd be blundering around in the twilight too tired to react quickly and more likely to get my head blown off.

The Red Bull offered me a bed for the night. I had a stroll round the town, then demolished a doorstop cheese sandwich washed down with a cool black stout. I batted away the enquiring glances and the pointed questioning of the handful of customers and mine host. I told them I was a travelling salesman, in encyclopaedias. That seemed to drain the life out of the conversation, but I'm pretty sure they had me down as a British agent.

The bed was softer than I liked but I was more tired than I knew. I plunged into sleep till the light of morning jolted me awake and left me baffled and disorientated. It took me a second or three before I recalled where I was and why. The why bit clenched my head with anger against Slattery and fear for Sam. I brought up a picture of the Dickson in my hands. I saw myself pulling the trigger and felt the tension ease the bands round my skull. I was on the road by eight o'clock and heading west again, my stomach swollen with Irish hospitality and my water bottle filled from the landlord's tap. I was about an hour's drive from my showdown with the Slattery boys. Were they to be my nemesis? Was this to be the violent conclusion to the journey I'd foreseen on that rocking sleeper to Glasgow? All roads intersecting at this murderous end point? And which, if any of us, would walk away?

THIRTY-NINE

The main road cut through Enniskillen. The town was thronged with traffic, much of it horse and cart. People were smartly dressed for a provincial town in the Wild West. Then the bells reminded me: it was a Sunday. I began to feel more and more conscious of the big Riley and its Scottish plates. I felt the crowd scrutinise me as I edged through. This close to Lisnaskea there was just the chance of running into one of the Slattery men and being recognised. I put my hat on and pulled it down on my forehead.

The faces outside were familiar, but not because I knew any of them; I'd seen those generic, whey-skinned, undistinguished features – like oatmeal biscuits – a hundred times a day growing up in the West of Scotland. The accents drifting though my side-light window were as impenetrable as the best of the Gorbals.

I threaded my way out of town and turned due south towards Lisnaskea. I waited till I found a farm track and pulled off. I cut the engine and let the silence sweep in, or at least what passed for silence in the country. The birds were singing for their lives all around me as I stepped out of the car and opened the boot. The smell of grass and hot earth seduced my brain and made me think of walking hand in hand with Fiona long ago by the Kilmarnock Water.

But I had other business this day. I unwrapped the cloth next to my coat and tossed the gutting knife up and down to get the feel of the balancing point. I chose a tree about ten feet away. I flung the knife. It clattered handle first off the trunk. I adjusted my grip and tried again. It flew straight and true and sank into the soft wood. I repeated the throw until I was satisfied I had the measure of the blade. I moved back another few feet and repeated the move. I cleaned the knife and slipped it down the side of my sock, point first. The metal chilled my leg and the sharp blade pressed sideways against the ankle bone as I moved.

I tore open a cartridge box and lifted out the Dickson. I broke the gun and slotted two shells in the chambers and clicked it closed. I put it up to my shoulder and aimed along its length at some circling crows. It was tempting to test its accuracy, or, to be honest, just feel the recoil and smell the cordite; it had been a while since I last held such a weapon. I tracked a pigeon for a while and went *bang bang* at it. It seemed unmoved by my play. I placed the beautiful piece down in the boot. I filled my left jacket pocket with shotgun cartridges, my right with .455 bullets.

I cracked open the Webley and checked each of the six chambers was filled with the heavy shells. I spun the chamber once for luck and snapped it shut. I took both weapons round to the open driver's door. I placed the shotgun on the floor under the bench front seat. With a slight lean forward I could reach it and swing it up fast if I needed to. The revolver went into the open storage compartment under my steering wheel, its vulcanised stock reassuringly close to my right hand. I got back in the car and went off to find the OK Corral.

*

257

Lisnaskea was the second town in County Fermanagh after Enniskillen. Its population was about two or three thousand, mostly land workers or quarrymen hewing the grey sandstone and limestone to build houses all over the North.

I had decided on sheer brass neck being the best way of finding Planner Farm. I drove straight into Lisnaskea and along a high street that bent suddenly 90 degrees for no obvious reason. Maybe the surveyor got drunk or perhaps they just got bored with a long straight road. In the town centre, where it widened out briefly, stood a market hall in good sandstone. In front of it was a tall stone cross that looked borrowed from another age. I rolled to a halt and stuck my head out the window as two old wifies staggered by, Sunday-best black coats on, Sunday hats perched on their grey heads, gloved hands clutching hymnals.

'Excuse me, missus. Can you help me? I need some directions.'

They smiled and came over, pressing forward so they could see who and what was in the car. The guns were too low for them to spot.

'And where is it you're looking for, young fella?'

If I hadn't asked the question I wouldn't have understood her wild accent.

'It's a farm. It's called Planner Farm.'

They stepped back as though I'd just exposed myself. And clearly, in their eyes, I had, in some way.

'And who are you after exactly, did you say?'

'Dermot Slattery.'

Their two heads turned and looked at each other knowingly.

'And what would you be wanting to see this fella Slattery for exactly?'

'I'm delivering this car to him. He bought it in Glasgow and asked me to bring it over to him.'

This lie seemed to satisfy them.

'Straight ahead and out of the town. About two miles outside. On the right. You'll see a sign.'

It was only midmorning and I would have much preferred to be doing this by moonlight. But if I thought it was an unsuitable time to be storming this castle, presumably so would the Slatterys. I was gambling on them thinking that they were already in a fortress, rural Ireland itself – and wouldn't be expecting a cold-eyed Scotsman to arrive, guns blazing, in their midst. On the other hand, with Sam as the trap, that might be exactly what they were hoping.

I watched the cog of the milometer slowly turn round. One mile, then just after the two mark I saw a sign and a driveway up ahead. There was no guard at the wooden barred gate, or at least none I could see. I gingerly slowed down and cruised past at twenty miles an hour. No one in sight down a long straight drive. I caught a glimpse of a slate roof and a whitewashed low building. There were trees behind and to its left. Then I was past.

About a mile further on was another wood. I drove towards it and saw what I was looking for: a grassy path cutting into the trees for forestry work. I bumped the car over the rough ground until I was well hidden from the road. I drove on and pulled into a small glade. My heart was hammering. I sat back and closed my eyes and let the picture crystallise as best I could. In the Seaforths we were trained to observe targets in the blink of an eye, like taking a snap with a fast-reaction camera that we'd then process. A straight drive, about 150 yards from the road to a square horseshoe-shaped building. The arms of the horseshoe reached forward towards the drive. Sheltering between the wings was a black car. There might have been a figure standing to the right of the car, but I wasn't sure. That was the best I could manage.

I couldn't see the plate from the road but it looked like the big Austin from Arran. It could take four, maybe five in comfort. Let's assume that it had brought Dermot and Gerrit, Dermot's wife and a bodyguard or two. The boot was big enough for a trussed-up prisoner. Or a body.

I got out of the car, tucked the revolver into its pocket inside my jacket and slung the shotgun over my right arm, its barrels pointing to the ground. I hooked the water bottle over my other shoulder and began walking back to the road. Depending on what I found at the farm, I would go in now. Hard. Or if there were vigilant guards all round the building I could at least get the lie of the land and make my attack this evening. What I feared were dogs. Bloody animals. A slight noise or a whiff of a stranger and they'd be barking their heads off till teatime. Not to mention taking a lump out of my backside.

FORTY

emerged from the wood and scampered across the road. There was little or no traffic around here but it would be stupid to be caught sauntering along this country road with a shotgun under my arm looking like a refugee from a private shoot. The wood continued on the other side of the road, the side the farm was on, and I melted into the cool arbour and started to track my way back to the farm and parallel to the road.

I soon ran out of trees. Ahead was open ground bounded by waist-high, dry stone dikes. I made sure the safety catch was on both guns and clambered over the first. I made steady but cautious progress until after a sweaty half-hour I'd reached another wood. By my reckoning, these trees bordered Planner Farm. If I was guarding the place, this would be the most likely direction I'd expect an assault to come from. So I slipped into the first line of trees and headed north to come round the back of the farmhouse, still in the treeline. The air was still and I reasoned that if there were dogs they'd hear me before they smelt me.

I kept glancing to my right. Here and there the woods thinned; they were only about a hundred yards deep. Occasionally I caught a glimpse of whitewash or grey slate. There was no sound other than the birds, and even they weren't putting their hearts into it. It was midday and unseasonably hot. A time to doze.

I heard a thunk from the direction of the farm and saw something move at the limit of my vision. I froze and waited. Movement again. Someone had come out, slammed the door and was walking away from the house. I heard voices, and then another figure appeared, heading back to the house. The door slammed behind him. Changing of the guard? I started walking again. I did a dogleg and came back at the house from its rear. I was still in good shade. I shuttled from tree to tree, and finally got on my belly and crawled. This was where the hardy tweed came into its own. All I needed was some boot polish on my face and some twigs in my helmet and I was back at the training unit we shared with the commandos at Spean Bridge in the Highlands.

Finally I stopped and made myself comfortable. I laid my shotgun out and placed the pistol alongside it. I flipped off the safeties on both. I had a clear view of the house and the clearing in which it sat. It was single storey, with white-painted stone walls and a slate roof. There was a back door on the left and windows either side of it. All were closed. Gravel surrounded the whole house to a width of about ten feet. About twenty yards closer to me was a square stone shed; no windows this side and a sloping corrugated roof.

Just then I heard footsteps crunching on the gravel of the house from the right. I ducked down and then peered cautiously through the brambles and grass. My old pal Fergie strolled round the corner and halted about halfway across the back. He was carrying a shotgun in one hand, but the barrels had been cut just past the action. Easier to hide about the body and great in a packed room, but useless if you were trying to hit someone with lethal intent beyond ten yards. The shot would simply scatter and spray out in a fast-widening funnel. It would still hurt, though. Fergie looked around casually before lighting a fag. He looked bored. He was in shirtsleeves and braces and should have completed the picture with a knotted hankie on his head to keep the sun off.

He left after ten minutes and returned about twenty minutes later. The routine continued until after an hour he was replaced by his pal who'd helped throw me over the rail on the good ship *Jeanie Deans*. I watched this pattern unfold through the afternoon.

Then about five o'clock things changed.

I heard a sodding dog bark, and voices from the front of the house. Gravel crunched and Dermot Slattery appeared, towed by a rough-looking hound on a lead. I couldn't make out the breed but it wouldn't win any medals at Crufts. Somewhere between an Alsatian and a lurcher, but big, toothy and mad-eyed. Dermot had a stick and he bent down, unclipped the lead and set the dog dancing and barking around him. He flung the stick directly towards me and the bloody animal bounded after it, straight at me. Fortunately he didn't have much of a throwing arm. The stick barely made it halfway to my hiding place.

The two bodyguards appeared and the three of them took turns to throw the stick until the dog was foaming and wild-eyed like an advert for rabies. Now I knew my odds: four to one if you assumed Gerrit was inside with a good book. Five to one if you counted Fido.

Dermot seemed to get bored. He turned and banged on a window. A few minutes later a white-haired woman hove into sight with a tray bearing three dark bottles and three glasses. I wondered if this was lady Slattery. She put the tray down on the table and left them to pour their own. I watched as they slurped back the dark liquor. I was thirsty as hell and hungry. I sipped from my water bottle and envied them their beer. I'd known many times like this: waiting for the off. This time was no different except that this time it was personal.

By twilight things had quietened down. Dermot and the Hound of the Slatterys had gone back inside and even the guards seemed to have disappeared. Did they think no one would attack after dark?

I got to my feet and moved back far enough so that I could do some stretching exercises. My body was numb from lying still. Carefully I checked the guns again. I moved forward and to the left where the shed was, keeping to the line of the trees. With the shed between me and the house I ran over the grass and stood against the shed rear wall. I inched round the corner, saw nothing, heard nothing and crunched across the ten feet of gravel to the back door.

My heart was pounding, waiting for someone to shout out or just blast me with the sawn-off. He wouldn't miss from this range. I could hear voices from inside, his and hers, probably in the kitchen to tell by the crashing of dishes. Should I try the door handle and burst in? I put the 12-bore in my left hand and was just reaching out with my right towards the handle when I saw a shadow fall long across the grass from the side of the house. He was walking silently on the soft turf instead of the gravel.

The extended silhouette of a man crept along the ground and then the man himself appeared. He was looking ahead but immediately turned towards me. It was Fergie's mate. His face was a picture as he saw me. His jaw opened and he began to turn towards me, lifting his shotgun to take aim. I'd had an extra two seconds to prepare. I hoped I'd made the right choice of weapon. Hoped, too, I hadn't lost the art.

My arm was already raised behind my head, my knife held tightly by the point. I flung it with all my force and watched it race towards his chest even as he pointed the gun at me. The knife had twenty feet to travel. His gun barrel only had an arc of two feet to rise to be level with my guts. The knife hit with a dull thunk, slap in the middle of his throat just above his rib cage. His eyes opened wide with the shock. He stumbled backwards, dropping the sawn-off as he fell so that he could clutch at the blade that grew from his neck.

He coughed and tried to shout but it came out like a grunt. I'd been running towards him even as my knife was in the air. I got to him as he collapsed. I kicked the shotgun away and bent down at his side. The colour was already leaving him, except on his shirt where red was spreading fast. He looked up at my face in bewilderment. I thought he was about to shout for help, so I stuffed my hand over his mouth and ripped out the knife. I stabbed it down again, into his chest. I felt the blade grate against his ribs. He moaned under my hand and I felt his last gasps, then a spasm as his body tried to sit up before falling back. His head sank gently into the grass and he stared up at the sky unseeing.

I wrenched out the knife. More blood pooled and ran down both sides of his shirt and into the earth. I wiped the sticky blade on the grass and then on his trousers before sliding it back into my sock. I picked up my own shotgun and stuffed the sawn-off in my belt at the back of my waist. It would come in handy at close quarters. I had a second to wonder at my coldness, at taking the life of a man with such clinical efficiency and with nary a qualm. It didn't seem to be troubling me. And that troubled me. But that was for later. Three to one, not counting the dog. The odds were improving.

FORTY-ONE

I took a tip from the dead man and ran silently down the grass at the side of the house until I was level with the end of one of the wings of the house. I stepped on to the gravel and tiptoed across it and round to the corner. I peeped round. No one, but the front door was ajar.

I drew back and picked up a handful of stones. I flung my arm round the corner and let go. There was a satisfying clatter as a rain of pebbles fell against the door and walls and the window. I heard a shout from inside and the dog started barking.

'What the fuck you playing at out there?'

The door crashed properly open and someone strode out on to the gravel. I waited and waited.

'Martin! Where the fuck are you? Stop playing silly buggers!'

Then I heard the deep growl of a dog about to attack and I knew I needed to face this, fast. I darted into the open and dropped to my knee with the Dickson raised and pointed. Fergie was standing twenty feet from me in front of the door. He held another of their trademark sawn-offs in one hand. Dermot was in the doorway, holding the hound by the collar.

Dermot reacted first. 'It's fucking Brodie! Shoot him!' At the same time he let slip the dog of war, which sprang past Fergie, heading straight for my face.

Its jaws were already snapping in anticipation of fastening on my throat. The beast bounded forward, all muscle and snarl, and took off about six feet from me. Not the normal clay pigeon shot. I pulled the trigger. The blast caught it full in the chest. It turned in mid-air and landed in a sprawling, writhing heap next to me. I was already diving to the side just as Fergie fired. I felt a rush of pellets shred the air around me. Then, lying on my side, I gave him the second barrel. I didn't miss.

He was flung backwards on to the gravel. His shotgun went up in the air and clattered beside him. I dropped my empty Dickson and ran forward, pulling my pistol out of my waistband. I fired at Dermot but missed. He dived back in the house and crashed the door shut. I heard locks fall and knew he'd barricaded himself in. I heard him shouting and the woman screaming at him. But there was no other voice; still no sign of Gerrit. Fergie was writhing on the ground, clutching his stomach. He was screaming in a choked, panting way. It was a painful way to die. I didn't pause to put him out of his misery.

I ran at the door and hit it with my shoulder. It was a tough old plank of oak and I bounced back. The locks held. I slid my revolver in my belt and drew the sawn-off. I stood back and blasted the area round the keyhole. I kicked the door in and dived through headfirst, rolling into the small hall. Dermot was well down a long corridor, dragging the woman into one of the rooms. She was shrieking her head off. I couldn't fire in case I hit her. He slammed the door and locked it. I heard furniture being dragged across. I ran down the corridor like an avenging angel. I stood to one side of the door in case there was a third shotgun in Dermot's hands.

'Dermot! You might as well come out! Or I'll come in and get you! I won't harm the woman. Unless, of course, you've injured a single hair on the head of Samantha Campbell! In which case all bets are off. Do you hear me?'

All the response I got was more sobbing and more crashing of furniture. Then there was a new sound, of hinges opening, followed by the sound of feet on the gravel. He'd got out the window. I sprinted back down the corridor and flung myself through the front door. Dermot had dived into the car and was starting it up. The motor whirred and caught and he flung it into gear. The car shot forward, sending pebbles flying back at my face. It accelerated down the 150-yard drive towards the wooden gate.

I dropped the sawn-off and gripped my revolver in both hands. I fired steadily, once, twice, three times, smashing the rear window but seemingly doing no other damage. I stuffed it in my waistband. I had one shot left in the sawn-off. I knelt, picked it up, and let fly. I blew a hole in the boot but the car sped on. Shit, shit, shit! I dropped the useless weapon and ran forward, maddened at my rotten shooting.

I snatched up the Dickson and broke it open. The two used cartridges spun into the air. I delved in my pocket and grabbed one shell. No time for a second. I rammed it home and slammed the gun closed. I knelt in the gravel, pulled the Dickson tight into my shoulder and took a deep breath. Then another. The car was racing for the wooden gate and escape. I took a careful bead on his head and then lowered the barrel. I needed him alive to find out about Sam. I squeezed the trigger. The gun jerked back into my shoulder. I waited. There was no time to reload and fire. He was within twenty yards of freedom.

At first I thought I'd missed and was regretting my generosity of not aiming at his head. Then I saw the car lurch to the side as a rear tyre blew. Slattery swung the wheel to counter it. Swung too far and was on the grass. Swung again, all the while accelerating, aiming to ram his way through the gate. But the big car pitched again and hit the solid stone pillar with an almighty crash. I ran down the drive, ramming shells into my revolver.

There was a great hissing and clattering as the engine kept trying to pull the car forward. But the fan was jammed and there was nowhere to go. I wrenched the door open to find Slattery sitting with blood all over his face, groaning against the steering wheel. His head had gone through the screen. But I was taking no chances.

I caught him by his shirt collar and tried to drag him out of the car. He was stuck. I looked closer. The steering shaft running from the front axle up into the cabin had been driven back with the impact. Like a long blunt-ended spear. At the same moment his seat had catapulted forward. His chest was impaled on the central column. The bastard was dying.

He wasn't getting off that easy. I grabbed his hair at the nape of his neck and shook him. 'Where's Samantha Campbell, you little prick!' I shoved the gun barrel into his ear. 'Where is she!'

Someone was running down the drive. It was the woman he'd used as a shield. Her legs were flapping as she stumbled forward in her bare feet. Her hands were clawing at her mass of white hair. 'Don't kill him! Oh, don't kill him!' she shouted, and flung herself at me.

I pushed her back and held her away from me, as she flailed at my head. 'OK, OK! Tend to your man!'

Her mad eyes searched my face and then she sagged like a broken doll. She dived into the car and held Slattery's bloody head. He moaned and red seeped from his mouth.

'He needs an ambulance!' she shouted at me. 'Get help! There's a phone in there!'

'Mrs Slattery?' I said quietly. 'He needs a priest.'

She stopped and turned to me, her eyes filled with despair. 'That's the last thing Derry Slattery needs. The very last thing.'

There was a sound from Dermot, a great groan. He turned his face to her and tried to speak. Only a moan came out of his broken lips.

'Oh, darlin', don't try to speak. You'll be fine. Just wait. We'll get the doctor to ye. Just you hold on.' She turned to me. 'Can we get him out? Make him more comfy?'

Together we tugged and pulled and manoeuvred his wrecked body out of the car and on to the grass. We laid him on his back and she cradled his head. She wiped the blood off his face as best she could, using her skirt. Then she rocked him gently like a child until Dermot Slattery shuddered once more and gave up his violent life.

I have no idea why I helped her, but I found myself dragooned into dragging his body back the 150 yards to the house. We passed the now still body of Fergie without a glance. We dropped Dermot on a bed and I sought the kitchen. I found what I was looking for. It was Irish, but it had the same effect. I poured a big glass and ran some tap water into it. I slugged it back in two gulps. Then I stood by the sink and rinsed the blood off my hands and off my jacket sleeves as best I could. I realised my legs were shaking. The day was catching up on me. The familiar pattern. When the fighting stops, the adrenalin drains away. I felt sick and leaned over the sink in case. For a moment I was flung back to the darkest days this past winter. Despondency swept over me, disorientated me. The smell of the foxhole in the Ardennes choked me. I'd lain in it for two days while the shelling and strafing went on. Just me and my dead corporal. It seems I'd only killed one dog out there. I sucked in air and clung to the sink until the nausea passed. I heard someone come in. I turned fast in case she was carrying a grudge and a gun.

She shouldered me aside and filled a bowl with clear water. She took a towel and went off again. Later she returned and flushed the bloody contents of the bowl down the sink. Then she rinsed her own hands.

'I'm makin' tea,' she said.

'Is that an offer?'

She shrugged.

FORTY-TWO

We sat opposite each other at the table, warily sipping the hot, sweet tea. It was a bizarrely domestic scene given that three men and a hellhound lay slaughtered within twenty feet of us. Sometimes only old rituals get you through.

'So, you're the angel of death, Brodie.' She said it like a fact, as though she'd been waiting for me, and was mildly disappointed at the guise I'd turned up in.

'You'll not believe me when I say I'm sorry for your loss, Mrs Slattery. But I am. I'm not sorry he's dead, though. He had it coming.'

'Do ye think so, do ye! An' what do *you* know of Derry Slattery? What do *you* know of *his* life?'

'I know he took the lives of others. Or arranged for it to happen. Do you deny that?'

She took a deep breath and let it out. She shook her head. 'It got out of hand. He didn't start this way.'

'Mrs Slattery, I don't have time for his personal hard-luck story, with all due respect. I'm trying to find Samantha Campbell. Advocate Campbell?'

'I know who *she* is! That bitch!'

I nearly flung my tea over her, but I needed help here. 'Why do you say that? What harm has she done you?'

'She's her father's daughter, that's who she is! Fiscal Campbell! He was always after Gerrit. Never letting him go. Always hauling him into court. He had to be stopped. It was all settled. And then she ends up disturbing our lives again!'

I gazed at her, and rubbed my suddenly dry lips. 'What do you mean: "He had to be stopped" and "It was all settled"?'

She turned up her mouth at me, like a sneer. Suddenly I knew with complete certainty what she meant. The sequence of niggling coincidences were nothing of the sort. The constant harassment of the Slattery clan by the Procurator Fiscal in the late twenties and early thirties came to an abrupt halt when Sam's parents drowned. *Were* drowned.

'Dermot killed her father and mother, didn't he? On the loch.'

She got up and walked over to the sink. She picked up the whiskey and two glasses. She poured them full and plonked them between us.

'It's all one now. Derry had no choice. Same old story. He had to protect his brother. It's how it's always been.'

I felt sick again. Maybe it was the last of the adrenalin oozing away, or the peaty whiskey. Maybe it was the long dark story that stretched down the years. The tale that started with the deliberate drowning of an old couple on a walking holiday and led to Sam's own abduction and possible murder. The brutal and callous removal of everyone who might give evidence against them. The final retreat to the old country that ended in violence and gore.

I asked quietly, scarcely daring to hear the answer, 'Where is Samantha Campbell? Do you know?'

She shrugged, as if it was of little interest to her. 'Gerrit has her, I expect. The boy was always daft, so he was. Mental.'

I gripped the table, my guts churning in a mix of outrage and fear. Gerrit – the rabid dog – had her. 'Where?'

She took a big pull on her whiskey. 'That would be tellin' now, wouldn't it?' she smirked.

I flung the half-full tumbler at the wall. It smashed to pieces and left a dark, reeking stain down the whitewash. 'Well, you'd better be telling! Right here, right now!'

I was ready to beat the information out of her, and she knew it. I'd wiped the smirk off her face and for a second fear lit her eyes. But then her face glazed into a tight mask. This wasn't the first tumbler she'd seen smashed off a wall. It wasn't the first threat she'd had. Mrs Slattery had seen the worst life could offer and wasn't about to turn into a quivering jelly at this late stage. I let the silence fill the kitchen. Neither of us moved. I got control of my shaking hands by clasping them together on the table as though I was going to say grace. I decided to try the long way round.

'You said, "It's how it's always been." What did you mean?'

Her mouth softened. 'Since they were kids. Dermot looking after his wee brother.'

'Tell me.' I reached over and topped up her glass.

She eyed me up. She'd been beautiful once, I imagined. The white hair would have been thick black curls, and the curves more subtle. She would have set Dermot Slattery's blood racing. I bet she was a dancer. That shrug again. Another big mouthful.

'Trouble with the authorities. That sort of thing.'

'Were they IRA, Dermot and Gerrit?'

She laughed. 'Sure, everybody's a wee bit IRA round these parts.'

I tried a long shot. 'What about the priest? Why did Father Cassidy have to die?'

Her already flushed face turned crimson round the neck. She rocked to her feet and stood swaying. 'That's it! I'll say no more!

Now, get out of this house. You've destroyed us all, so you have! Just you get going!'

I stood up to face her, just as much at the end of my tether. 'Where is Gerrit Slattery? Where is he keeping Samantha Campbell?'

She tottered and nearly fell, then caught the edge of the table. Her speech was slurring. 'It's likely too late. Gerrit's a devil, so he is.'

'I need to try. For pity's sake, woman, just give me an address,' I pleaded. 'Enough folk have died, have they not?'

She looked out of the kitchen window as the darkness grew. She wiped her face and turned back to me.

'Gerrit brought all this down on us. He didn't deserve a brother like that.' She nodded towards the room where her husband lay. 'Derry was a good man. It could have been different for us. Him and me. But always, always, that bloody maniac threw everything up in the air. Just for the fun of it half the time. Or for his dirty treats. And now my Derry is in there. And he's out there laughing at us all.'

'Out where, Mrs Slattery? Is it right that Gerrit lives on and your Derry doesn't? After all that Derry did for him?'

She gazed at me through bleary eyes. She knew what I was doing, what I was saying.

She sighed, 'He'll be in one of two places. The cottage in Arran, or the den in Dumbarton. Him and his pals. And they'll get you this time, Mister smart murdering angel-of-death Brodie.'

'Well, you won't mind giving me the addresses, then, if they're going to kill me?'

She squinted at me, the logic sifting through her fuddled brain. Then she grinned. 'That's right. Send you to hell, so I will ...'

She told me, and my stomach turned over at the thought of Sam being captive so close to me in Glasgow while all the time I had been chasing the wrong target. I collected myself and started making for the door. I faced her again.

'What about …?' I nodded towards the room where Slattery lay oozing on to the bedspread.

'We'll take care of our own.'

'And the ones outside?' I felt no guilt about these deaths. It had been them or me. But there was the small matter of the police. All she had to do was pick up the phone and I'd be explaining this evening's work behind bars until I turned old and grey. Or they hanged me.

'I know some folk. We'll do it our way. The quiet way.'

I believed her, but to make sure, I made her make one phone call to a local number. She asked for two men. They would be round directly. I ripped out the phone from the wall and tore the cable away. Then I picked up my Dickson where it lay outside and walked off down the driveway in the warmth of a fine spring evening. I ejected the spent cartridge and filled both chambers afresh. I stepped round the big black saloon whose lifeblood was ebbing into the gravel in a glistening mix of oil and water and fuel. I climbed over the gate and walked off into the humming darkness.

FORTY-THREE

I drove through the night and got to Larne harbour in the wee small hours. I parked, slept fitfully in the back of the car and woke to the sound of chains and horns. I caught the first ferry back to Stranraer. I found a baker's open and bought a couple of soft rolls filled with some nameless paste. I stopped a milkman finishing his rounds with his horse and cart and acquired a couple of pints of milk. I chewed and drank as I drove. By eleven o'clock I was coaxing a garage in Girvan to let me have a couple of gallons without coupons. He took double the price but money wasn't my problem. Time was. Eighty miles to Glasgow.

I hammered the Riley up the A77 shore road past Ayr and then cross country through Kilmarnock. I was doing seventy down the Glasgow road, overtaking everything in sight like a madman. I reached the Jamaica Bridge by one o'clock and headed out west towards Dumbarton. I'd decided to start with this den she'd talked about. If I found nothing there, I'd cross the Erskine ferry and catch the boat to Arran.

Initially I passed rank upon rank of swinging cranes on either side of the Clyde where the shipyards were dinning away. Then there was the long stretch of Clydebank where a town used to sit next to the yards. The community was blitzed to rubble in '41. On along the Dumbarton Road past the Erskine Ferry until the big rock of Dumbarton castle shunted into the clear blue morning. It was a perfect site for a fortress and had held the pass through the Clyde estuary for centuries. Kings of Scotland and, before them, Pictish kings had been crowned here and ruled the surrounding fertile valleys. But not even a Celtic seer could have forecast the Luftwaffe.

I eased the car down the long sloping road into the town and began to look for Bute Street. Finally I stopped and asked a road sweep. I took his directions and found myself passing through the town on a shore road that ran back towards Glasgow. The quiet road finally petered out into a farm track with grass down the middle. Ahead I could see a glimpse of water through the trees.

I paused. There were eight wooden huts slung along the lane – four either side – and peeping out from the trees and shrubs. Each had its own mud path running off the road up to the front door. They were more like wooden caravans than houses, with clapperboard walls and corrugated flat roofs. There was no smoke coming from any of the rickety chimneys. They seemed abandoned but were probably just holiday homes.

I parked the car on the tarmac road and got out. I slid my revolver into my waistband and closed my jacket. The Dickson was harder to hide but there was no one around to see it. I checked the new cartridges were sitting neatly in their chambers and clicked it closed. I stepped up to the entrance to the lane and looked down the tunnel of foliage, peering into the mint-fresh greenery. In front of each hut was a simple stake with a number on it. Some of them also had crude names hanging from them. According to Mrs Slattery I was looking for number 4. I just hoped she wasn't lying. There was no sign of telephone cables linking the huts to civilisation so I assumed she had no way of contacting her brother-in-law. But I'd soon find out if I had a reception committee or not.

The hut to my left was number 1, the next number 2. Number 4 was at the end of one row. It sat at the river end of the glade and well back from all the others. It looked as if it had about double the land around it compared to the rest. The windows were blacked out and there was no sign of a car.

I flicked off the safety on the Dickson and slid into the trees behind the left-hand huts. I crept round through the patchy undergrowth until I was behind a tree within thirty feet of number 4.

No sign of life, but Gerrit could be in there with at least two of his thugs, and possibly Sam Campbell. I stood listening. Apart from spring birdsong it was quiet as a morgue. The hut had a front door square in the middle. I guessed it would also have a back door. I shuttled round until I could see. There was a little wooden porch and a door. I eyed it up. Standard panelled job, one big lock and a smaller Yale above it. No sign of reinforcing.

My old sergeant in initial training told me that when in doubt, just bleedin' charge the bastards, shouting your bleedin' head off. I skipped the battle cry but dashed across the open clearing, bounded once on the wood terracing and drove at the door with my shoulder.

There was a satisfying crunch, the wood splintered and tore, and the door half opened. I hit it again and crashed through, raising my shotgun as the door slammed back against the wall. I kept running straight through the kitchen into a front room. It was pitch dark and empty. I raced down a corridor, kicking the doors back as I went. Nothing. I went back to the front room, chest heaving, and looked around me. It was too dark. No electricity, so no light switches. I fumbled my way across to the windows, pulled back the heavy blackout curtains and took in the room. Nondescript couch and a couple of easy chairs whose inners were spilling from cracked seams. A silent wireless and plenty of ashtrays. A couple of oil lamps.

I wandered back through the house. At the front a lounge, to the rear the kitchen that I'd entered through. Off the short corridor two bedrooms facing each other. But at the far end of the corridor was a locked door that I hadn't noticed in the dark. The door wasn't just locked but it was secured on the outside by heavy bolts top and bottom. To the right of the door a large key hung from a nail embedded in the wall. Below it an oil lamp hung from another nail. I listened again and could only hear the blood rushing in my ears.

I propped the shotgun against the wall and took down the lamp. It was there for a purpose. I shook it: plenty of paraffin. I struck a match and lit the wick. It caught quickly and I trimmed it and lowered the glass. I put it on the floor and took down the key. I slid the big bolts back and put the key in the lock. It groaned and turned. I took the lamp in my left hand and the shotgun in my right. I used my left hand to turn the handle, and kicked the door open. At first I could see only floor, then as I paced forward holding the lamp up before me, I could see and smell more than I wanted.

I knew this place. One of my interrogations had taken place in the SS commandant's house outside the camp near Bremen. He'd made himself at home. It was a pretty house from the outside. Inside it had comfortable armchairs and Alpine pictures on the walls. The curtains were rich red to match the sweep of good carpets. It also had a cellar. They had unchained the young women by the time I got there.

*

This was no flashback. The stench hit me first. Fetid and heavy, the outpourings of bodies racked by pain and incontinence.

A mattress lay sprawled in one corner of a bare wood floor. Nameless brown stains mapped its filthy surface. I lifted the lamp higher. Two heavy hooks dangled from wooden beams of the ceiling. They weren't for hanging game. Confirming my fears was a pile of coiled ropes and chains on a wooden table by the wall.

Completing the sordid picture was a contraption that looked like the wooden horse we used to jump over at PT in the Army. Two crude A frames joined by a horizontal spar about waist height. A thin mattress had been slung over it. It too was stained.

I backed out of the room, gagging with nausea. I fled down the corridor and out into the back yard, gasping for air. I stumbled over to the shrubbery and threw up. I fell to my knees and emptied my stomach on the grass until the dry heaving convulsions were past. My body was covered in sweat and I walked back to the wooden terrace and sat down till the perspiration cooled on my body. The pressure began lifting behind my eyes and I took out a cigarette and lit it.

All along I'd been wondering where they kept Rory before dumping his abused little body in Hugh's house. This place fitted the bill. This was where he'd been violated and finally murdered. And if so, Rory wouldn't have been the first. The set-up of the room wasn't a one-off. This was planned by Gerrit Slattery, who would have been just at home running a Nazi death camp, taking pleasure and pride in his work. Where he got his 'dirty treats', as Mrs Slattery so nicely put it.

It was handy having the Clyde at the back door: some rope, some weights and the evidence is gone. A way to get rid of opponents and have some fun in the process. A place to bring abducted boys and abuse them before dumping their tortured bodies in the river. Somewhere to bring an interfering advocate whose father had been a constant thorn in the side? To punish her, make her beg for mercy or death, before dumping her slim body in the grey water? I punched the ground.

But why not dispose of Rory's body the same way? Why bring it out into the daylight? Maybe they'd been feeling the heat? Maybe even the Glasgow police force were getting interested? So Gerrit needed a scapegoat. Someone disposable to take the rap until things died down. He used Rory to frame poor old Hugh. Pitiless murdering bastard.

I had another fag and walked back to the car. I turned it round and headed back towards Glasgow and the Erskine ferry. En route I stopped at a call box and dialled 999. I told the police where to come and what to look for, and to bring a forensic scientist from Glasgow University to identify the stains and look for prints. They might also need a boat and a frogman.

I crossed the Clyde and headed west to Ardrossan and yet another ferry. I should have bought a season ticket, or a boat.

Dumbarton had been a fruitless detour. It was always likely that Gerrit would have put as much distance and water between himself and retribution as possible. But I hadn't wasted much time checking out the mainland den. If I'd started with Arran it would have cost me at least a day. This time I knew where I was going and what I had to do there. My clarity had returned. After what I'd seen I wasn't expecting to find Sam Campbell alive. Either way, someone was going to die. I hoped it wasn't going to be me.

FORTY-FOUR

bumped off the ferry at Brodick and headed south, back towards Lamlash and Whiting Bay. Kildonan was on the southern point of the island looking down the Firth of Clyde towards Ailsa Craig and Ireland. Mrs Slattery had described the place: about a mile beyond the village, a white house standing by itself on a piece of land that jutted out into the water. It had its own moorings. Gerrit fancied himself as a bit of a sailor and had a boat, though it had always made Dermot seasick. But it was a handy route between Northern Ireland and Scotland if you didn't want close scrutiny from the exciseman or the police.

I looked at my watch and the clear sky. It wasn't the best time for a frontal attack on a well-defended peninsula. In truth there was never a good time to attack a redoubt protected on three sides by deep water. Not unless you were Royal Navy. I could either wait till morning and make a dawn raid when Gerrit and his merry men would be at their lowest ebb. Or I could just get on with it now, and make the best of the fading light and the element of surprise. Always assuming it would be a surprise; Mrs Slattery would have had her phone fixed by now.

Passing through Lamlash, I made a brief detour. I found the Catholic chapel tucked behind the line of the main street, small and discreet, unlike its Protestant counterpart at the village end with its tall square tower looking out to Holy Island. I picked up the Dickson and walked towards the front entrance framed by pretty panes of glass that glowed in the afternoon light. I pushed open the heavy door. I stepped into the hushed hall lit by candles and daylight pouring through the glazed Stations of the Cross. A figure in white knelt in front of the altar, praying.

I felt completely calm. I walked towards him until I was six feet away and close enough to hear the droning repetition of his litany. I broke the shotgun and closed it again with solid clunk. The supplications stopped. He turned and climbed to his feet. He looked older. His eyes were red and staring. His floor-length white robe was belted by a dark cincture like they'd used to truss Cassidy before hanging him. O'Brien didn't look much like the man I'd met on the beach at Lamlash so long ago now. My instinct to trust him had been wrong, so wrong. He looked at my shotgun and then back at my face. He didn't look scared or surprised.

'Are you here to kill me?'

'Not necessarily. I'm here for information. I don't have much time so I want answers right now.'

He shook his head. 'There's nothing I can tell you.'

'You haven't heard the question. And you haven't heard what I have to say.'

'I don't want to.' He was sullen, stubborn.

'I'm going to tell you anyway. There've been more deaths. More blood. Perhaps on your hands, eh, Father? They've been covering their tracks, the Slatterys. Three days ago Gerrit strangled a high court judge. Now why would he do that? Then he kidnapped Samantha Campbell. Brought her here to the island. I'm going to find her and then I'm going to kill him.'

Father Connor O'Brien's face contorted as if he'd been kicked in the belly.

'There's more. I tracked Dermot to his lair in Ireland. He's dead and so are his two minions. Afterwards his wife and I had a bit of a wake, if you like. Over a glass or two she told me that her darling husband murdered Samantha's parents back in the thirties. Drowned them in Loch Lomond to stop him making life difficult for young Gerrit. So, on top of all the others – Hugh Donovan, Mrs Reid and her daughter and sons, and of course the good Father Cassidy – a lot of folk have died to keep a wee secret, wouldn't you say?'

He had his hands up to his mouth as though he was going to be sick. I pressed on.

'And I haven't mentioned Rory Hutchinson. And the four others that are missing, presumed raped and murdered. Gerrit's work, I imagine. I found his torture chamber. Did you know about that, *Father*?'

'What do you want?' he screamed.

'What was the link between the Slattery boys and Patrick Cassidy?'

He shook his head.

'I don't have time for this, Connor.'

I lifted my shotgun, took careful aim, and fired. He dropped to his knees as the shot echoed round and round amidst the sound of glass falling and breaking. O'Brien turned and looked behind him. A large section of stained-glass window had vanished, leaving St Paul not just blind but headless. A real Damascene conversion.

'That's blasphemy!'

'No, Father. What Cassidy and Slattery have been doing is blasphemy. Now, what's your next favourite?' I raised my gun again and pointed it at the Virgin Mary.

'Stop! Stop! In the name of God, stop!'

'God seems to have lost interest, lately.' But I lowered my gun anyway.

The priest sagged against the altar. 'He regretted it. You must know he bitterly regretted it.'

'Who regretted what?'

'Father Cassidy. He told me he couldn't help himself. It was when he was teaching at the Nazareth House in Belfast. He got close to some of the boys. He transgressed ...'

'You mean he buggered them?'

He winced. 'It wasn't like that. The Slattery boys were sent there by their father. The father had been abusing them for years. Dermot was strong. He got over it. But Gerrit ... Gerrit got changed by it. He grew to like it, may God have mercy on him. He seduced Patrick. He corrupted a good man. You must believe me!'

'Go on.'

'Patrick fled to Glasgow and tried to put his past behind him. The Slatterys appeared one day, and from then on they blackmailed Patrick to help them. Provide cover for them. Patrick was doing good work in the Gorbals. A sort of penance. He couldn't let them take that from him. Gerrit continued his perverted ways in Glasgow. Finding young boys. Harming them as he had been harmed. He found others like him. He procured boys for them. There was a group of men, some senior in civic life.'

Oh, shit. 'Chief Justice Allardyce?'

'I don't know their names. It's possible.'

'Senior policemen?' I didn't need to hear his answer. Muncie and Silver hadn't just been worried about looking stupid if they admitted they'd got the wrong man. It was likely they'd colluded in rape, torture, murder, perjury and perverting the course of justice. They'd as good as murdered Rory Hutchinson and his father, Hugh.

He stood there in his virginal white with a face like a martyr, *what could I do?* I had an almost uncontrollable impulse to give him his wish. To tarnish the white with his own tainted blood.

'So they got rid of Procurator Fiscal Campbell and replaced him with the biddable Allardyce? Perfect.' Then it occurred to me. 'How do you know all this, Connor? How are you involved?'

'I'm not – as you put it – involved! Patrick was my tutor. He confided in me.'

'But why are you protecting him? I wouldn't go this far for my old Latin teacher.'

He looked down. Then he ran a hand over his face from brow to chin as though washing himself. I should have felt disgust. All I felt was weariness at the way we were blown and driven through life by our natures. As if we had no choice.

'Not in the confessional box, then? More like the bedroom, eh, Father?'

'Don't say that! I was the only one he could turn to! It was a burden too heavy for one man!'

'Believe me, Father, if you knew all about this *burden* and didn't tell the police, you *are* involved. And your relationship, all the sordid details of it, will come out at the trial.' I thought he was going to throw up or have a heart attack. I pressed on. 'What about Hugh Donovan? Was that part of the "cover" Cassidy provided?'

He was tugging at his cincture as though it was cutting him in half. 'It was Patrick's lowest moment. It drove him mad. Slattery wanted a scapegoat, someone who'd take the blame for the missing boys. Donovan was a drug addict. He depended on Gerrit to supply him. Gerrit saw Donovan with the boy and had the boy picked up. Then he arranged for the evidence to be planted.'

He saw the look of contempt on my face.

'Donovan's life was meaningless compared to Patrick's work. You must see that!'

The fury rose in me like bile. 'I thought your God took those sorts of decisions?' My gun came up and I aimed at O'Brien's head. 'Who planted the evidence?' I asked quietly.

The priest stared at me as if I really was the avenging angel. Perhaps he hoped I was.

'Who planted it?'

He swallowed. 'Father Cassidy.'

The wind whipped in from the hole in the window. It stirred the folds of cloth on the pulpit and sent the candles fluttering and waving. I lowered my gun, turned and walked away, my heels clicking on the wood floor.

'What are you going to do?' he called after me. I didn't turn.

'What shall I do?' he screamed.

I opened the chapel door and stepped out into the cool of early evening.

FORTY-FIVE

I drove slowly into the tiny village of Kildonan, letting my anger cool, trying to find that still, calm centre I needed before action. It was illusive. I felt the mounting pressure in my head that presaged headaches and despair, as though my life force was draining away, leaving me bereft. O'Brien's forced confessions had depressed me more than I expected. Was nothing untainted? I thought I could trust him when I first met him. It seemed like I'd lost my ability to judge folk. I wasn't too surprised about his revelations about Cassidy. But their relationship …

I was getting more naïve as I got older, not less. I thought I'd seen and heard the worst of mankind in the eyes and from the mouths of the SS officers I'd interrogated. I'd seen their handiwork in the camps near Bremen and put it all down to an aberration of the Hitler-inspired Reich. That he'd been a messiah to the minority: the loonies and fanatics; the psychopaths and criminals; the inhabitants of the seventh and eighth circles of hell. That while the rest of the nation had been asleep in the back seat the fiends had grabbed the wheel and driven Germany over the Rheinfalls. I truly hadn't expected evil to be a commonplace. That I'd find it here in the soft hills and sandy shores of my own country.

*

I stopped the car, rolled down the window and lit a fag. The views drew the eye. Away to the east was the mainland of Ayrshire. To the south, about half a mile out in the bay, was a small wedge of an island. A lighthouse jutted phallically from its midpoint. Far out to the south east sat Ailsa Craig, the peripatetic lump of granite. Beyond that, but out of sight, lay Ireland.

Kildonan itself was a scattering of white houses and a fine beach. It would be a pretty place to spend a few days – a bit of fishing perhaps, paddling, and reading a good book in a deckchair on the sliver of fine sand. Was it a good place to die? As good as any. The odds were probably worse here than Lisnaskea. And I'd given up on finding Sam alive. I was weary of it all, sickened by endemic wickedness, careless of life. I was ready to trade it for taking Gerrit Slattery with me.

So, did Kildonan have what I needed today? It was early in the year and they might not have geared up for tourists. There was a hut on the beach and in front of it, lying tipped in the sand, were four wooden boats each with a two-stroke engine strapped to its stern. I drove forward and drew up opposite the hut. The boats would take three or four people each for a spot of light fishing. A chain linked each of them through a ring on its prow. The chain was tethered to boats one and four by padlocks. A sign offered them for hire by the hour for 9d or, for the day, 2/6d. Fishing gear could be hired separately. Trips to the island of Pladda could be arranged with tours of the lighthouse. There was no sign of the boat owner. It was nearly six o'clock. Perhaps two more hours before sunset.

The village was quiet, teatime quiet. I drove on and out, looking for a turn-off about a mile outside. The coast dipped in and out at this point. Past the bay of Kildonan the land cut back in and the road followed it. To my right a second bay opened up, much smaller than Kildonan. On the promontory partly obscured by trees was a white house, a two-storey job with windows all round. A jetty extended into the sea. A good-sized yacht stood alongside, rocking gently in the waves. It was two-masted, with the mainmast forward. The sails seemed to be lying folded along the booms. The hull had a simple beauty of line that suggested effortless speed. No bulking cabin cluttered the deck. In the driveway leading to the house stood a car. Its distinctive sloping rear suggested a Standard Twelve. There was no sign of activity.

It was all still, until I saw a figure walk past a downstairs window. If my sums were right, Gerrit Slattery would have three of the remaining gang members with him. And one of them would still be nursing a hole in his foot. But that wouldn't stop him from firing a gun at me. I had to assume they were armed at least as well as Dermot's team. I checked the line of fire in front of the house from the driveway leading up to it. No cover, simple to defend, permitting good triangulation of fire on attackers. My old unit had a term for it: Victoria Cross Posthumous – VCP. It would be VCP level of futility to make a full frontal. It wasn't that I was scared to die this day; it would just be such a waste to go without having a fair crack at Slattery.

I toyed with the idea of driving the Riley full tilt at the house, maybe aiming to put the front through the downstairs lounge window. But the walls looked solid and I'd likely end up sailing through the windscreen and smearing myself on the white walls like a giant dead fly. It was definitely plan A, the sea. Or was that what I was supposed to think?

I turned the car around and headed back into Kildonan. I parked about a hundred yards from the hut. I armed myself as before: revolver in my waistband; knife tucked down my sock;

and shotgun held pointing down inside my jacket. It wasn't hidden but only obvious if you got up close. There was no one around to examine me. I dropped down on to the sand and walked to the hut. I kept it between me and the village as I walked over to the first boat. I made short work of the padlock and slid the chain out on to the sand. I walked round to the outboard motor and looked in the tank. Empty. I walked along all four, all empty. Damnation.

I propped the Dickson in the first boat and trudged back to the hut. Same padlock type and just as simple to open. I stepped into the dark interior and waited for my eyes to adjust. On a shelf was a ball of fishing twine, finest catgut: could be useful. I pocketed it. There in the corner was a pair of cans. I opened them and savoured the sharp stink of petrol. I lifted one and turned to go out when a shadow fell across the floor, a giant shadow.

'A bit of night fishing, is it?' asked the man, about my age, big red beard and corduroys, as if he'd left his fiddle somewhere.

I placed the can back down. 'Are you the owner?' I felt for my revolver.

'Of the boats, the hut, the can in your hand? All three.'

'Look, this is an emergency. I can pay you.'

'An emergency fishing trip? Caught sight of a big one out there, have you?'

'Look, I'm really sorry, pal, but I don't have time for the sarcastic chit-chat. Fun though it is. There's a woman's life at stake and I need a boat.' I pulled my gun out my belt and levelled it at him.

'Why didn't you say so?' he said, looking down at the muzzle and calmly holding his hands up.

'Oh, put them down for God's sake.' I stuffed the gun back in my belt, disgusted at my antics.

'Is there really a woman in bother?'

'If she's alive, she's in bother.'

He stared into my eyes. 'Can I help?'

'Sure.'

He picked up the can and headed towards the first boat. He saw the long lethal shape of the Dickson resting on the stern and raised his eyebrows at me.

'Shark hunting,' I said.

'Would they be Irish sharks by any chance?'

'The white house, round the bay? With the yacht?'

'The *Lorne*. She's a ketch. By Dickies of Tarbert. A pretty craft. Too good for that scum.'

'Is that what it is? Two masts? Taller at the front?' My brain struggled for the right words.

'You're not a sailor, then.'

'Tried it once. I prefer ferries. Will anyone be on board or do they all stay in the house?'

'Depends.'

'I don't want anyone to get away.'

He nodded. 'Here.' He put the can down and knelt in the sand. He began drawing. 'It's simple. Main mast is for'ard, mizzen is aft. She's gaff rigged, fore and aft.' He sketched square-shaped sails whose top edge was suspended from a wooden spar instead of tied directly to the masts. 'Makes it easier to handle. You get more sail up for less mast. There's also a jib.' He drew a triangle without spars, that ran from the top of the main mast to the bow. 'You can sail her fine on a mizzen and a jib. When it's moored they just drop the sails onto their booms and lightly reef them. Quicker to the off.'

The vocabulary started to come back to me. 'Steering?'

'Tiller. Helmsman stands thigh deep in a cockpit between the stern and the mizzen mast, under the boom.'

'Cabins?'

'I've not been on board but she'll have six or eight bunks and a galley. Access from two hatches.'

'A handy boat for a round trip to Ireland?'

He nodded. 'Are you just yourself?'

'Me and Dickson here.'

He sized me up. 'Army?'

'2nd Seaforths. 51st Highland Division.'

A grin split the red beard in two. His hand came out. 'The Highway Decorators. One of Tom Rennie's boys. Me too. Black Watch. Tobruk?'

I smiled. 'You were on our left flank. Christ, it was hot.'

'Hotter in France.'

'The first time or the second?'

He looked at me quizzically. 'Just the once. We were 9th Highland. Territorials. Rebadged as the new 51st in time for Africa. Sicily *then* France. You?'

I sighed. '*Deux fois*. BEF in '40. Then Africa, Sicily and back to bloody France.'

'St Valery? I thought you all went on a nice German holiday? You escaped with Rennie?'

'A few of us didn't fancy the tour guides. A crofter from Lewis taught me how to sail a fishing boat we pinched from the French. Three days of rope burns and a headache. I thought he was talking Gaelic all the time. It was just fancy boating terms. It's why I prefer big boats with engines and a canteen.'

He looked me up and down. 'Christ.' Then, very deliberately, he saluted. 'Wait here.'

He went back to his hut. He came tottering back with another outboard motor, a much bigger version than any of the ones clamped to the boats. It took him five minutes to replace one with the other and to fill the tank.

'You should get ten, maybe eleven knots from this yin. It might help.'

He placed another can of fuel inside the boat, and we began to drag the boat down the sand and into the shallow water. He held it steady while I clambered on board. He stood with waves lapping against his hips while I settled myself. He explained how to start the motor, priming the carb and using the throttle. I held the top of the motor, gripped the handle of the cord and tugged. The engine coughed, spluttered; I opened the throttle a little more and it fired up and moved into *pop pop* mode.

'What's your name, friend?'

'Eric. Eric McLeod.'

'Brodie. Douglas Brodie.' We shook hands. 'Well, Eric the Red, I'm truly grateful. If I don't come back, or it gets damaged, well ...'

'Never mind the boat. Find that lady of yours. I'd come with you, for the laughs. But I've the wife and bairn now,' he said wistfully.

I turned round to face the open sea, twisted the throttle-cum-steering handle and revved away from the shore. Dusk was settling across the water and the waves grew choppier as I headed out past the point. A northerly was picking up from the shore and I began to worry about getting swamped when I turned side on to it.

Far off, at the point of the next bay, I could see the distant house and boat. I took a wide arc out towards the Ayrshire mainland and buzzed and splashed my way for half an hour. I tried the boat at full pelt to see how fast it could go. Quick enough for me to get drenched and on the verge of capsizing as the wind buffeted me from the shore.

I settled down to a steady three or four knots, butting into the waves. When I was opposite the house a good three or four hundred yards out, I turned about and started heading land-ward. I sat lower in the boat, relying on the gathering dark and the grey, swollen sea to make me invisible. I just hoped the bad guys were all pointing their guns at the road.

FORTY-SIX

dropped speed until the engine was down to a low-key throb. But it still sounded as loud as an ice-cream van on a Sunday, without the pleasurable anticipation. Finally I had the bulk of the jetty between me and the house. The *Lorne* was bigger than I'd thought from afar, perhaps a 50-footer. The jetty was about forty feet long so that the ketch stuck out well beyond the end. Hefty wooden pillars propped up each side of the jetty and stood a good three feet proud above the deck. Halfway along the deck stood a wooden locker about six feet long, three wide and high.

As each swell rolled through, the ketch swung from side to side and the halyards flapped and clanked. I cut the motor and nudged against the pier, and sat there clinging to the wood for a long minute to make sure no gangster with a grievance was about to blow my head off.

I tethered the boat to a pillar on the opposite side from the *Lorne.* I scrambled to my feet, praying none of my weapons would end up as buried treasure in the murky waters below. Slowly I raised my head above the deck of the jetty. I could see into the back room of the house about thirty yards away. There was a big bay window with wonderful sea views, or in this case wonderful me views. Lights were already on and I could see one figure standing up talking to someone else, sitting down. He turned and talked to someone else. I think I recognised the curly-haired guy I'd shot in the foot. I hoped it still hurt.

I climbed back down to my boat and lifted the can out. I placed it on the deck and then laid my shotgun, knife and revolver alongside it. I carefully climbed up and on to the jetty and crab-crawled along it. Then I made my preparations.

The fire caught quickly and roared into the air above the wooden locker. The flames themselves were enough to attract the attention of the house. But just in case I'd left the can, with its cap tightly screwed on, on top of the locker. I watched, tucked down behind the last pillar as the flames enveloped the can. I started to fret. If the fire ate through the wooden lid too fast, the can would drop through and just lie there. I looked up at the house. Three figures were at the window, gesticulating. Then they vanished. From a side door, two came running, or rather one was running, the other hopping. The third figure stood in the doorway watching.

The two coming fast towards me had handguns. They should have had buckets of water. The faster of the two sprinted on to the deck and crashed on his face like a felled tree. His gun spun away from his hand. Behind him, Hopalong did a more leisurely but nevertheless acrobatic tumble and came to rest nursing his shoulder and head. Neither had seen the tightly drawn fishing line stretched across the first two pillars. The downed men were about three feet from the roaring flames.

They were both struggling to their feet when the can exploded. I ducked behind my pillar as the shrapnel flew. Bits of red-hot tin sliced the air and peppered their faces and bodies. Globules of burning petrol and oil stuck to their bodies and roasted their flesh. They screamed like girls, fell over and rolled, trying to snuff out their flaming skin and clothes. Finally, in desperation, one after the other, they leaped into the sea. A second or two later they were screaming again as the salt water licked at their wounds. I looked over the side and raised my shotgun to put them out of their pain but lowered it again. They were no longer active participants in this game. I'd keep my powder dry for Slattery.

I peered through the wall of flame but couldn't see Gerrit. I made my move. Revolver in my belt, knife down my sock, Dickson to my shoulder, I charged through the wave of heat. I heard my hair singe and smelt it burning. As I passed through the fire, knowing I'd be silhouetted against the flames, I dived to the left and ducked behind the jetty's pillar nearest the house. I peered out from behind it. There was no sign of anyone. If I were Slattery I'd be heading for the car – cautiously, mind, not being sure if there was a frontal assault as well. I had to get round the front and cut him off.

I got to my feet and ran to the left and up towards the house. I got to the side and ran forward again. The car was about ten feet away from the front door. I dived forward and hit the grass, rolling and rolling till I was on the car's flank, protected from the house. I drew my knife and stabbed the tyres, one after the other. The car settled on its rims. It wasn't going anywhere, at least not in a hurry. I sized up the house. Two large windows at the front on either side of the main door. I decided to go in through the front to keep Slattery pinned with his back to the water. I lifted the shotgun and took aim. The blast echoed loud and long, followed by the smashing and tinkling of glass as the right-hand window exploded.

I dashed forward and up to the window sill. I moved to the side and, protected by the window frame, looked into the room. Nothing. I cleared the shards of glass from the frame and climbed up and through. I dropped into the room and stood waiting. Quiet. I moved forward in the darkness, got to the door on the right-hand side and threw it open. I was in the hall. There was the second room door opposite me, and down the corridor a door into what I assumed was the big back room where I'd first seen them. There was a staircase up on my left. Again I stopped and listened. All I could hear was the sound of distant crackling as the fire burned itself out.

I decided to clear the ground floor first, and then start on the upper floor. I pressed forward. Then I realised that the stairs not only led up, they went down. After a run of five or six downward steps was a door. It was gaping open. Light came from the cellar. I inched my way down, step by step. Was this a trap? Was Slattery waiting for me in the cellar, gun aimed? Or was he above me, waiting to slam the door on me?

I put half my body round the corner of the door frame and could see into the cellar. It was about fifteen feet square. And to prove it was a Slattery residence a single grubby mattress lay on the floor next to some cords. Suddenly I knew what was happening. I leaped back up the stairs and into the hall. Without hesitating I hit the closed door with my shoulder and stumbled through. The room was empty and the side door was open. Out in the fluttering light from the last embers of the fire I could see the masts of the ketch. Instead of bare poles, a jib fluttered from the mainmast and its mizzen sail was nearly fully raised and already filling. The bow was edging away from the jetty and with the steady off-shore breeze it would soon pick up pace and vanish into the night.

I ran madly out into the back yard and on to the jetty. He had already cast free. The mizzen sail was firmly in place. The yacht was already a full length away and gathering speed. Facing back, with his left hand on the tiller, Gerrit Slattery grinned at me in malice. He held a pistol in his right hand but it wasn't aimed at me.

I raised my shotgun to blast his wicked head off, when he shouted: 'Fire, and she's dead, Brodie.'

I stepped forward and saw where his gun pointed. Sam was lying curled at his feet in the cramped cockpit.

FORTY-SEVEN

Sam was on her back, her hands tied behind her, and her feet roped. Her legs were tucked up to her chest because of the narrowness of the cockpit. She looked groggy, but at least her eyes were open. Her mouth was gagged and her head lolled as the yacht moved. I lowered my gun.

'That's right, Brodie. You'll play my tune now, so you will. Come after me and she's dead.'

'You can't hide, Slattery,' I shouted. 'I tracked wee Dermot down and he's gone to hell!'

'You're a fucking liar, Brodie! Nobody fucks with Dermot Slattery.'

'Well, the worms are fucking him now, Gerrit! The worms at Planner Farm.'

I saw his face change, saw his gun arm come up and I dived to the deck as he fired once, twice, in fury. I got off a shot but missed. He swung the tiller across and the boat turned smoothly and accelerated into the dark. Beyond him and to his left a light flashed. He was steering west of the Pladda light and south-east on a line that would take him back to Ireland.

I watched him go until I was sure he could no longer see me, then I ran to the side of the jetty and dropped into my boat. I landed with a crash and nearly capsized. I stowed my shotgun, steadied myself and got the engine going. Then I headed out into the sea, throttle full open. Slattery was going to kill her whether I came after her or not. If he hadn't already done so. She would simply be ballast that went overboard. I wondered how soon he'd try to get the mainsail up and how easily he could handle it. With all canvas up he'd leave me for dead.

I aimed for my last sighting of the sail to the west of Pladda's sporadic flash but for long minutes could see nothing. I squinted along the wave tops. There! In the brief flash something waving. I adjusted my bearings and headed after her. The crisp breeze was still nicely behind the ketch. He could stay comfortably on this line running downwind until he made landfall on Ireland, perhaps trying for Belfast and what he saw as safety in the city. By my reckoning, he would be making six or seven knots to my ten or eleven. Unless the wind picked up even more. Or he got his mainsail up. Or I ran out of fuel.

The clouds shifted and the moonlight ran across the heaving water like mercury. We were well past Pladda. The *Lorne* was in plain view. She was still running on mizzen and foresail. I pressed on, hoping my engine noise wouldn't be heard above the splash of his bow wave and the wind through his rigging. I made steady inroads on the gap. Two hundred, then one hundred. I could see Slattery clearly, standing with his back to me, both hands pushing the tiller to keep the ketch on course. I wasn't sure, but I think I saw the glint of Sam's pale flesh and white blouse. I looked longingly at the Dickson lying in the bottom but realised I hadn't reloaded. I needed one hand to steer. I drew my pistol.

I was within twenty yards when he heard me. He turned and looped cord round the tiller to lash it in place. I fired the big Webley. It kicked and crashed but missed him. I fired again but the boat was too unsteady. He pulled his own gun out of his belt. He bent over and dragged at the body lying at his feet. There was resistance. He yanked Sam to her feet by her bound hands, making her face contort with pain as her arms were wrenched up behind her. He stood with Sam as a shield and held the pistol to her head. She looked as if she would slump to the deck. He used his left arm to hold her close to him. He shouted something at me but it was blown away by the wind. Then he tore down the gag round her mouth and said something in her ear. She tried to shout, but I heard nothing. She tried again. All I heard was 'Back', then 'Go back, Brodie'. I saw him grin and he waved his gun in front of her face.

I was close enough now to see her expression. I expected terror. Instead it was pure, undiluted anger. I saw her hunch a little as if to gather herself. Then her blonde head struck like a mamba. Her fine white teeth sank into his wrist and, in surprised reflex, Slattery dropped the gun. He flung her from him and she fell out of the shallow cockpit to sprawl helplessly on the deck. I twisted the throttle and felt the boat leap forward like a seal.

Slattery was scrabbling for his gun when the ketch lurched. He'd been sloppy lashing the tiller. With no counterforce, the rudder swung back and the ketch rounded up with a jolt. It staggered through 90 degrees and threw Slattery across the deck and into the gunnels. He lost his grip on the line controlling the boom and the freed sail flapped uselessly in the wind. With its speed slowed to a near stop I crashed into the hull, just managing to turn the boat side on as I did. I dropped my pistol, grabbed the little anchor and rope in the bows and tangled it round the taut rigging lines. I cut the engine, drew my knife and leaped on the deck of the wallowing *Lorne*.

Slattery was getting to his feet, blood running from a deep cut in his head. He looked concussed. He wiped the gore from his eyes and saw me stumbling towards him. At the periphery of my vision I could see Sam lying still against the lifelines. Slattery made another scan of the deck for his gun. Then he stooped and came up with a six-foot grappling pole. Its point was a combined spear and wicked hook, just the thing for landing a big fish or gutting a boarder. He swung at me and missed my ducking head by an inch. He held it like a lance and lunged at me. I sidestepped and tripped as he passed. I tumbled into the cockpit and broke my fall across the swinging thick bar of the tiller. I jerked back as the spiked pole drove past my chest and glanced off the tiller. I half fell, half jumped out onto the deck. I was winded and wondering if I'd cracked a rib.

Slattery stumbled round the tiller and flailed the pike at me. I took it across my arm and shoulder. I felt the pain and then numbness in my arm. This fight wasn't going to last long . A man with a weapon always trumps a one-armed man. I danced away from the vicious flail, trying to keep the cockpit between us. I did one full circle then fell back and back towards the stern. I kept moving my left arm to try to get some feeling back. Fire shot along it. Better that than no feeling at all. I was near the stern now, still retreating. Slattery was back to his annoying grin again, as though he could smell my blood. He kept jabbing at me, and was surely going to jab me all the way overboard. My mind blinked. We were fighting outside Caen. Flushing a German platoon out of a barn. Suddenly a frenzied Kraut broke cover ten feet from me and charged me with fixed bayonet, screaming like a lunatic. For the first time in this chase fear gripped my guts.

My training cut in. When in doubt, attack. I dived into a somersault and shot up under his weapon, almost into his face. I stabbed with my knife but he dropped the near end of his staff to block me. I went in close and tackled through him, my left shoulder screaming in pain. We both crashed to the deck and rolled around kicking and lashing at each other. He dropped the pole. It was no use at close quarters. He was like a thrashing maniac, all fists and knees and teeth. He got hold of my knife hand and beat it on a metal stanchion till I dropped it. I managed to twist round and kicked it out of the way. If I couldn't have it, neither could he.

We got on our knees then managed to stand upright on the pitching deck, glaring at each other and panting. The boom of the mizzen sail suddenly swung back on board and we both ducked. I ran at him and we locked arms like drunks holding each other up on a Saturday night. He was blinking blood out of his eyes. His small moustache was thick with it. I drew my head back and smashed it forward into his face. I felt his nose crunch. I shifted my grip to put him in a headlock. The boom came swinging back, trailing its retaining line.

Instinctively I grabbed the line and looped it round his neck. I put a quick half hitch in it and yanked tight. I made a second half hitch for luck. The boat gave a lurch and I pushed Slattery and the boom. He stumbled on the gunnel and I gave the boom another shove. Slattery went over the side clutching at the boom. His feet dragged in the sea. His hands tore at the wooden spar to stop from falling. He made one frantic effort to hold himself up with one arm round the boom while he clawed at the rope round his neck.

A big wave broke over his chest. He lost his grip and was left dangling by the rope round his neck.

For a long moment he tore at the line in terror, trying to loosen the wet knots. His weight and the rolling waves made it impossible. His feet thrashed in the water as though he was trying to run on it. His face turned to mine in horror. His mouth screamed but nothing came out. I stood panting and watching him hang by the neck until he was dead.

His body gave a last twitch or two then sagged. The ketch slowed and the boom dipped, trailing its human sea anchor. I ran forward and unhitched the foresail line so that jib flapped. The *Lorne* finally stopped and lay wallowing in the water. I came back and used the grappling iron to pull the boom close to the side. Slattery's blotched face stared up at me, eyes bulging with accusation. I felt no remorse. I dragged the body half over the bulwarks and onto the deck face up, so that only his feet were being washed by the waves. I tugged the knots loose and made the line secure on a deck cleat but with plenty of give. I wasn't ready to try and sail her until I worked out what I was doing. I felt sick and trembling.

Behind me, I heard a groan.

FORTY-EIGHT

broke open a hatch and with the last of my strength carried Sam down the steps into the cabin area. I laid her on a bunk, cut off her bonds and wrapped a blanket round her shaking body. I rubbed at her hands and feet to get the circulation going. Her face was bruised along one side and her limbs were battered from her fall. Her eyes stayed closed and she lay quietly moaning as though in a bad dream.

I looked around and found cigarettes and a bottle of Scotch. I raised her head and let her suck a mouthful or two from the bottle. She choked but swallowed and her breathing grew stronger. I took a couple of gargles myself and never recalled Whyte & Mackay tasting so good. I wrapped a blanket round my own shoulders and sat on the facing bunk. My hands were shaking like palsy as I tried to light up. I coughed and spluttered and took another mouthful and another drag. The nausea was passing, leaving me numb. I had no sense of triumph, no sense of anything. It was over. I listened to the slap of waves on the hull and felt the ketch wallow and drift, rudderless and directionless. It didn't take much of an insight to see the parallels.

I stirred myself. My arm and shoulder were killing me, but at least I could use them. First, I had to do something about the sails. As I'd explained to Eric the Red, my last seafaring adventure involved pinching a 15-foot dinghy from a French fisherman to escape a POW camp. I often wondered how the rest of the 51st had got on as they were marched off to Germany. Those who made it would have been brought home by now. I hadn't dared try to get in touch. I didn't know what to say. I was confused at feeling guilty at escaping. It wasn't as if I had five easy years. So why should front-line service seem a better result than idling away in a POW camp?

Private Donald MacLennan, sometime crofter, fisherman and poacher, who later bought it on the beach at Normandy, taught me the rudiments of sailing in those three endless days after St Valery. My challenge now was to transfer the dimly recalled skills to something three times the size and with two masts instead of one. I wasn't about to try to raise the mainsail. I'd follow Slattery's lead and stick to the mizzen and foresail. I clambered back on deck and looked around me. A flash of light broke the dark. Unless it was some other lighthouse, that was Pladda to the north. I could see where we'd come from. The wind was still blowing from the north, but not as strong. I decided to keep it simple and run for a while before the wind. If I wanted to head back to Arran I'd need to have my head clear to cope with the tacking. Slattery's body lay flat on its back as if he was star gazing. His head lolled with the waves. I'd deal with him shortly.

I stepped down into the cockpit and grabbed the tiller. It came alive in my hand. I pushed it round until the flapping mizzen sail filled. The ketch began to slip and pitch through the waves. The thrill of it coursed through me. I lashed the tiller properly to keep on the southerly course and hauled in the mizzen boom. The sail tightened and the ketch heeled a little. I laced the line round a cleat and fumbled along the deck to find the foresail line. I hauled it in and let the sail billow and catch. We were off!

The *Lorne* may only have been doing six or seven knots but it felt like twenty poised above the great dark sea. I tinkered with the tiller until I was happy about her trim and direction and turned my attention to Eric's little motor boat. I untangled its hastily wrapped anchor and rope and let the boat slip down the side until it lay directly behind the ketch. I made it secure and let it ride like a tender behind us. I was duty bound to return it to Eric the Red and buy him a very large Scotch. We had to compare notes about the Highway Decorators, discuss where Rommel went wrong in the Western Desert, and exaggerate the hard slog across France to the Rhine. In truth it sounded like a two-bottle session.

I turned to Gerrit Slattery. His strangled corpse would require a fair amount of explanation if I moored at Arran or the mainland. I could just dump him over the side like his pals had with me. But there was the chance of his body washing up on Barassie Beach and frightening the kids, not to mention getting the attention of the police. I went down into the cabin. Sam was lying looking sick but at least her eyes were open. She tried a smile. It didn't work.

'Just rest. It's all right. Slattery's gone.'

She nodded and closed her eyes.

I rummaged around the cabin and found a heavy metal toolbox and a coil of rope. Perfect. I flung the rope over my good shoulder and dragged the box on deck. I cut off a good slice of line and tied one end to the handle of the box and the other round Slattery's waist. Water gurgled from his mouth as though he wanted a last few words. I didn't mind if he did a Lazarus on me. I'd enjoy having to kill him all over again.

I propped the box against the low rail, ready to be pitched over. I got under Slattery's shoulders and lifted him into a sitting position alongside the box. His backside was still on the deck and his legs dangled over the side. With a great heave I lifted him up so that he was sitting on the bulwarks for a brief moment. A final push and he was over the side in a clumsy dive. His body dragged and bumped along the side tethered to the box. I could feel the effect on the *Lorne*. I quickly got under the box, balanced it on the edge and shoved it over. It hit the surface with a splash, filled with water, and sank like, well, a metal box. Body and box were lost to sight in a heartbeat.

I rummaged around the deck until I found Slattery's gun and my own knife. I stowed them safely on the second bunk in the cabin along with my guns.

I inspected Sam. She was awake and had a little more light in her face.

'Douglas Brodie, can I just say thanks, for the moment? I'm too … too …'

'Shattered, battered, hammered? Not to mention chloroformed. You've been through it, lassie. It was a brave thing, biting that bastard's hand. You saved my life.'

'Don't be so bloody ridiculous. *I* saved *your* life, indeed. Pass me the bottle, Brodie.'

'Why don't you lie down? We can talk later.'

A spasm ran across her poor white face. 'Is he …? Is Slattery …?'

'He's gone, Sam. I put a spanner – or two – in his works. He won't be back.'

'His brother?'

'Dead. Car accident.'

'You know Gerrit did those awful things? To the wee boys?'

'Yes. I found his den out by Dumbarton.'

'He said it was the priest's fault. Father Cassidy. He was there – at the Nazareth House where the boys were sent. He …'

'Whisht, I know, I know. It's no excuse for anything. But I've seen it before – damaged people damaging other people. Bullied kids in peacetime becoming camp guards in wartime. Dermot spent the rest of his days looking after his wee, abused brother. I don't know where the start of all this was. But I imagine it was why Dermot killed his father. And the ripples have been swamping innocent people for years.'

She nodded and pulled the blanket tighter round her. Maybe now wasn't the time to tell her. But, then, she'd coped with worse, surely, these last few days.

'There's one other thing, Sam. Your mum and dad. When I talked about ripples ...'

'I know. He couldn't resist telling me. He threw them overboard in the middle of the loch and just waited till they couldn't swim any more. Drowning people seems to be their specialty. How could anyone do that?' The tears were blinding her again, and I wished I'd made Slattery – both of them – suffer longer.

'There's also Allardyce ...' I began.

'He'll swing for this, so help me! He just stood there, inside his room, and Slattery came up behind me, and stuck a hankie over my mouth, and it was foul, and I don't remember ...' She punched the mattress again and again.

'Sam, Sam. He's dead. After he knocked you out, Slattery killed Allardyce in the hotel.'

She shook her head, and her eyes widened as her brain went into overload. She started to shake again. I held her tightly and stroked her hands and arms until she calmed. I made her lie down. I pulled another blanket over her from the second bunk. She lay staring up at the bulkhead for a while as I held her hand. At last she closed her eyes. She was asleep in moments. We could talk it through properly when she woke. If we needed to. I stared at her face as it relaxed and took on its familiar gentle contours. I wondered how I'd ever thought her plain. Or why age had anything to do with beauty. I pushed back the errant blonde curl that fell across her forehead. She twitched but then settled and was already far from me.

I let the *Lorne* run for a while, enjoying the speed and getting the feel of her. At last I pushed on the tiller and swung her round. I reset the sails and put her head north-east, back towards the Ayrshire coast. I could see Arran's dark bulk cluttering the sky-sea horizon ahead and to my left. The boat rocked gently as it parted the waves. The sound of the bow cleaving and slapping the furrows soothed the restive core of me. I could feel the knotted anger drifting away like sand in a timer. For the first time in weeks I was no longer in pursuit of anything or anyone. And no one was pursuing me. Was this what hope felt like? It would do for a while.

The sail above my head and the foresail rippled as I headed closer to the wind and I felt the boat prance like a live animal under me, ready to dart and sprint. It would take us a while to get back, much longer than the outward journey, tacking against the wind all the way. I wondered if I could get the mainsail up. I didn't have the compass bearings for Kildonan but could follow the flicker of the Pladda light.

A tempting thought scampered across my mind. I remembered long ago, in the hot slouch of an English lesson, listening to our teacher intoning the rhythm and imagery of Tennyson:

> *... for my purpose holds*
> *To sail beyond the sunset, and the baths*
> *Of all the western stars, until I die.*

I smiled, standing at my tiller. I brought her round on a deep tack, heading west, knowing that if I spun her another few degrees we would sweep past the Mull of Kintyre and out into the wide open Atlantic. The next stop would be America. I felt the wind tugging me round, urging me towards the open sea. And I wondered how many chances a man gets to take off into the westering sun in a fine yacht, with a pretty wee blonde.